ALSO BY JUDITH CHERNAIK

Double Fault

The Daughter

Leah

The Lyrics of Shelley

LOVE'S CHILDREN

LOVE'S CHILDREN

A NOVEL BY

JUDITH CHERNAIK

Alfred A. Knopf

NEW YORK

1992

THIS IS A BORZOI BOOK
PUBLISHED BY ALFRED A. KNOPF, INC.

Copyright © 1991 by Judith Chernaik

Originally published in Great Britain as Mab's Daughters by
Macmillan London Limited in 1991.

Library of Congress Cataloging-in-Publication Data
Chernaik, Judith.
Love's children : a novel / by Judith Chernaik. — 1st American ed.
p.   cm.
ISBN 0-394-51325-8
1. Shelley, Percy Bysshe, 1792–1822—Fiction.   2. Shelley,
Mary Wollstonecraft, 1797–1851—Fiction.   3. Clairmont,
Clara Mary Jane, 1798–1879—Fiction.   4. Shelley, Harriet
Westbrook, d. 1816—Fiction.   I. Title.
PS3553.H354M33   1992
813'.54—dc20   91-35722
CIP

Manufactured in the United States of America

For Laura, David and Sara

Yet, human Spirit, bravely hold thy course . . .
Shelley, *Queen Mab*

CONTENTS

PREFACE

There once were four women, three of them sisters, who fell under the spell of a poet with a passion for reforming the world.

The poet was married, at different times, to two of these women, and they bore his children; the other two women loved him as a friend and brother. One of the sisters pursued and captured a second poet, a satirist of the same world which the first poet longed to reform.

All four women were educated and literate, in the haphazard fashion of the early nineteenth century. They browsed in their fathers' libraries and favoured sentimental novels; they attended boarding schools for young ladies, where they learned a smattering of French, geography, music, and drawing. They devoted at least an hour each day to writing letters, and they kept journals in which they noted the weather, visits received, visits paid, journeys taken, books read. In private signs they recorded the dates of their periods, missed periods, the birth of a child, the death of a child. Everything they wrote was carefully preserved.

Their names were Mary, Clare, Fanny, Harriet; the poets with whom their lives were entangled were Shelley and Byron. Gossip provided material for a dozen novels (including several by the chief persons and their friends), half a dozen plays, and, in recent times, films and television drama.

The bare outlines of the story are familiar enough.

Fanny Godwin was the illegitimate daughter of Mary Wollstonecraft, author of A Vindication of the Rights of Woman, one of the first works to argue that all civil and political rights and duties should apply equally to men and women, without regard to sex. Mary Godwin, born three years after Fanny, was Mary Wollstonecraft's daughter by William Godwin, author of An Enquiry Concerning Political Justice, popularly known as 'The Anarchist's Bible' because of its defence of pleasure as the chief ground of human activity, and freedom as man's chief good. Both Godwin and

Wollstonecraft attacked the institution of marriage as a means of enslaving women and placing fetters upon love. But upon discovering that Mary was pregnant they set aside their principles and married quietly in a private ceremony in St Pancras Church. Soon after giving birth to her second daughter, Mary Wollstonecraft died of puerperal fever, and Godwin then adopted the three-year-old Fanny and gave her his name.

Three years later, Godwin married Mary Jane Clairmont, his neighbour in the Polygon, Somers Town. He hoped thereby to provide a home for his two motherless girls. Mrs Clairmont had a three-year-old daughter, Clara Mary Jane (father unknown), who was called, at different times, Jane, Clara, and Clare. From the time that Mary and Jane were three, and Fanny six, they were brought up together in Godwin's household, living first in the Polygon, then moving to a house in Skinner Street, in Holborn, close to St Paul's Churchyard and the publishing heart of London. There Mrs Clairmont opened a small publishing house of her own, featuring children's books of an enlightened tendency, written by Godwin and tested on the children, who now included William Junior, born to Godwin and Mrs Clairmont soon after their marriage.

It was at Skinner Street that Godwin was first visited by an ardent young disciple of his libertarian philosophy, the poet Shelley, who brought with him his young wife and fellow disciple, Harriet Westbrook, daughter of a prosperous London tavern-keeper. It was also at Skinner Street that Shelley met and fell in love with Godwin's daughter Mary, then sixteen years old. Harriet was at that time expecting her second child by Shelley; their daughter Ianthe was a year old. After a few weeks of tormented indecision, and against the strong objections both of Harriet and Godwin, the lovers eloped to France, accompanied by Mary's step-sister Jane.

These events happened in July 1814, a few months after Napoleon had been defeated and exiled to Elba. The travellers were thus among the first to set foot on French soil at the end of the wars that had devastated the continent of Europe for twenty years. It was at this time that Mary and Clare first realised that the journals they had kept since childhood might have an interest beyond the merely personal.

Shelley, Mary and Clare returned to England after only four

weeks, homeless and penniless. Harriet fully expected Shelley to return to her, but this was never a real possibility.

Our story begins two years later, during the summer of 1816, when Shelley, Mary, their six-month-old child Will, and Clara (as she was now called) shared a small villa on Lake Geneva. They were a few minutes' walk from the Villa Diodati, where the celebrated Lord Byron was nursing his bruised feelings following his separation from Lady Byron, on grounds too horrible to be named in public – though rumour whispered tales of incest and sodomy. The previous March, Clara had introduced herself to Byron (a director of the Drury Lane Theatre) as E. Trefusis, an aspiring actress and playwright eager for his advice; by June she knew that she was carrying his child.

A year later, through the offices of Shelley's good friend Thomas Love Peacock, Shelley, Mary and Clara were settled with their children in the town of Marlow, on the Thames, thirty miles west of London. Their lives during that time of public and private crisis were charted day by day in journals and letters which eventually came into Peacock's possession. Shortly before his death, Peacock presented these papers to the Library of East India House, where he had worked for more than forty years; they have remained there, forgotten by the world, until the present time.

TO THE READER

I often think that if I had been able to persuade Shelley and Mary to remain in Marlow, they might have achieved the happiness that was the theme of our daily intercourse. But they had convinced themselves that Shelley would die of consumption within weeks if they stayed on at Albion House. True, it was damp and insanitary; there was something wrong with the drains, and for nine months of the year it was dark and sunless. But Shelley longed to be of use to his country; he wanted above all to awaken Englishmen and women to a true understanding of their condition, and he left England only under the strongest compulsion. He was to drown in Italy only four years later, just short of his thirtieth birthday. It was the cruellest of ironies.

Then again, by that time he had begun to despair of life, of love, of any hope of realising his vision of a liberated humanity. His last poems were a sustained cry for death, and it may be that he welcomed its release.

Even if Shelley's health had not been at risk, they would have left England sooner or later, for Shelley lived in terror that the courts would remove his children from him, as a self-confessed atheist. In any case, Miss Clairmont would have prevailed upon them to travel to Italy as soon as Lord Byron agreed to receive her child. The sunny Italian skies beckoned; and they could not know that the children would not survive the rigours of the southern climate. The little boy was three when he succumbed to a fever in Rome; the baby girl lived for only a year, and Miss Clairmont's child died in a typhoid epidemic at the convent where Lord Byron had sent her to be educated in the Catholic faith.

When they left Albion House, Shelley entrusted me with their personal papers and possessions. Their departure was as sudden as all their comings and goings, and they took nothing from Marlow except their clothes and two writing desks. After Shelley's death, when Mrs Shelley was preparing his works for publication, she asked me to send her any of his writings still in my possession. It was only then that I discovered the private journals kept by Mrs Shelley and Miss Clairmont during their last year in England. I did not read them through; but neither did I return them. I regarded them as material held in trust for my lost friend. It came as a surprise to find Fanny Godwin's journal among Shelley's papers, but it seems to have been in the suitcase he brought back from Bristol on his fruitless attempt to discover her whereabouts. Miss Godwin's journal too I continued to keep under lock and key.

I still believe that I was right to withhold these journals from Mrs Shelley, who had evidently forgotten their existence. They would only have added to her grief at Shelley's death, and they would most certainly have exacerbated the burden of guilt she carried with her until her death ten years ago.

The papers of Shelley's first wife, Harriet Westbrook, came into my hands much later, when Harriet's sister Eliza summoned me to her lawyer's rooms in Gray's Inn, and solemnly presented me with a box containing Shelley's early poems, family letters, and Harriet's notebooks. Harriet's daughter Ianthe was to be married, and Miss Westbrook wished these last reminders of a buried past to be in my safekeeping – for I had maintained relations with the Westbrooks after Shelley's death, and I defended Harriet's reputation in public when the first biographies of the poet appeared.

The pages that follow may help to elucidate the most puzzling mysteries in the tangled relations of the Shelley circle. They constitute an intimate chronicle of the Geneva summer and that last fateful year in England, its joy and heartbreak, its triumph and failure.

It occurs to me that I cut a rather lamentable figure in these journals; for all my good intentions, I was largely ignorant of the inner drama of my young friends' lives. I fear they saw me as no more than an amusing companion. But the events described here occurred more than forty years ago. The chief actors, Shelley and

Mary, are both dead, and I have allowed the material to stand as written. Publication is interdicted until fifty years after the deaths of those of us who are left: Miss Clairmont, Mr T. Jefferson Hogg, and myself. We have agreed to leave these uncensored records to the judgement of posterity.

Thomas Love Peacock
London, 1860

ONE
Summer 1816
Geneva/London

Man's love is of man's life a thing apart;
'Tis woman's whole existence . . .

Lord Byron

MARY
June 1816, Montalègre, Geneva

Tuesday, June 18th Rain all day; we stay indoors. L.B. comes down to Montalègre at 4 to talk with Shelley. They go out in the rain to secure the boat.

I would like to describe L.B. to Fanny, but I cannot do justice to his beauty of mind and spirit. He is a Poet in the grandest sense. Life has been cruel to him, he has been vilified by his former associates and caricatured in the press – and yet he is the most sympathetic of human beings. I find that my deepest thoughts have been perfectly expressed in his poems. Shelley and I are always quoting lines to each other. And he is so kind, so courteous, such a cheerful companion and generous host. S. says L.B. thinks very highly of me – I cannot imagine why, for I have hardly said more than two words when we are together.

Thursday, June 20th After supper last night we went up to Diodati with 'Clara', newly christened – 'Jane' we must banish. We reclined on cushions and thick rugs in the *grande salle* that stretches the full length of the balcony, candles flickering in the great bronze candlesticks, a log fire ablaze in the fireplace, which is large enough to roast an ox, lightning from across the lake suddenly illuminating the entire scene without and within, then terrific rain beating in on us, as the poets discoursed on a dozen topics, including poetry, politics, the vegetable diet, galvanism, and ghosts.

The storm showed no sign of diminishing in force, and L.B. pressed us to stay the night. As the great clock struck midnight he recited Coleridge's lines about the Lady Geraldine, 'hideous, deformed, and pale of hue'. He declaimed the last line with the most powerful effect, whereupon Shelley shrieked and covered his eyes with his hands, then he took up a candle and fled from the room.

I hurried after him, followed closely by Polidori, L.B.'s physician. We persuaded him to lie on the sofa and bathed his face with cold water, then Polidori administered some ether, and after a few minutes, when he was able to speak, he said, 'Oh Mary, hold me, don't ever leave me,' and sobbed, catching his breath. I tried to calm him but he kept breaking into short sobs. When he could speak again, he said that while L.B. was reciting, he saw or imagined that my dress had fallen away. He gazed at my breasts and to his horror my nipples turned into eyes, which regarded him with a fixed expression. It was this vision which caused him to run from the room.

'Does your husband often have seizures?' asked Polidori, who seemed quite alarmed.

I told him that S. is subject to fits in which he is unable to distinguish between reality and the creations of his overheated brain. I did not tell him of my suspicion that these attacks are brought on by the laudanum which S. takes almost daily. After a quarter of an hour he seemed to recover, and insisted he was well enough to return to the company. But we retired soon afterwards, and I held him in my arms all night.

In the morning he said, 'Ah Mary, you will have to be the strong one, I fear that I shall die.'

'That is nonsense,' I said. 'You are not going to die, you are young and in good health, there is nothing the matter with you.'

'Yes,' he said, 'but I have enemies who are bent on destroying me.'

'There are no enemies here,' I said. 'You are surrounded by friends and you have nothing to fear. Why do you torment yourself needlessly?'

He kissed me and said I was right, and he would try to be better.

Wrote to Fanny asking her to send Coleridge's poems.

On Monday Shelley and L.B. leave for a boat trip round the lake. I pray that the weather improves. If there is a storm, Shelley said, he will cheerfully return to his natural element. 'What, and leave me and your sweet babe?' I said. 'Never fear,' he said, 'L.B. is a strong swimmer and will save me.' Fine thoughts to have on the eve of a journey.

Tuesday, June 25th Only two days gone, and Clara has been languishing as if bereaved. I suggested that she read Rousseau. She said she loathed Rousseau.

'It's easy for you,' she said. 'You know very well that Shelley loves you. But I have no idea whether I will ever see Albé again. If I do not see him for a day, it is as if there is no connection between us, and never has been. Each minute is precious. I cannot afford to lose a day, certainly not an entire week. It is a lifetime to me.'

I suggested that she could hardly expect to monopolise his lordship's leisure hours. There was no point in fretting.

'But I feel wretched – really I am quite ill.'

'You are making yourself ill,' I said. I sometimes think I preferred her company when she was Jane.

As if to prove her point, she suddenly went pale, retched, and rushed out of the room. She was gone for a long time, and when she returned she was carrying a book – *Udolpho* by Mrs Radcliffe. 'Are you really unwell, Clary?' I said.

She tossed her head. 'Not exactly.'

Suddenly a light dawned – how stupid I've been! 'Oh, Clary,' I said. 'You should have told me.'

'I thought you would guess.'

No wonder she has been fretting – this was not part of the grand plan.

'How long have you known?'

'Long enough.'

'And you have kept it to yourself? You haven't told him?'

'No – not yet.'

Then: 'Oh, Mary, do you think he will be pleased?'

I was appalled. What on earth could she be thinking about? Does she imagine for one moment that L.B.'s feelings for her will be affected in the slightest by this news?

'I doubt it,' I said.

'You know, I think he cares more for you than he does for me. He respects you – I don't think he respects me at all.'

This may well be true, but I did not like to say so. 'I imagine he will want to provide for the child.'

'Oh, I am certain he will. He will want to be a proper father to his child. He has not seen his daughter Ada since she was a month old, and he feels the loss more bitterly than anything else. He will want to have the child with him, I promise you.'

I could see the direction her thoughts were taking. If L.B. were to take the child, might he not take the mother as well? This is certainly a delusion, but I thought it might be prudent to let it pass unchallenged, before the truth sinks in. I can see that we will have to have a frank conference when Shelley returns.

Thursday, June 27th Fine all week, but today there are storm-clouds scudding across the lake. Elise assured me that the weather on our side of the lake is no guide to the weather at Evian, where Shelley should now have arrived.

'Madame must not worry,' she said. 'There is no need.' Then she smiled her crooked smile, to acknowledge the courtesy of 'Madame'. If little Will were not so fond of her, I could cheerfully dispense with her services. But, alas, she has become indispensable.

Clara has purchased silk thread and needles in town, and is teaching herself to crochet. She has not said anything further about her dream of living happily ever after with L.B., but she seems more contented. This morning she asked me what it was like to give birth.

I tried to remember. 'It's like nothing else in the world.' Therefore it is very difficult to describe. I was suddenly assailed by the memory of the seven months' child I carried and lost after my Beloved and I were first united, exactly two years ago. Poor little thing, so frail, the fine skin transparent so that you could see the thin bones, and the tiny mouth, gasping, trying to suck. Two weeks struggling to keep a faint hold on life. Oh, it was cruel of Clara to ask me to remember, for I cannot think of one without the other. Darling little Will was sitting on the floor at my feet, playing happily, as sunny and healthy a child as one could wish for. How true it is that we are pawns of Dame Fortune.

6 *Mary*

'I cannot describe it to you,' I said. 'But I shall try to write down what I can remember. One thing I can tell you now – it is like being torn apart by wild animals.'

Clara looked dismayed, and I felt a twinge of remorse. 'But it may not be the same for you,' I added.

Neither of us mentioned a similar exchange we had some months ago.

Jane, as she then was: 'Tell me what it's like.'

'You will find out in good time.'

'I want to know now.'

'In a way, it is . . . nothing much.'

'I don't believe you. When you come home you look different. You look as if something has happened. Something tremendous. I always know.'

'If you know, why do you ask?'

'I want to know what he does.'

'All right, then. Listen to me carefully. I'll say it in French. *He makes love to me, with his mouth, his hands, his body. He enters me, again and again, and I move with him, and I entrust myself to him with my whole being, heart and mind and soul.*'

'Does he hurt you?'

'No. Never.'

'Does he say anything?'

'Sometimes . . . sometimes he cries out my name. Sometimes he seems to be in pain – in anguish. I would do anything for him, then.'

Clara looked at me enviously. 'One day I shall trade notes with you,' she said.

Which we have not done. There are things I would prefer not to know, especially as they concern L.B. But I shall try to write down an account of childbirth, as I promised.

The pain begins in the back, very low, and passes through the belly and the womb, rising in intensity, on a slow, inexorable curve. Then it decreases as mysteriously as it began. Instinct tells you that it is better to receive the pain by relaxing your body than to fight against it. The pain starts again a few minutes later, and so on, repeating, until you seem to grow accustomed to it as to a regular visitor; in between the pains you can rest, talk, walk about, even read. But then the pains begin to come closer together, and each one is like a wave of pain filling you, crashing over you, and you feel that your entire body has become a vehicle for this pain, you no longer exist except as the pain, you are the pain that is tearing you apart. The strange thing is that it is not at all natural, it is a violent invasion of your inmost self. It would be natural to be reading a book, or talking with friends. But this pain that has taken over your body is inhuman, it is your mortal enemy.

To this account of childbirth I am tempted to add a recurring dream which I had before William's birth. More a nightmare than a dream, I woke from it each time determined never again to allow it to enter my thoughts. But perhaps if I try to set it down here I can exorcise it once and for ever.

In the dream I hear my baby crying, and I go to take it up and suckle it, and when I reach into the cot, I find – oh, it is impossible to describe what I see – I recoil in horror, unwilling to believe the evidence of my senses – it is a monstrosity, hideous, deformed, yellowish in colour, with coarse black hair, inhuman – and crying, crying with hunger. My breasts are full, I tell myself that I must try to feed it, but I cannot bring myself to touch the creature. Then in my dream I think: I cannot love it, it is not mine. Still it cries, and I know I must feed it, but it has grown, it is enormous, I cannot possibly nurse it – yet there is no one else, I must try what I can – and at this point I wake in horror and self-disgust.

Mrs Mason, to whom I told this dream, said it is common to all pregnant women, there is even a name for it in Greek. She thinks it is a way of protecting oneself against the possibility of losing one's baby, for if the baby is a monstrosity, it is better that it should die. She said that since I lost my first baby, I would be even more fearful about the second.

Then it occurred to me that the dream might have a different meaning: it might be a way of guarding against the possibility that one might not love one's child. For this too is a common response to motherhood, though few women will admit it. If the child is a monster, one cannot really be expected to love it.

It is painful to give utterance to these thoughts, but I feel better for having written them down.

Tuesday, July 2nd Joyful reunion yesterday at Diodati. We hear an account of the Castle of Chillon and the prisoners formerly kept in the dungeons there. S. describes Meillerie and the groves sacred to the love of Julie and St Preux, and, most harrowing to me, L.B. provides a full description of the squall and near-overturn of the boat, which was exactly as Shelley predicted, including his calm resolution in the face of death, and L.B.'s readiness to sacrifice himself for his friend. Fortunately there was no need for heroics, on either side.

S. told us that in the guest register of the inn at Lausanne, inspired by the spirits of Rousseau and Gibbon, he inscribed himself in Greek: *democrat, lover of mankind, atheist*. He was extremely pleased with this. L.B. said it was a foolish jest, and he would undoubtedly regret it.

Our own news waits. Clara has promised to speak to Shelley at the first convenient moment. But she could not hide her joy when we left her at Diodati; her eyes were bright and her cheeks glowing, and her expression could only be described as triumphant.

Thursday, July 4th Rain all yesterday and today, so we are confined indoors. We exchange ghost stories. Much speculation on the origin of life, and the possibility of creating it in the laboratory.

My dream: I am feverishly assembling my creature, who is stretched out on a table, larger than life. As I prepare to administer a final electrical stimulant to the nerves, I see his extremities twitching, manifesting the first signs of vital movement. I recoil in horror, willing the thing to relapse into inertness. The slight motion appears to cease and, partly reassured,

Mary 9

I withdraw to my chamber and prepare for sleep. But then I waken suddenly, and the creature is standing by my bedside, looking down on me through the parted curtains with yellow, watery eyes . . .

I start up terrified, and Shelley awakens with me. I tell him my dream, and he says, 'Why, that is your story. You must write it, you shall begin tomorrow.' And so I shall.

Friday, July 12th Shelley and L.B. on free will. Shelley argues that men have the power to change their lives but lack the will to do so. L.B. insists that we are creatures of circumstance, subject to our own dark nature and a fate over which we have no control.

S.: History is made by men, acting alone or in combination. Change is always possible. But human beings find it difficult to imagine a world different from the one they inherit. They accept existing evils only because they have never experienced anything better. Once they can imagine the possibility of living in a different way, then they have taken the first step towards changing their lives.

L.B.: My dear friend, you talk Utopia. Each age repeats the errors of the preceding age. And why? Because men break free of one set of chains only to bind themselves in another. Even you, my dear Shelley, must recognise that happiness is fugitive, while suffering is constant. If you study the last fifty years in France, paying close attention to the works of our friends Rousseau and Diderot, you must see that the best efforts of the wisest men are no more likely to contribute to the sum of human happiness than are apathy and indifference. Where did the enthronement of Reason and the proclamations of liberty lead, but to the slaughter of the Girondists, the tyranny of Robespierre, and the crowning of Napoleon as Emperor? These are not coincidences, they are part of a single process, which we must try to understand if we are to see ourselves and our fellows clearly. I am fully prepared to fight for freedom and against evil, but in the clear knowledge that my efforts and yours are utterly futile.

S.: You cannot expect a population that has been enslaved for centuries not to relapse into barbarism. This is what despotism feeds on – ignorance and fanaticism. You see this as a reason for despair; I see it as proof of the necessity to extend the benefits of enlightenment to the masses.

They argue until four in the morning, L.B. remaining per-fectly cool, Shelley becoming more and more agitated, until he is almost stammering with the effort to convince our aristocratic friend that he is mistaken. But it is not a matter of right and wrong; rather it is that Shelley has faith in humanity, L.B. has none. I sit listening, quiet as a mouse – but I cannot agree with L.B. that all men are prisoners of their age. When I am with my Beloved, all things seem possible, if only we remain united and continue to love each other.

Monday, July 15th Clara has had her long-postponed talk with Shelley. He says that she will not listen to reason. She is cheerful and happy, and indifferent to the perils of her situation. But sooner or later she must discuss the future with L.B., and reality will break through, as it always does in the end.

Sunday July 21st – Saturday July 27th Our expedition to Chamounix and Mont Blanc by mule. Here Shelley keeps the Journal. Past St Martin we come upon a beautiful scene, the river foaming below and the rocks and glaciers towering above. Thence to Montanvert and the Mer de Glace – a most desolate place, an inhuman world, inaccessible peaks of ice rising to a blank heaven. It is impossible to conceive of life surviving here, impossible to imagine a purposeful or beneficent Author of this primeval wilderness. S. writes a poem on Mont Blanc.

We return to Montalègre, and I embrace my darling Babe who does not seem to have missed me. Elise says he was very good. I transcribe Shelley's Journal to send to Peacock. Write to Fanny asking her to send *Clarissa Harlowe*. I think L.B. is somewhat in the character of Lovelace, torn between his brooding sense of wrong and his true generosity of mind and spirit.

Friday, August 2nd Shelley and L.B. sit on the wall before dinner; they talk for over an hour. Clara walks nervously to and fro. I write my story, and decide to give it an Alpine setting. After dinner, Shelley goes up to Diodati with Clara, returning alone at 11. Clara back at 6 in the morning. Tears. Love thou art a great deceiver, and we poor women are ever thy fools.

CLARE
June 1816, Geneva

Tuesday, June 25th I am convinced that Albé is a sentimentalist at heart. His coldness is only a pretence, a form of self-protection. What he fears most is any constraint upon his liberty. He is fond of saying that we are creatures of the moment; any reference to the past or the future irritates him beyond belief.

He told me that he has succumbed to the 'grand passion' in the past, two or three times at least. But now he is used up, exhausted. *He wants nothing.*

How well I understand him! From being the darling of fortune, he has become her plaything; he has been forced to leave his family and his country; his name has been dragged in the mud. Bitter and resentful, he broods over revenge. It seems to his injured pride that everything he touches turns to ashes.

Still, I am convinced that there is a small corner of his heart that is mine. He knows that he can say anything to me, he can be cruel or unkind and I will not protest. He accuses me of being insensitive, but then he enjoys teasing me. 'Out of my sight, woman!' he roars, but a minute later I am nestling by his side, his lordship pretending to ignore me, but he knows perfectly well where I am, and into whose lap his hand is straying.

They have been gone two days. Dismal conversation with Mary. Examined my chin closely in the glass: the spot is inflamed and painful, it feels as though some foul poison is working its way to the surface. Mary says to apply a paste of soda and water to draw the pus, but as usual she speaks confidently on matters about which she knows nothing; she has always had the clear skin of a three-year-old child. Mama would know exactly what to do. Why are some so fortunate, others cursed with bad luck? Shelley says the Goddess Fortuna is capricious, but we must try to ward off despair. Out, damned spot! I conjure thee by the holy gods of unwed maids . . . Otherwise I feel a surprising sense of well-being. No visible signs of change.

Thursday, July 4th I record this now so that I shall not forget events that have forever changed my life. I have never before nor do I expect ever again to be as happy as I am at this precise moment, 10 in the morning on Thursday the 4th of July 1816. I love passionately with every fibre of my being the kindest, best, wittiest, handsomest of men. I love his voice, which is deep and manly, with a hint of laughter. I love his features and especially his profile in repose, his mouth with its melancholy downward curve, his fine aristocratic nose, his brilliant greenish-blue eyes, now and then shooting a glance of fire or scorn, reflecting his impatience with the pretensions of mankind. I love the dark brown curls which frame his exquisitely proportioned head, as in the Greek sculptures in the gallery of antiquities. I love the way he takes me on his knee and calls me his little fiend, and tells me I deserve to be whipped for my impertinence in following him halfway across Europe, and I love him when he grasps my wrist and bends my arm behind my back, and whispers into my ear that I'm a fool to trust him for he knows he can do what he likes with me. 'Are you sure I am so easy to win?' I say, my heart beating fast.

Then he regards me with a steady look so melancholy that my own eyes fill with tears, and he releases me and sends me off. 'Go back to the others, swear you will have nothing more to do with me. I bring disaster to anyone whose life touches mine. You should fear me as you would polluted flesh.' I fall to my knees and embrace him. 'No,' I cry. 'Do not send me away. Trust me, let

me help you. I ask for nothing, only for the right to serve you. I'll
be your comrade, your page.'

To my amazement, he softens. 'You're a foolish girl,' he says,
'but I suppose I can't send you out into the night. Now, you
understand: there is to be no talk of love, no talk of the future,
no sentimental cant.' I nod agreement; yes, I understand. 'Well,
then, you might as well know certain things about me, if only to
clear the air. First . . . *primo*. I love one woman and one woman
only, whom I shall love until the day I die. That is my sister,
Augusta. Second . . . *secondo*. Anything that passes between us,
between you and me, is purely and simply for the pleasure of it. It
has nothing whatever to do with love. I find you amusing, I like
your friends. I can lie single or I can lie with you – it's all one to
me. In short, I have no objection to having you in my bed now
and then, upon invitation. But on one condition: that you
understand that there is to be no pretence of love between us.'

I agree entirely, I say. No love, no talk of love. No pretence.

'I might add that I'm not the man I was in London' – a shadow
of a smile, then the brooding look. 'I feel half inclined to be done
with all that, once and for all.'

I thought it best to say nothing. But after a moment I assured
him again that I expected nothing, I understood his feelings – his
lack of feelings, I should say, for he seems to me someone who
has suffered so much humiliation at the hands of a heartless
public that he is numbed.

Then I took a tremendous risk. I think at heart I am a
gambler. 'If you really want me to leave, I'll go now,' I said. I was
sitting at his feet, he reclined on a low divan covered with
oriental cushions and embroidered cloths. I seized his hand,
which is fine as a woman's, the nails immaculately filed and
trimmed, indeed I think he takes greater care of his person than
either Mary or I have ever done. I pressed his hand to my lips.
'Send me away, if you insist. I'll do whatever you like. I should
hate to be a burden to you.'

But he was in another world, brooding on his wrongs, his
noble profile turned away from me, his eyes hooded, unseeing.
'Go or stay, it's all the same to me,' he said wearily.

I leaned my cheek on his hand, which lay listlessly in my own. Then, reckless, inspired, I drew his hand to my breast, to my heart, pressing it against the fine silk (I was wearing Mary's long pale green dress which Shelley had made for her in Bond Street). He seemed unconscious of my daring act, but he did not draw his hand away, and after a minute or two his fingers began to stroke and fondle my breast as if absentmindedly, and I was sure he would not send me away.

'I promise that I will not stay the night,' I murmured. 'I'll be gone before morning.'

'You can have Poli's room,' his lordship said, then he called rudely, 'Poli, here, Poli,' and Poli appeared instantly, as if he had been waiting just within earshot, but of course that is his duty, as personal physician to his lordship. 'Poli, will you let Miss Clairmont have your room. She'll be staying tonight.'

'Certainly, your lordship,' said Poli, blushing crimson. His lordship's hand was quite visibly straying in my bosom. And where I wonder was poor Poli to sleep? On the hearthrug, no doubt. 'Come to bed, then,' said his lordship, and he took a candle and led the way upstairs, with me following demurely, and Poli a few steps behind.

'I'll just remove one or two things,' Poli said, still acutely embarrassed. His room is adjacent to Albé's, with interconnecting doors, and a separate door to the hallway.

'Poli doesn't want you to read his diary,' said his lordship. 'Isn't that right, Poli?'

Again Poli blushed, poor thing. I felt quite sorry for him. 'I'm sure Miss Clairmont could have no interest in my diary,' he said, but he must have removed it, because when I went into his room later it was nowhere to be found.

Albé set the candle down on a low table next to the bed and tossed me a silk nightshirt and a thick Turkish robe. I stood there holding them, feeling foolish, not knowing whether he wanted me to undress and change into night clothes or to stay as I was. His bed like the divan downstairs is covered with oriental cloths and cushions, and the sheets and pillow cases are silk, for he will have nothing next to his skin but the finest cloth, silk or cashmere. He began to disrobe . . .

I am now called away by Mary, who must tell me about a dream she has had – why this can't wait is a mystery to me.

Sunday, July 14th Too much has happened, too quickly, for me to record in any sensible order. We all had dinner at Diodati again last night, then I stayed behind as usual when Mary and Shelley returned to Montalègre, no questions asked, everyone in high good humour, including Albé. I am now copying the stanzas Albé wrote during his trip round the lake with Shelley; this is my regular chore, and also my excuse for coming and going as I please. (I wonder for whom these rituals are enacted!) I have the use of Poli's room, which has a fine writing desk and supplies of pen and ink, whenever I like, or, I should say, for as long as Albé remains so disposed. For let me have no illusions, my present happiness is entirely a function of his lordship's whim, and can alter as his whim alters.

Shelley addressed me very sternly on the subject this morning, when I returned from Diodati. I was longing for a bath, for although his lordship tells me to make myself comfortable, I cannot ask Fletcher to bring hot water at six in the morning. But poor S. was so serious that I could not put him off, and I followed him meekly into the little room he uses as his study and seated myself opposite him, waiting to be lectured. My anxious friend was pacing nervously, combing his wild hair with his fingers, determined to convince me of his sincerity. And, oh dear, he is so kind and concerned, and has so little notion of the true dimensions of this affair . . .

'I want you to know, Clara mia,' he began, 'that you can count on me. Also on Mary – No, do not turn away from me – '

'It is very good of you to offer advice,' I said. 'But you need not worry about me.'

'So you say. But life is unpredictable, dear girl. The truth is, whatever his virtues – and we agree that they are very great – you cannot count on Albé in the same way that you can on us. To us you are sister, friend, comrade – to me you are more than all these.'

'How little you trust me!' I exclaimed. Then I added, 'You have no idea how happy I am . . .'

'Ah, Clara – I can see you are happy.' This rather mournfully.

'But you insist on telling me that it will not last. And what if I don't care whether it lasts?'

Earnestly taking my hand: 'You are a wonderful girl, Clara. I would not presume to advise you. But I am deeply interested in your well-being – in your future. If you need me, I am here. You are the dearest person in the world to me, next to Mary.'

I threw my arms about him and kissed him. 'And you are one of the very dearest people in the world to me.'

How surprising it would be if Albé were to say, 'I want you to know that you can depend on me, always,' or, 'You are the dearest person in the world to me.' How grateful I should be if he said, 'I'm growing rather fond of you, Clara mia.' But his attitude seems to be: you as well as another. And the truth is I am happy to serve him; I would follow him to the ends of the earth. Oh, Clara, Clara, where have your fine ideals gone, your belief in freedom, equality, independence? Vanished into thin air. I am in a state of bondage which I would not exchange for any form of worldly power and dominion. For hours after he – makes love to me, I would say, but if I am to be honest, I would have to say, after he has his way with me – I am in a state of high exaltation. Nothing can touch me, nothing can alter this strange wholeness of being, which has its centre in my sex, and radiates outward through my entire body.

Yet it is a contradiction of every principle I hold sacred to allow myself to be so much in the power of another human being. I revel in the feeling of self-abasement – yet I do not feel demeaned, or injured; on the contrary, I feel privileged above other women, and men too, who would give their soul to be in my place.

Shelley insists on the need for equality between men and women. Unless there is equality, he says, the 'inferior' one is perpetually insecure and resentful, and the 'superior' one tires even of adulation. Where there is equality, love of the 'other' is securely founded on self-love and self-respect. Mary solemnly agrees, and they both quote copiously from the sacred writings of Mary Wollstonecraft. But I do not see much equality in their relations; on the contrary, Mary leads him by the nose. They are equal only in their refusal to see what is so obvious to any outsider.

Where do the great philosophers stand on this issue? I do not think that 'equality' figures at all in Plato's discussion of love. If, as Plato says, the essence of love is to long for that which we do not possess, then love must be of the lesser for the greater. We worship that which is beyond our grasp. Shelley concedes that it is natural for a man to love qualities in a woman which he lacks – beauty, serenity, clarity of intellect. But he will not admit that it is equally natural for a woman to love those qualities in a man which she can never possess: physical strength, a spirit of devilry, above all, worldly knowledge and experience. S. assumes that a woman can experience life as fully and freely as a man can. Everything in society teaches us otherwise. Even if a woman is compelled to keep herself, she will seek out a protector; she cannot set forth cheerfully into life as a man can, trusting to his wits to survive, meanwhile gaining experience of life in all its infinite variety.

In any case, how could I presume to compare myself to Albé, the greatest poet of the age, the darling of society, 'the glass of fashion and the mould of form'? Shelley himself is in awe of Albé, defers to him, is at his beck and call. There must be such a thing as *natural* superiority, which men and women alike recognise and love when they are in its presence. It is only the artificial superiority of money and rank which is wicked, and must be resisted.

No, equality in love between a man and a woman is a chimera. Either the man idealises the woman, investing her with qualities that are purely a product of his imagination, or he treats her like a toy, uses her and discards her. As for the woman, she would grow bored if she felt the man was no more interesting than she was, had not felt more, experienced more, thought more deeply on life.

Yet if there is not equality, there may be a balance of complementary qualities, which works to the advantage of both the man and the woman. I have noticed that men of genius often have a terror of going mad (as if from excess of mental activity) and at the same time are drawn irresistibly to those mental states of exhilaration and heightened perception which tend to approach madness. Such men indulge in a kind of reckless experimentation, a readiness to try anything new; they take each experience to its furthest limit, even if it means risking death. This is very marked in Albé, who more than once has announced to the world: Well if I die, so be it. I am convinced that women are far more prudent than men in this respect. Mary and I, though so unlike in other ways, are alike in this, that we both have our feet solidly on the ground, we both observe very closely the distinction between reality and fantasy.

When Shelley takes laudanum, for instance, as he does almost daily for the pain in his side, he actually welcomes the blurring of the line that separates the real and the dream worlds. The other night he tried to describe the sensation to us. He said he drifts into a timeless world in which colours and sounds have an intensity which is physically painful. Yet, having once entered this world, he longs afterwards to return to it. For compared to the sharpness, clarity and brilliance of the dream, ordinary life is dull and lacking in focus.

Albé does not take laudanum or spirits, but his vision and hearing are extremely acute, and I am sure he sees and hears things that pass me by entirely. I am just an ordinary little woman whose sole distinction lies in the power to love one person, and so to participate, however briefly, in his world, his being, his thoughts. Shelley pities me, Mary is appalled at my lack of pride – but I tell myself a hundred times a day that I am the most fortunate of women.

FANNY
July 1816, Skinner Street, Holborn

Monday, July 1st Today I gathered up my courage to tackle Papa on the forbidden subject. I made an appointment with him for seven in the evening.

At seven precisely, I knocked on his door, and after a minute he asked me to enter. He was sitting at his desk, which was covered with books and papers; he had wrapped a plaid shawl over his shoulders, which he brought from Ireland fifteen years ago, when we were little. As usual, there were books spilling out of the shelves and on to the fireside chair and piled in stacks along the wall. A coal fire glowed in the grate (he has complained bitterly of the unseasonable cold; everyone says it is the worst summer in memory). His thin grey hair was combed down severely on his forehead. I could tell immediately that he was in a bad mood.

'I must speak to you, Papa, whether or not you listen,' I said.

'I am listening.' He would not look directly at me, but fiddled with his pen and papers.

'I do not like to disobey you, Papa. I have always tried to do as you asked. But I cannot go on in this way. I must ask you – how long do you mean to stop us from mentioning my sister's name?'

He frowned and looked as grim as possible. 'I told you before. I do not want her name to be spoken in this house.'

I came behind the desk, threw myself at his feet and clasped his knees. 'I beg you to relent, Papa dear. You are making us all miserable. I implore you, forgive her, take her once more to your heart – for her sake, for the sake of her little boy, for your own sake.'

'There is nothing to forgive. She has made her choice, now she must live with the consequences. I have told her that as long as she persists in her folly she is not to consider herself my daughter.'

'But, Papa dearest, she is your daughter, your darling, and she loves you and reveres you above all others. She doesn't speak of it, she is too proud to ask you to change your mind. Indeed, she is very much like her Papa in her pride. But I know how terrible it is for her to be forced to choose between the two people she loves best in the world. Her child is your namesake – and you have never seen him, never held him in your arms. And oh, Papa dear, what if she has another child? Unless she is reconciled to you I truly believe it may kill her.'

I lifted my eyes to the portrait above his desk. *As childbirth killed our mother*, I would have said, but I did not dare.

He set me aside, rose and paced angrily to and fro.

'You understand nothing of these things, Fanny,' he said. 'She has placed herself under the protection of a man who abused my confidence and my hospitality. A man I trusted and loved as if he were my son. I have made my position clear. There is nothing further to say.'

I fought back tears. I know how he despises women when they use tears as a form of blackmail. 'If they return to England,' I said, keeping my voice steady with a tremendous effort, 'they will want a home, and the support of loving friends. Mary is my sister. I shall offer her a sister's love.'

Now he looked at me, with a look of thunder. 'What you do is your own business,' he said. 'I do not wish to know anything about it.'

And so the tears would come, do what I could to prevent them. Total and utter defeat. He knows as well as I do that what Mary needs is the love not of a sister but a father.

Tuesday, July 2nd This morning, my copying was set out as usual. No reference was made to what had passed between us. I gave William Jr. his lessons, losing my temper once when he stumbled three times running in his Latin conjugations. He looks more and more like his mama, red-faced and sullen, without a spark of imagination. As for his mama, she barely speaks to me nowadays, except to give orders for dinner, or the cleaning.

In the evening I was summoned to Papa's study. 'I have had a letter from your Aunt Everina,' he said. 'She writes that they require a teacher for their school in Dublin.'

My heart was pounding. They want to send me away! I waited for him to continue. His brow was furrowed and his mouth set in a thin line. Though he was talking to me, he regarded only the papers on his desk.

'They can pay only thirty pounds a year, but you would have your room and board and you might be able to take one or two private pupils as well. You would be in charge of a dozen girls, aged nine to fourteen.'

I said nothing.

'We must take some decision about your future, Fanny,' he said at last. 'You cannot stay at home indefinitely; you can see how pressed we are. And it is time that William went to school.'

'I did not know you were thinking of school for William.' I could not conceal the note of reproach in my voice.

'He should have the company of other boys. It is not right for him to be brought up in a house of women. And you will not always be here to tutor him.'

Why, where then should I be? I thought.

'Your aunt will be coming to London in two weeks. The decision is entirely up to you, of course. But I would point out to you the advantages of earning your living. You have a facility for teaching, you are industrious and hard-working, and I am sure you would do well.' He did not have to add: You can see all around you the disadvantages of dependency.

Thursday, July 11th Letter from Mary requesting Coleridge's Poems. In the hallway, as I am on my way out, Madame Spy calls from within the shop.

'Are you going somewhere, Frances?'

Her face is high-coloured, her eyes small and spiteful.

'I have some errands to do, Mama,' I say.

'For your sister?'

I remain silent.

She is in the hallway, hands on her hips. 'You are not honest with us, Frances. Your father dislikes dissimulation above all.'

'I have tried to speak frankly to Papa. He will not listen.'

'He knows that you disobey him. You sneak out behind his back. You are in constant communication with them.'

Thank God for that, I whisper under my breath.

'We cannot go on like this much longer, Frances.'

'What do you want me to do?'

'It is not up to me. But we are arranging for William to start at Dr Burney's Academy in Greenwich in September, and you will need to discuss your future with your father.'

My future . . . what future have I in this house? 'I shall do as he tells me,' I say.

'You are a strange girl, Frances. You appear dutiful and obedient, but underneath you are as stubborn as the others.'

I longed to walk out of the house. It was a battle of wills between us; she was determined to keep me standing there as long as she could. Finally I asked if she wished me to do any errands for her.

'No, but I should like your help in the shop. I trust you will be back before noon.'

How cruel, to insinuate that no one needs me, now or ever, and to keep me tied, bound hand and foot! I fled the house into the busy street, with womanish tears coursing down my cheeks. Nobody appeared to notice. Am I to be denied the right to serve the only people on earth I love, the only people on earth who love me?

Monday, July 15th I have determined to make a study of my mother's writings. Papa has supplied me with her 'Thoughts on the Education of Daughters', which she wrote when she was a governess for Lady Kingsborough, and a book of Lessons written after I was born and including a history of my first months of life, which she intended to apply to my early education. He has also given me *Mary: a Novel*, which he says she wrote as a warning to women not to devote their lives to service to a man – enslavement was the term she used – but rather to become full human beings in their own right. Papa says that the events in the novel are all drawn from circumstances in my mother's life or the lives of her friends and acquaintances. Papa said that when I am finished with these he will give me *The Wrongs of Woman*, which was the last thing she wrote before she died, and this too, he said, contains material drawn from her own life.

I asked Papa if he would give me fifteen minutes of his time to discuss these writings as I finish reading them, and he promised that he would set aside a portion of next Friday evening for this purpose.

I should like to conduct my life so as not to be unworthy of such a mother.

Saturday, July 20th I finished all the books Papa gave me by Friday afternoon, but at six he sent me a short note (which Willy delivered) saying that unfortunately his services were required elsewhere, and putting off our discussion to next week. Willy obligingly told me that Papa was going through some papers with Mama, which I suppose accounts for the services required elsewhere.

Mama says that Mary and Jane laugh at me because I take everything so seriously, and because I weep over novels. It is true that I have many faults of character, of which the worst, probably, is a tendency to feel sorry for myself. Indeed, I feel such a heaviness at my heart, such a lethargy of spirits, that any activity seems a chore. This has been true since Mary and Jane left me alone in this house, or virtually alone, two years ago – for I have no one I can confide in, no sympathetic ear, no heart to which I can unbosom my feelings. Still, it is unkind of them to laugh at me. Jane has always had a sharp tongue, and often used to call me a crybaby. But happiness should make people generous, and Mary surely could spare a tender thought for her unhappy sister.

Monday, July 22nd Papa allowed me exactly fifteen minutes of his time.

'You will have observed that your mother's guiding principle of life was independence,' he said. 'She wanted her daughters to think for themselves, to grow into strong, confident women. She believed in a healthy diet, regular exercise, a balance between study and play, and the continual fostering of curiosity about the natural world and human society. She also believed that economic independence was essential for women if they were not to be either the slaves or the playthings of men.'

I nerved myself to ask the question that was trembling on my lips from the time I entered Papa's study.

'Then why, Papa, were we not brought up according to our mother's principles?'

'Because, Fanny, your stepmother did not see eye to eye with your mother on all things. As she was to have the chief care of raising the children, I did not think it right to interfere.

'Also, the times have changed. Your circumstances are very different from your mother's. Her father inherited a modest fortune, but dissipated it in gambling; he was violent and abusive, dissolute and tyrannical. Her mother was a slave to her husband and worn out by childbearing; she doted on her eldest son and ignored the other children, and the eldest son became a deputy tyrant in the father's absence. Your mother's only chance of freedom was to escape from her family, and then to assist her younger sisters to escape. But you have been raised among congenial people of liberal thought and affectionate manners; no one has ever restricted your ideas or forbidden you to do anything you desired. Isn't that so, Fanny? Correct me if I am mistaken.'

I remained silent, for the very good reason that I did not trust myself to speak. But several questions rose to mind: Why, if my mother believed independence to be essential for women, have I not been trained to earn my own living? Why am I limited to the same bitter choices that she faced, to be a governess, a teacher, or companion to an elderly widow?

'I wish I felt more independent,' I said. 'I do not feel at all confident of being able to make my own way.'

'Your mother was a very remarkable woman,' he said. 'But you must not think that she was cold and ambitious. She was a woman of passionate feelings, tender-hearted and emotional. She was also exceptionally fortunate in some ways; she met

Johnson the bookseller just when she needed a friend and benefactor: he encouraged her in her writing, and she had the start she needed. Mary seems to have inherited her gift for writing, and I trust she will be able to turn that to advantage.'

'Do you think I have inherited any of her qualities?' I asked.

He bit his lip angrily; I think he must have remembered that he had forbidden Mary's name to be mentioned.

'She had a tendency towards melancholia, which I fear you may have inherited,' he said. 'She was also very fond of duty, at least in her early years, before I knew her. I am not sure that you can inherit a love of duty, but I believe it is a strong element in your character.'

'Do you think it is a fault in my character?'

'It is a matter of balance. An excessive attachment to duty would not be desirable. I am sure your mother would have wished you to enjoy a healthy self-esteem and to have a proper regard for your self-interest.'

'Do you say I am lacking in self-esteem?'

He hesitated. 'I do not wish to answer with a yes or no, Fanny.' He glanced at his watch.

Instantly I rose from my chair. 'Thank you for your time, Papa,' I said.

'Not at all, Fanny.' He turned to the papers on his desk.

'May I have the other writings, *The Wrongs of Woman*, and any others that I have not yet read?'

'I shall leave them for you in the shop tomorrow,' he said. I was dismissed, and left quietly, shutting the door behind me.

Upstairs in my room I flung myself on my bed and wept. I know he does not mean to be cruel; he believes that women, like men, are rational beings who are capable of acting in their own best interest, rationally conceived. But talking to him is like talking to a stone. At last I washed my face and considered my position. I made some resolutions which I have written down, as follows:

I will try to be more cheerful.

I will read my mother's writings for an hour each day.

I will also read the works of Rousseau and Thomas Paine.

I will stop eating meat, for Shelley says that animal food impairs the faculties and coarsens the blood.
I will walk for at least an hour each day.

Wednesday, July 24th Today is the first day of Aunt Everina's long-expected visit. Everyone is in a fever of irritability. Aunt Everina has grown even more prune-faced and angular; she has a booming, stentorian voice which sets everyone on edge. She is accustomed to ordering her pupils about and she makes no distinction between her young charges and her relations, even Papa, who is not accustomed to such treatment. She wears a coarse black dress, black laced boots, and a black bonnet which she could not be persuaded to remove even in the dining room. She does not seem in any way to resemble my mother, though she is my mother's sister and her nearest relation.

At dinner she launched into an examination of Papa on the conduct and present whereabouts of his daughters. 'But is it true that they are both living with a married man in Switzerland?' she demanded. 'It may seem extraordinary that my eighteen-year-old niece should be gossiped about on the streets of Dublin, but I assure you that is the case.'

Papa frowned and looked very severe indeed. 'I would prefer that the subject not be discussed at my table,' he said.

'No doubt that is what you prefer,' Aunt continued. 'But I keep a respectable school for young ladies in Dublin, and I cannot afford to have my nieces gossiped about, especially if one of them is to become a teacher at my school.'

I looked resolutely down at my plate.

'I am sure that Fanny is not being gossiped about in the streets of Dublin,' Papa said icily.

Aunt sailed on. 'That is all one to me. I cannot afford to have any of my nieces gossiped about, and I insist that you see that the girls return home at once.'

Mama was turning quite red with the effort to remain silent, and finally burst out: 'You seem to have no regard to our feelings in this matter, my feelings in particular as a mother.'

'Your feelings are of no interest to me,' Aunt boomed. 'I am addressing my remarks to William, and they are for William to answer.'

'Perhaps we should withdraw to my study,' Papa said in his calmest, most reasonable tone.

'With pleasure,' said Aunt, and swept before him, leaving us to the debris of the table, the boiled pork and cabbage congealing on the platter.

'Are you not eating any dinner, Frances?' said Mama.

'I have decided to take a vegetable diet,' I said.

'Well then, you must go hungry, or shift for yourself. I do not propose to spend money for meat which you leave untouched on the plate.'

'I am sorry if I put you to extra expense.'

'But you do put me to extra expense, Frances. Like anyone else you must have clothes and linen and soap, you too must be able to travel and to go to the play – '

'Go to the play!' I exclaimed under my breath. 'When do I ever go to the play?'

'Never mind. I certainly do not begrudge you your pleasure. But pleasure costs money, and money is the one thing we do not have. You might put your mind to the problem, Frances, instead of shutting yourself up in your room and reading sentimental novels.'

Suddenly I could bear it no longer, and I rushed out of the room, downstairs and out the front door, just as I was. I took several deep breaths to calm myself, then I walked past Newgate Prison, averting my head from the dreadful sight of the prisoners being brought in, shackled one to another, then down to Ludgate Hill, and I stood outside the coffee house where Mary and I met Shelley so many times. I wished that I had the courage to go inside and sit by myself at a table, but I was afraid of being stared at. Instead I went into St Paul's Cathedral and sat at the back for half an hour, where it was dark and cool, and I kept thinking Oh what am I to do, how am I to earn a living, for Aunt Everina I am sure will not want me to teach at her school.

Thursday, July 25th At last a letter from Jane, which I shall answer this afternoon.

4th July, Montalègre

My dear Fanny,

We are happily installed in a little villa by the shore of Lake Geneva, I do not know how long we shall remain here but it is a kind of Paradise at the moment, and I am very sorry to think of you remaining in cold and rainy London while we are enjoying fine sunny days (at least we did until two days ago, since when it has rained in torrents without stopping) and genial companionship.

I am so sorry we had to leave for Geneva without telling you fully of our plans, but secrecy was essential and we did not know until the night before that we were actually leaving. Mama is quite wrong to say that you are the butt of our laughter, indeed we love you dearly and speak of you most affectionately.

I shall try to describe Lord B. for you, but it is impossible to convey an adequate notion of his genius and charm. We see him every day, sometimes twice a day, and he has asked me to copy out the Poem he is now engaged upon. I have a corner of the Villa Diodati to use for my copying. He calls me 'Clara' (upon my instruction, you will guess), which I consider far more European than 'Jane', and I have prevailed upon Mary not to betray me – there is no need for Skinner Street to know, though Mama has Swiss relations, and I hope to meet them (as Clara, *bien sûr*) if we should travel to their *canton*.

Lord B.'s villa is very grand indeed, more like a palace than a villa. It is furnished with antiquities and Eastern rugs and tapestries. He has an entire menagerie of birds and other creatures wandering about in the gardens and even in the house; they are quite tame but still it is rather startling to come upon a peacock as one is turning a corner of the stairs. Lord B. looks exactly as he does in his portraits; he has dark brown curly hair and brilliant green eyes with long graceful lashes (the contrast between his light-coloured eyes and the long dark lashes is very beautiful), a Roman nose and sensuous lips. He is of average height and his limp is not very noticeable, although he is extremely sensitive about it and makes a great effort to keep his 'good' side to his walking companion. He prefers riding to walking, and swimming to both. He has a very melancholy streak and sometimes lapses into a brooding silence which is quite terrifying as one does not dare to interrupt it with a foolish question, but most of the time he talks to us with the utmost frankness, and he takes a great interest in Shelley whom he regards as his particular friend. Shelley says he is the greatest poet of the age, and he cannot understand why he (Lord Byron, that is) is reluctant to undertake a project worthy of his genius. Shelley would like him to write a poem on the French Revolution, which S. thinks is the great topic of the times. I often congratulate myself on being the agent of their meeting, for I knew that they would have much to talk about, which has proved to be the case, and Lord B. (who did not know Shelley's poetry before) has made a point of reading all that S. has given him, and has commented most favourably on it.

Well, Fanny dear, you will not be angry with me any longer, will you? Try to be more cheerful, and write to me as soon as you can, with news of everyone. Mary and Shelley send their most affectionate regards; they have promised to write separately, so you can expect a regular parade of letters with news and gossip.

Your affectionate,
Clara Mary Jane

Friday, July 26th I decided to skip dinner again, and so have a slight headache, but I am sure it is good for me to eat less. Shelley says he can live for an entire day on raisins and a loaf of bread. In the afternoon I compose an answer to Jane.

My dear Jane,
I was very pleased to receive your letter, which took less than three weeks to arrive, and I shall try not to be angry, though I do think you and Mary could have taken me into your confidence more than you have. Things here are as they were when I last wrote, though after a spell of unusually cold days we have had a

few days of fine weather which always makes life more bearable. I am afraid the fine weather has not been felt within-doors, however. Your Mama goes about in a state of perpetual annoyance, and Papa is oppressed by his debts and can see no solution to his difficulties unless Shelley can come to his aid. This seems to me a most unreasonable hope unless he can bring himself to unbend towards Mary, but you know how stubborn he is, and he refuses to see any connection between the two things. And so we go on in the same round.

I have tried to imagine what it must be like to listen to two poets conversing about the subjects closest to their hearts. I wonder if I might beg a favour: do you think you could make a second copy of the poem you are copying for Lord B., and if he could inscribe it for me that would be most gratifying. I do think there is nothing more sublime than poetry, which enables us to forget our own small worries in the contemplation of beauty.

Would you tell Mary that our Aunt Everina has been to visit, and there is talk of my going to Dublin to teach at her school, but I suspect nothing will come of it.

Mr Owen has been here to talk with Papa about Equality. He believes that if one small community in which property and duties are shared equally among all members can be shown to be successful, then the example will spread everywhere within a very short time, and the rich will all be persuaded to give up their property to the poor. Alas, the contrast between Mr Owen's optimism and the misery only fifty yards from our door is very striking – ragged children begging on the street and their poor half-naked mothers selling their bodies to wealthy men from the City or sailors who have just been paid, and everywhere vice and degradation. But such is London, and such it has been and such it will be for many years yet.

Well, I do seem to run into melancholy thoughts however cheerfully I begin. Tell Mary I will answer her letter as soon as I receive it, and give little Willmouse a special hug from his Aunt, and believe me,

ever your affectionate
Fanny

Thursday, August 1st I am definitely conscious of a decrease of appetite. For three days now I have followed a strict regimen. For breakfast, a dish of coffee and hot milk; for dinner, cheese and a piece of fruit; for tea, a slice of bread and butter. A slight headache on the first day was replaced yesterday by feelings almost of weightlessness. I find no diminution in my energy or strength, indeed I have more nervous energy, and less need for sleep.

Letter from Mary today, but she adds nothing to Jane's letter, only anxious enquiries about Papa. Of course I write immediately.

1st August, 1816.

My dearest Mary,

I cannot give you good news about Papa. He is worried to death by tradesmen, and unless he can lay hands on £300 he says that all is over for us, he must go to prison and his house and goods will be confiscated. I cannot believe that things are as bad as this, but Mama also goes about with a face of gloom, and does not hold out hope for the usual miracle. However, both Lamb and Mr Owen have been to see us, and I am sure that money will somehow be found, at least to tide us over.

You are not to worry about this, as there is nothing you can do – unless Shelley suddenly comes into his fortune, which I am afraid Papa is secretly counting on in his heart of hearts. You and I know better, but I cannot speak frankly to Papa, he is as stubborn as ever and will not listen.

Aunt Everina has been and gone. There was talk of a post for me in her school in Dublin, but much to my relief the subject was dropped. Still, I wonder what I am to do for money. I do not see why I could not advertise for pupils, but Mama says there is no room here to give lessons; still I could go to people's houses if necessary.

I have prevailed upon Papa to provide me with our mother's writings, which I have been reading every day. I am full of admiration for her genius. She had a rare combination of intellect and feeling which manifests itself in every line. Is it not strange that we should have known so little about her earlier life and her writings before Shelley told us of them? My greatest wish is to live my life in such a way as not to dishonour her example.

I am delighted to hear of Willy's progress. He is an enchanting little man; do tell him his Aunt Fanny said so, and kiss him for me again and again. You do not need to apologise for Shelley. I do not expect him to write to me separately, but I am very glad to hear that he is recovering from the pain in his side and I trust that the clear mountain air and the beauty of the natural scene will soon restore his spirits. I have asked Jane if she could copy out Lord B.'s new poem for me. Perhaps you could also procure copies for me of the poems Shelley and Lord B. composed during their boat trip around Lake Geneva. I have several of Lord B.'s poems by heart, and it would please me greatly if you could let me have a detailed account of his manner, his countenance, and his speaking voice, which for me is always a good indication of character.

Mary dear, both you and Jane accuse me of a want of cheerfulness, but I assure you I am trying very hard not to give in to melancholy, which Papa says is our family curse. I have embarked on a diet according to Shelley's plan which seems to be providing some relief, and if it were not for the scenes of sorrow which are to be witnessed daily both on the London streets and at home I am sure I could be as gay as Wordsworth's linnet, 'Scattering gladness without care.'

Please write to me again as soon as you can spare the time. Letters seem to take ten days to two weeks on the road. Believe me, ever,

your affectionate sister,
Fanny

Saturday, August 24th At last a letter from my dear sister, written at the end of July.

Dearest Fanny,

We shall be leaving here the first week in September, arriving in Portsmouth (we hope) by September 9th or 10th. If you can procure the following supplies, I should be very grateful, since it is impossible to buy anything of quality here, and we shall arrive virtually naked and penniless.

5yds cambric muslin, which you can get at Maltby's in Holborn, the smallest and plainest pattern you can find.

5yds fine white linen, from Mr Horrocks in Bond St.

2 suits of warm clothes for Willy – I leave the choice to you.

Overmantles for Jane and myself, blue or green velvet (Smith's of Holborn carries these), hats to match if possible.

I should also like to have the volumes of *Clarissa Harlowe* which you will find on the top left-hand shelf in Papa's study. *Do not tell him they are for me.*

We shall have news to impart when we see you. Probably Jane and I shall not go directly to London, but Shelley will certainly do so, and will let you know where you can deliver the above to him at the earliest convenient time.

In haste,
Mary

Yes, my darlings, everything you need shall be ready for you. And oh my heart, poor throbbing heart, in less than a month my darlings will be in England, and I shall leave this place for ever.

HARRIET

1815–1816, Chapel Street, Grosvenor Square

To Mrs Boinville,
Bracknell.

15th January, 1815.

Dear Mrs Boinville,

It is as you predicted. How I wish I had taken your advice, but what was I to do? I have seen Mr Shelley once since poor little

Charles came into the world two months ago; he is interested only in obtaining money from me. Yet how often he professed undying love and tenderness to me and to our dear Ianthe. I believe he is bewitched by Miss Godwin.

I am still at my father's, which is very wretched. I cannot bring myself to leave my room, yet I do nothing but brood on the past, and when I see Ianthe watching me with her great sad eyes I cannot stop my tears. Eliza says the children will be better off in the country, away from me. We have a nurse for Charles, but he remains very sickly and cries a great deal.

When I shall quit this house I know not. Everything goes against me. I am weary of my life. I am so restrained here that life is scarcely worth having. I wish I could come to you – I would do everything to make you happy. For myself happiness is fled, I live for others. At nineteen I could descend a willing victim to the tomb.

Is it wrong, do you think, to put an end to one's sorrow? I often think of it – all is so gloomy and desolate.

Please write and tell me what you think of this, and be assured that you are ever in the thoughts of

your unhappy Harriet S.

7th February, 1815.

Dear Mrs Boinville,

Thank you for your kind words. You are right – I shall live, it would be selfish to think only of myself. I am a mother – my children depend on me – I must not give in to the temptation to seek an early grave. Yet how hard it is to live without love, to waken each day to the knowledge that I am not loved. I would like to return to Ireland, perhaps in the spring I can persuade my sister Eliza to accompany me. I believe I still have friends there, and I am sure a change of scene will revive my spirits.

You do not say whether your chest is better. I trust you keep flannel on at all times, and you must be sure to keep out of draughts. Here we have a fire in each room, and one does not like to go out of doors, the air in London is so thick and dirty.

Eliza has prevailed upon me to send the children to friends in Shropshire; this will be for a short time only, I trust, to enable me to regain my strength.

My sister joins me in sending her warm regards. Please believe me your ever-devoted and grateful friend

Harriet S.

To Mrs Catherine Nugent,
St Stephen's Green,
Dublin.

20th April, 1815.

Dear Mrs Nugent,

I cannot tell you how happy it made me to see your beloved handwriting again, after two years of silence. I am so glad that you and your sister are well, and that your sister is fully recovered from her lumbago. Your cottage sounds delightful, and I trust you will both enjoy many years of good health in the mild climate and pleasant environs of Galway.

Your letter brought back to me vividly those happy weeks we spent together in Dublin. Oh, my dear Mrs Nugent, my life is very different now, how changed you can hardly imagine. Mr Shelley has gone – he has left his two small children and their mother to fend for themselves, and if it were not for my dear sister Eliza I do not know what would become of us. We are living in my father's house at Chapel Street, near Grosvenor Square, and the children are staying for the present with friends in Shropshire, where they have fresh air and country food. My father has settled an annuity on us, and he is very good to me, though he cannot disguise his anxiety, and my sister tends to all my wants – but nothing can supply the place of a husband and father. I am sure you remember Mr Shelley with the warmest feelings. Nobody who knew him could help loving him; surely no human being ever was more sympathetic to those less fortunate than himself – he was always ready to rescue the poor and the oppressed, his actions were always good and selfless, his enthusiasms those of a noble heart. I pray nightly for his return – but I have seen him only once during the past six months, and since that time not a word has he sent me, not a single enquiry as to the health and well-being of his beautiful children, except through his solicitor Mr Whitton. Little did I suspect that a man so tender in his feelings would ever be capable of such cruel neglect. But we must bear our fate, however hard.

Dear Mrs Nugent, please write to me again with news of yourself and your family. How I wish I could see you and fold you to my heart!

Believe me, ever,
your unhappy Harriet S.

12th June, 1815.

Dear Mrs Nugent,

Yes, I agree entirely that we shouldn't have made peace at such a price. France is to continue the slave trade for another seven years, and I cannot bear to think of the misery which the poor Africans will suffer as a consequence of Lord Castlereagh's treachery – husbands and wives, mothers and children forcibly torn apart, never to see one another again, shackled and imprisoned, then sent to their death or to a horrible enslavement across the sea. Do you think it would help if we refused to take sugar with our tea? I for one would be happy to take honey instead, if I thought this could contribute to the ending once and for all of such a despicable practice.

I am afraid I am as before. Mr Shelley is living with the two daughters of Mr Godwin, one by Mary Wollstonecraft, the other the daughter of Mrs Clairmont, Mr Godwin's present wife. It is all because of Mr Godwin's book *Political Justice*, which though it was my Bible too for a time is full of pernicious ideas attacking marriage and preaching free love.

A year ago Mr Shelley spent a month alone in London trying to raise money to pay Mr Godwin's debts. Mr Shelley believed that his expectation of inheriting his grandfather's fortune conferred upon him the strongest duty to help his friends; he never regarded this money as his own by right. When he saw that Mr Godwin, whose entire life was devoted to furthering the cause of

Harriet 37

political liberty, justice, and equality, was being hounded by
creditors, he felt it was incumbent upon him to rescue his friend
and mentor.

Alas, it was during this time that Mary, the younger daughter,
who was educated in the wicked ideas of her mother and father
regarding marriage, met Mr Shelley and determined to seduce
him. Disregarding the fact that he was already a husband and
father, she insisted that he accompany her to her mother's grave
in St Pancras Churchyard, where she produced a bottle of
laudanum and threatened to kill herself unless he promised to
elope with her to France. Terrified by her passion, he agreed to
all her demands. He wrote to me urgently, asking me to come at
once to London from Bath, where I was then residing with my
sister. I hastened immediately to London, and protested most
vehemently against his mad plans. I believe that Mr Godwin,
rather than supporting his daughter, also urged Mr Shelley in the
strongest possible terms not to proceed with an act of folly which
would have irreversible consequences for all concerned.

Mr Shelley insisted that he still loved me, and he proposed
that we might all live together, I as his sister and Mr Godwin's
daughter as his wife. He said that his love for Mr Godwin's
daughter was founded on an ungovernable passion, while his
love for me had always been founded on friendship and respect.
He had wished to form my mind and guide my heart, and he
wished still to do so if I would consent. He was haggard and
feverish, and his aspect was wild, and I feared to incense him
further and perhaps to risk convulsions. I said that I would
remain his friend, and I assured him that I did not blame him for
his actions, hurtful though they might be to me and to our year-
old daughter, darling Ianthe, but I could see that he was in the
grip of an irrational frenzy, and I sincerely hoped that it would
pass, and that he would return to me, his true wife.

You can imagine the effort it cost me to remain calm and self-
possessed, and indeed on my return to Bath I was laid up in bed
for a fortnight. Alas, my pleas and my tears had no effect, and
news soon arrived that he had gone off with Godwin's daughters
to France. I wished to die, I begged my sister to procure lauda-

num. She remonstrated with me that my first duty was to my precious Ianthe and also to myself. For although Mr Shelley claimed that I was no longer his wife, he was still a husband to me, and I was with child by him.

I agreed to live; thanks to an excellent constitution I survived. Mr Shelley visited me the following November, a week after I was safely delivered of a son. He was in desperate need of money, for his expectations were tied up in law suits, and he was unable to procure any funds even on post-obit. I gave him fifty pounds, which was all the money I had on hand. He has since been to see me only when he needs money. He cares not for his children or for their mother. He is not well; he complains about a pain in his side, and is convinced that he is suffering from the late stages of tuberculosis. Indeed, I fear he is not in his right mind.

Dear Mrs Nugent, how I wish I could visit you and pour out my troubles on your kind bosom. You were ever more than a mother to me. Though I am living in my father's house I am alone and solitary; my sister has taken the children to friends in Shropshire, where they will be boarded for the summer and perhaps longer, for London does not agree with them, and I find that I am too nervous and agitated to nurse them. My father is much occupied with his business and my mother is confined to her bed. I trust you do not find this letter too long and too melancholy, and I sincerely hope you will write again to
your affectionate and unhappy
Harriet S.

Harriet's dream. From her Journal. April 16th, 1816 I dreamed that he came to me about 11 in the morning; I was alone in the house. We sat upstairs in the drawing room on the sofa. He was carrying a bunch of violets.

'These are for you, Harriet,' he said. 'I bought them for a penny from a gypsy at Covent Garden. She said they will bring good luck.'

'I think they will be strewn on my grave,' I said.

'My dear child, why must you be so gloomy?'

'What have I to live for? I have no hope for the future, I can see nothing ahead for me but sorrow and loneliness.'

He took my hands between his.

'Look at me, Harriet. Look at your friend, who cares truly for your welfare.' His tone was indescribably kind. His eyes were bent upon mine, they were filled with tenderness. 'You have everything to live for,' he said. 'You are young and beautiful, and good and true. If only you would trust me once again to help you.'

I could not bear his unaccustomed kindness, and began to weep. 'No,' I said. 'You do not love me, you are merely pretending.'

He folded me to his arms. 'Of course I love you, you silly goose,' he said. 'I have never stopped loving you.' He kissed my tears, my eyes, my lips. Then he murmured, 'Still cold to me?'

I only wept more. But my heart was beating fast. He slipped his hand under my handkerchief, into my bodice.

'I have been very unhappy,' I said.

'No more, my darling,' he said. He unfastened my dress.

'Not here,' I said. 'Let us go up to the bedroom.'

We rose and walked upstairs, and all the time he was supporting me on his arm, for I was half fainting from the intensity of my love, and the pain and delight of discovering that he still loved me. I turned back the covers of the bed and we undressed and lay together, and when he came into me I thought I would die from the joy of it, and all the time I thought with wonder, how could I have been so mistaken? And he was inside me for the longest time, moving and then still, and moving again, and when he finished he looked at me and smiled and said, 'Now do you believe me when I say that I love you?' and I said, 'Yes, I believe you.'

But then I woke up and I was crying and I knew that it was only a dream, and nothing had changed.

TWO
Autumn 1816
Bath/London

Misery – O Misery,
This world is all too wide for thee.
                              Shelley

MARY
September 1816, Abbey Churchyard, Bath

Wednesday, September 11th Shelley has gone to London, and Clare and I are settled in lodgings at Abbey Churchyard, in the shadow of the great cathedral, Clare as Mrs Clairmont, myself as Mrs Shelley, with Elise and little Will our chaperons. We have two bedrooms and a sitting room, and our landlady, Mrs Andrews, will provide dinner. We know nobody in Bath, and propose to keep quietly to ourselves, reading and writing as usual. The city is very genteel and charming, with pleasant vistas of fields and wooded hills rising beyond the graceful stone terraces and crescents. Elise expressed satisfaction with the beds, thank goodness, and is pleased to be in the centre of a town. Clare has been very good so far; whether her pleasant humour will last I very much doubt.

After everyone retired, I wrote my story. To my surprise, it is still fresh to me after a sea voyage of 27 hours, and two days of coach travel on terrible roads. But as soon as I take up my pen I am once more in Geneva, with the lake in turmoil and the storm clouds concealing then revealing the dark frowning Jura. How astonished Papa would be if he knew that I am writing a novel! How I would love to talk with him about the progress of my tormented hero and his creature – I have the example of his *Caleb Williams* always before me – but alas this is not to be, now or ever.

I am sure Papa suffers from his proud unbending nature even more keenly than I do, but he will never admit that he is wrong. I understand him very well. Shelley is confident that they will meet like rational beings, and agree to a reconciliation. After all, what is past is past; Papa hurts nobody but himself by his stubbornness, etc., etc. But I know exactly what will happen. Papa will refuse to see Shelley, but will insist on having the money which he now regards as his right, and will send Fanny to negotiate. Fanny will weep and protest, and in the end will do as she is told. Well, there is nothing to be done.

Thursday, September 12th However unhappy I am at Papa's behaviour, I am forever in his debt, as I realise afresh each day when I sit at my little table, composing my story. He always impressed upon me the necessity of devoting part of each day to reading or writing. It was for this reason that he and my mother kept separate lodgings even after they were married. They wrote in their own apartments for three hours each morning, and again in the afternoon; in the evenings they met only by appointment, and they never went into company as a couple but only as two single people who happened to be together on the same occasion. Whether these arrangements would have lasted long I cannot say. Certainly Papa's arrangements with Madame C. are very different. Madame C. runs the shop and supervises all business arrangements, printing and sales; she presides over her table and her house, but Papa is permitted to entertain his friends in private in his study, to which Madame C. is not allowed entry. I have always suspected that she goes there secretly, when he is out paying visits, or dining with his friends, to spy on his correspondence, and generally to keep herself *au courant*. She would be perfectly capable of rearranging everything precisely as she found it to conceal her presence. It is not jealousy, though Papa was always attracted to women, and remains devoted to the women friends of his youth; it is rather a zeal to manage her household. I shall never be able to understand how Papa, who is so disciplined and methodical in his mental habits, so stern in his personal morality, can be so weak and complaisant as a husband. But so it is, and from that complaisance all our sorrows follow.

Friday, September 13th Clare is a continual source of amazement to me. This morning she set off alone for the Pump Room, having failed to persuade me to accompany her. 'And in your condition,' was on the tip of my tongue, but I would not give her the satisfaction of showing my disapproval. I did remind her, however, that we had agreed before coming here that we would keep quietly to ourselves. 'That is all very well for you,' was her retort, 'but I cannot settle anywhere until I have made a survey of my surroundings. I am like a cat in my habits.' And off she went, having borrowed my green silk dress, which is now extremely tight on her, and my paisley shawl. Meanwhile I must finish unpacking our things, and provide strong coffee for Elise, and arrange for William to have his daily walk, and negotiate with Mrs Andrews for our meals, laundry, etc. It is always the same, I must take responsibility for all of us, and Clare does exactly as she pleases.

Tuesday, September 17th Shelley writes that Papa has refused to see him, which does not surprise me in the least. He has met twice with Fanny, who paints a melancholy picture of life at Skinner Street. She says that if Papa does not have £300 by the 15th of next month he will go to prison, the house and shop will be repossessed, and they will all have to fend for themselves as they can. Papa has cried wolf so many times that it is hard to take this seriously. On the other hand, if S. can secure the money he is determined to do so. Poor Fanny would like to break free, but she is afraid of Madame C. and she will not hurt Papa's feelings. She could certainly advertise for pupils, or for a post as governess or companion, but she must account to Madame for every minute of her time, and any suggestion of putting her own needs first would meet with charges of ingratitude. Shelley says she looks very pale and has no appetite, and he fears she is unwell, and very unhappy.

Wednesday, September 18th Excellent work on my story; wrote three pages today. It is a strange thing, but while I am writing, the persons who constitute my real life – little Willmouse, Shelley, Papa, the nuisance of Clare – recede and take on the unreality of a dream, while my characters, insubstantial creatures of fantasy, become real to me, and assume vivid personality as they move inexorably towards their terrible fate. I am no more than a witness, set here to record their movements. If all else were to disappear, I would still have my pen and paper.

CLARE
September 1816, Bath

Thursday, September 12th I knew from the moment we arrived, tired and bedraggled, looking more like a crew of gypsies than respectable folk, that I would love this enchanting city. Each day confirms my belief that I could not have found a more perfect setting for my new state of life. On our arrival we stayed at a hotel in the Crescent, most elegant and commodious, and affording a splendid view of the Park and the bustling town below. Now we are comfortably installed in lodgings just by the Abbey. Mary has arranged everything, as she always does, and although she is not the pleasantest company, she has exercised noble self-restraint throughout, complaining only once about the prices, once about the food, and once about the damp sheets. She introduces me as her sister, Mrs Clairmont, and we are both treated (my condition becomes more noticeable by the day) with as much deference as a pair of princesses.

Friday, September 13th This morning Mary declined to go abroad with me, pleading her work and a headache, and so I went alone to the Pump Room, where there is a promenade of fashionable society each morning. I slipped in behind an overdressed couple (he in grey frock coat, she in red silk and ostrich feather fan), and their four giggling daughters. I observed that in all that gaily dressed company, I was the only female who was unaccompanied; each young woman was attached to a sister or an aunt. The gentlemen too went in pairs, though I noticed a few who appeared to be alone, or rather, who lounged about as if waiting for the other half of the pair, male or female, to appear at any moment. The ladies promenade clockwise, the gentlemen counter-clockwise. I was determined to make a circuit of the room, and so I set off alone, looking neither to the right nor the left. I held my head high, thinking to myself: If anyone here knew that I am carrying the son and heir of the chief poet of the age, what looks I would receive of outrage or envy! On my second circuit I decided to nod to every third person that I passed, and several people nodded back. As I suspected, people are more afraid of being accused of snubbing an acquaintance than of being thought over-familiar. I am sure that if I chose to make the effort, I could have as large and devoted an acquaintance among these people as any woman of fashion.

I then walked in the Park, observing the nursemaids and children at play, and I grew quite melancholy. How hard it is, to be told I must not write to Albé, must not think of him, must try to forget him utterly, as if thought can be controlled and rationed, diverted from one track into another by willing it. Surely I can allow my thoughts to roam freely, and it is very unfair of Mary to look at me sternly and say, 'I know what you are thinking. You must stop thinking of him and reconcile yourself to the facts.' As if facts are immutable and fixed, as if facts are not subject to change, like all things.

Saturday, September 14th This morning I ventured into several shops, though having no money in my purse I was unable to make any purchases. The shopkeepers are without exception extremely polite, and the subject of money did not arise. I selected two pairs of gloves and a new bonnet, and had my feet measured for new boots; I also had three yards of good cloth set aside. Mary was shocked, and spoke grimly of being forced to leave Bath for another town, but I assured her that I could claim the goods at any time within six months, or leave them if I could not pay for them. I shall certainly need new boots, as my feet have increased in size; the bonnet and gloves I may have to dispense with. There is a fine lending library, but it costs a guinea to join, and Mary says we have enough books.

Wherever I go I am accompanied by a strange fluttering, which I would mistake for dyspepsia if I did not know its cause, and if I did not feel so extremely well and energetic. How strange that a new being has attached itself to my inmost self, is already part and parcel of my life, as dear to me as life itself. I asked Mary if she had felt set apart from other women during her pregnancy and she laughed at me and said she had felt exactly the same as she always felt. She says that it is important to continue one's activities as before, and not to attach too much importance to the changes taking place in one's body. 'They will take their course in any case, for better or worse,' she said. I wish I had her fortitude, and her powers of discipline. I am hungry all the time, ravenous, in fact, and I cannot pass a tea-room without longing for a bun or a cream-cake. But I should hate to grow fat and swollen like the women one sees approaching their time, waddling like great sows, gasping for breath if they have to walk up three steps.

18th September, 1816.

Dearest,

I have promised my friends not to write to you, but I know you will be pleased to learn that we arrived safely in Portsmouth (after a journey so harrowing that it will be kind to spare you the details) and that your manuscript has been delivered to Mr Murray, all in good order. (I know that Shelley will write to you as well, but it cannot hurt to be told such reassuring news twice.) Mary and I are now resident in the charming city of Bath, where we expect Shelley to join us shortly, and we plan to live here quietly for the next few months, and to pursue our usual course of study, reading and writing.

Seriously, you will not object to hearing news and gossip from me now and then. I think of you continually and shall always regard you as my dearest friend. I expect nothing from you in return, but I shall be happy to think of you reading my words and setting the letter aside with perhaps a smile, and the thought that *she is a good girl after all.* You would certainly smile to see me parading about among the local belles. Society here is hardly what you were accustomed to in London; it is a mixture of retired colonels, solicitors and gentleman farmers from Somerset, with their overdressed wives and daughters. Everyone is looking for society but they see only reflections of themselves and must make do with what they see.

Mary continues to write her story; she has the most astonishing powers of concentration. I wish I could follow her example. But if I were to write a story I think it would be like my life, a series of episodes without any definite direction, though with a good deal of interest along the way.

I wonder if you have yet set out on your travels with Mr Hobhouse. I was very jealous of him for taking up most of your time during the last week of our stay, but I forgive you for that as for all things, my dearest friend. I shall always feel the warmest affection for you and I continue to feel happy even in my solitude, for 'I have that within' which exercises a holy claim upon my love, and I shall take care of myself all the more for *his* sake, whose future must be all my joy.

Think of me kindly, and rest assured of my tender feelings towards yourself,

Your
Clara

Monday, September 23rd Tomorrow Mary goes to Maidenhead to meet Shelley, and they will walk to Marlow to see a house which Shelley's friend Peacock has found for them. I shall stay here until little Lord B. is born, whatever they decide.

FANNY
September 1816, Skinner Street

Friday, September 20th To my great disappointment my sisters are not here, nor am I likely to see them or little Will for some time. But I have seen Shelley twice, and we are on our way to an understanding. We met at the Coffee House near St Paul's, and do what I would, the tears came, and it was five minutes before I could bring myself to speak. But Shelley was very good, as always; he took my cold hands and chafed them, and talked to me of Geneva, and Lord B. and their trip around the lake, and one thing and another, until I recovered. My sisters had no time to make me a copy of Lord B.'s poems as I had requested, they are very busy as usual, but Shelley promised that he will secure a copy for me as soon as they are published.

I had first to tell Shelley that Papa will not see him, nor will he receive letters on any subject other than the immediate pressing one of money. On that subject, I explained that Papa must have £300 by the 15th of next month; he is counting on S. to secure this sum.

'That will not be possible,' Shelley said.

'Well, then, Papa is convinced that it will be prison for him this time, and the house and shop will be repossessed.' I had promised Papa to convey this information exactly as I have set it down.

Shelley turned pale. 'They will not send him to prison,' he said. 'There can be no question of prison for him. What of his friends, Lamb, and Mr Owen?'

'He has already applied to them; they have given all they can. He is depending on you to help him.'

'But Fanny dear, I have written to him explaining precisely what my situation is. He knows that I cannot lay hands on the sum required; it is doubtful that I can find £50. Does he want his daughter and grandson to starve?'

'He is not hard-hearted,' I said. 'He does not imagine that

Mary is in danger of starving. He can see only his own trouble. He knows that he is poor and in debt, and he thinks you should be able to borrow against your grandfather's estate. It seems to him that you are under a moral obligation to help him. You yourself have said so, many times.'

'And he sends you to tell me this, and refuses to speak to me, or to embrace his daughter! It is very cruel, Fanny – cruel to you, unspeakably cruel to Mary.'

'I am afraid he cares nothing about that. He wants simply to know if you will supply the money.'

'He knows I will do all I can for him. A year ago I secured a loan of £1,000 for him against my inheritance; in April before we left for Switzerland I sent him £500. There will be more money; he knows that I am negotiating now for a full settlement. But I cannot borrow on my grandfather's estate while the deeds are in the lawyers' hands.'

I did not know Shelley had advanced Papa so much money. Poor Papa! He must appear to everyone to be a sieve, or a bottomless pit – I certainly could not explain where the money goes.

'Why can he not manage better?' Shelley asked.

'He tries very hard; you know he spends nothing on himself. We live very frugally.'

I did not like to call attention to my own frayed cloak and bonnet, my worn leather boots, patched and resoled more times than I can count. Yet it was from my own private store that I purchased the items Mary asked for, which came to six guineas, eight shillings, ten pence and which I have already sent on to her by diligence.

'You see, it is a never-ending circle,' I said. 'Each time Papa convinces himself that it is the last time, and he will make a fresh start. But then he is overtaken by events. Also, Mama is convinced that the shop will make money, but it can only make money if she invests in stock and continues to publish. They both work very hard; Papa sits at his desk each day until he has finished at least one new chapter of the Children's Encyclopedia, and Mama is in the shop from morning until night, dealing with tradesmen and customers. Then Papa is also working on a new novel, and he is sure that this one will bring in some money. Indeed, when he is feeling very gloomy about the future he says he will not mind going to prison, since he will then be able to finish his novel in peace, without the interruption of tradesmen's duns, children, and quarrelling women. The rest of us, he says, will have to manage as we can.'

'He tortures you, Fanny; it's very wrong of him.'

'He does not mean to torture me; I think he would help me if he could. He would like me to establish myself as an independent person. He has been very good to me – he has given me my mother's works to read, and we discuss them as I finish reading them. I am sure he would have been a very different person if my mother had lived. He had noble ideals when he met her; now his ideals have been defeated by worries about money.'

'It must be hateful for you. I wish we could offer you a home!'

At this my eyes filled with tears, and I bowed my head. I hope and pray that he could not read my thoughts.

Our second meeting was little better than the first. I could not sleep the night before, and I had the strangest feeling of apprehension in the morning before we met. Again we met at the Coffee House; I was there first and steeled myself to walk inside, past the elderly gentlemen reading their newspapers, to the back where it was quiet and empty. I was convinced that something terrible had happened to little Will, or to Mary, or even to Shelley himself. Indeed, I was so relieved to see him appear, his usual eager, boyish self, that I leaped up and threw myself into his arms and hugged him tight.

'Why, Fanny, is something wrong?' he asked. 'Why do you weep?'

As soon as I could speak, I reassured him that all was well. 'Not well, but no worse than last week.' Then I told him of my fears, and we talked about these strange premonitions, which have been reported by many people from the earliest days to the present.

Shelley said the ancient Greeks paid as much attention to dreams as they did to their waking life. He said they were not superstitious but were rather preternaturally attuned to all phenomena of thought. 'If we trust memory, which we know is unreliable, why should we dismiss signs and signals of changes to come?'

'Papa always taught us to laugh at superstition,' I said.

'He takes a stricter view of the matter than I do. Why should we assume that consciousness is fixed in the present moment, and can move neither backwards nor forwards? In every age there seem to be certain persons who have the gift of seeing into the future, prophets, and seers; they are the true poets. The world calls them mad, but we need not agree with the world.'

I looked at him with admiration – his eyes were brilliant, his voice thrilling. He is so kind, so gentle! He is the most truly poetic soul I know.

If only we could have remained as we were, at our dark table, in the back of the Coffee House, talking about dreams and the ancient Greeks and signs and portents! But I had my instructions, and money was to be my theme. 'Papa has had your letter,' I began. 'He says that on no condition should you allow your estate to revert to your brother John; that would be absolute folly. He says that you must hold on to your full right of inheritance, as eldest son and grandson, and take your father to court if necessary. Meanwhile, you should be able to borrow £300 on post-obit from Toby & Sons, the Jews in the Minories, with whom Papa has done business before.'

'But, Fanny, he cannot have read my letter. I explained everything – the agreement I have come to with my father, the arrangement we have made regarding my brother, the quarterly sum my father is advancing to me. There is nothing further I can do – it is sheer obstinacy that makes him persist.'

'I am sure that he has read your letter. He believes that he understands the situation better than you do.'

'Then, Fanny dear, you will have to tell him that he is mistaken.'

Tell Papa he is mistaken! The very thought made me wince. Suddenly I doubled over in pain. 'I cannot bear it!' I cried. 'It is too much. You will kill me between you!'

Poor Shelley was not a little alarmed. He urged me to take some water, but I was quite unable to swallow anything. My hands were shaking and my legs were trembling.

'What are we to do?' S. said. 'It is intolerable that he should torment you like this.' He finally persuaded me to drink some tea and he ordered a dish of plum cakes.

'I think I should like to walk a little,' I said when I had recovered somewhat. I had the odd fancy of going to St Pancras Churchyard to see my mother's grave. Shelley agreed to accompany me, though he said he had promised to see his lawyer in the afternoon. I had a great terror of being seen by Mama, so we took the long way around, behind St Bartholomew's Hospital to Chick Lane, up Saffron Hill and across to Grays Inn Road, thence to Pancras Road and the burial ground. It was drizzling lightly; I felt rather faint and clung to Shelley's arm, and when we arrived at the church after about an hour's walk we were both wet through. We stood by the grave and I recited, 'We are as clouds that veil the midnight moon.' Shelley was surprised that I knew it, but I could only say the first four lines. He promised to write it out for me. We went into the church to stay out of the rain and sat down at the back. There were only a few people in the church; a beggar-woman sat in the corner with her bags and satchels, and a drunken man was sleeping on one of the pews.

'You must take better care of yourself,' Shelley said earnestly. 'You must try to eat regularly, even if it is only bread and fruit.' I said I was grateful for his concern. I could not promise to reform; I cannot eat if I have no appetite.

Our conversation turned to my mother's writings. 'I cannot understand why we were not given her works as children,' I said. 'I know they are difficult but I do think her works were ours by right; I feel defrauded to come upon them only now.'

'Your father may have wished to protect you and Mary.'

'I think there were reasons,' I said.

Shelley looked startled. Does he think I am too delicate to be told the truth? 'What reasons?' he asked.

'Perhaps there were things he wished to conceal from us.'

'Why, Fanny, there is nothing in your mother's life that

reflects badly upon her. She acted simply and honestly in accordance with what she felt – and she seems to have been the most affectionate and loving of women.'

'Do you think Mary has inherited her character?' I asked.

'Oh, I am certain she has. Her character, her intellect, her beauty . . .' He was about to continue, then his expression changed. 'And I think you must have inherited something of her nature too, Fanny.'

'Do you think so?' I asked. 'Truly? Please do not lie to me.'

'Yes, truly. I am sure you have something of her . . . genius, her light and shade.'

'Do you know, I think I can remember my mother. I seem to remember sitting at her knee, listening to her read from her book of Lessons. I have a distinct impression of her pale face, her soft voice, her scent . . . and her difficulty in moving when she rose from her chair. She must have been close to her confinement. It must have been within the last month of her life. I seem to remember her as heavy, and very tired, leaning on a chair, holding one hand to her belly. It is the only clear memory I have of her. I would have been three. She was wearing a loose brown gown, with a white kerchief about her throat, as she is in the portrait above Papa's desk.'

'I know the portrait very well – it shows your mother as a revolutionary heroine, her eyes flashing with the spirit of courage and independence.'

'Papa says the only thing I have inherited from my mother is her melancholy.'

'Oh, Fanny – that cannot be true. Melancholy is not a trait of character, it is a response to particular circumstances.'

'No, I think it may be a trait of character. It is a kind of cloud that descends, and blocks out the sun; it has very little to do with particular circumstances. It has always been so. When we were little, Mary was the clever one, Jane was the naughty one, and I was the sad one. I could be counted on to burst into tears at the least trifle; I was always being teased for it.'

'You are very sensitive, Fanny. But that is not a fault. It was wrong of them to tease you for it.'

'Papa thought it was a grievous fault. He wished us to be stoical and even-tempered, and to bear our little trials and misfortunes with grace. I am afraid none of us would oblige him. Mary used to sulk, and Jane had tantrums. And I was the cry-baby.'

'But you can laugh about it now.'

'Oh, yes. I have learned to conceal my feelings, from Papa at least. But as soon as he shows the least sympathy, I weaken, and the tears will come. I am talking too much. Stop me if you think I am talking too much.'

I knew he had an appointment, but I was reluctant to leave the darkness of the church, where we could talk undisturbed. How comforting it was to sit unseen on the hard wooden bench with the dim light filtering through far above, and an atmosphere of peace, such peace . . . the peace of death and burial, and the beauty of the psalms . . . *Thou art my refuge and my strength, a very present help in trouble.*

'I must go, Fanny. Do you wish to stay here awhile?'

I knew Mama was expecting me. 'I shall go with you.' The rain had stopped, and we walked quickly, in silence. Shelley offered me his arm, which I leaned on, and I adjusted my steps to his. In spite of my melancholy, I felt relieved at having opened my heart to my dear friend and brother. What must he think of me, I wonder? Silly Fanny, complaining about trifles . . . We parted at the top of Snow Hill. 'Goodbye, Fanny dear,' he said, and pressed my hand. 'I will try to find the money – tell your father I shall write to him.' Again my eyes filled with tears, and my voice trembled as I said goodbye.

Next Tuesday he is going to meet Mary at Maidenhead, to view a house in Marlow. When they are settled there, he promised that I shall come and visit, for as long as I like.

HARRIET
September 1816
Elizabeth Street, Hans Place, Knightsbridge

To Miss Eliza Westbrook,
23 Chapel Street,
Grosvenor Square

Thursday eve, 12th September, 1816.

My dear Sister,

When you return from Shropshire I shall be gone from Chapel Street. Please do not seek for me, you would only try to persuade me to return, which I must tell you is impossible. You have always been my closest friend and best counsellor, but you must allow me to go my own way. Rest assured that I am well – as well as one can be who has very little to hope for in life, very little to live for if it were not for my precious Babes. Please tell Papa that I am in the country with friends. You can direct to me care of Mary Ann Phillips, at the Fox and Bull. I hope you will let me know from time to time how my darlings are. Please send Mary Ann any letters that may come for me.

Your affectionate sister,
Harriet S.

To Mary Ann Phillips,
the Fox and Bull,
Knightsbridge

Thursday eve.

Dear Mary Ann,

Thank you so much for all your many kindnesses to me. I am comfortably settled in Hans Place, thanks to you and our good Henry, and I am reconciled to remaining here for some time at least. I have written to my sister Eliza asking her to direct to you at the Fox and Bull, and I have asked her not to try to find me, it would be useless. I know you will not breathe a word of this to your father or anyone else. This is the best course for me, though my tears flow at the thought that I must not see my darling children, must not speak with my dear sister or my papa, must entrust myself to the care of strangers. I hold fast to your promise that you will come each week and bring news of my dear ones, or if you cannot come yourself, you will send Henry. Mrs Thomas seems a good soul, she will prepare dinners and attend to laundry, and you can be sure my wants are few. The rooms are very pleasant; I am only a few minutes' walk from the Park, and I think I shall be quite comfortable here. Henry told Mrs Thomas that my husband was abroad, she has got it into her head that he is in India with the regimental army. I shall not disabuse her.

I have arranged to pay by the month, in advance, which seems the most sensible way. I go by the name of Mrs Harriet Smith.

I shall stop writing now as my head is sorely troubled.

Your affectionate friend,
Harriet S.

Sunday, September 15th I write this to settle my thoughts. Solitude cannot be good to one in my state and yet there is no one to whom I can talk freely.

The summer is well and truly gone; from my bedroom window I can see the great sycamores in the gardens, which are already losing their leaves. At dusk they are invaded by flocks of starlings, which set up a most tremendous clatter and cry, then after a few minutes fly off in great clouds to settle in some other public square, more to their fancy. A fine rain is falling and it is all I can do to prevent my own tears falling on the page. Exactly two years ago I was pregnant with my poor little Charles, waiting anxiously to hear news of his absent father. Alas the only news I had at the time came in the form of frantic pleas for money, both from him and from Miss Godwin on their return from France. She cannot have loved him then to cause him such anxiety; she cannot love him now – I truly believe she is a sorceress and has enchanted him.

Two years ago I awaited my lying-in at my father's house. Then too it rained almost every day, and as the days grew shorter, the darkness and the fog and mist seemed to be a weight on my mind. I remember my feeling of desolation as my time approached, and I am sure this is why Charles was so weak and puny, he was an eight months' child and we had to have a nurse for him, and he is delicate to this day. Still, I had my dear sister close at hand, and my sweet Ianthe. I was not alone, as I am now, and am likely to be for the foreseeable future.

Yet I know that I must be secret, and patient. I am terrified each time I walk abroad that I shall meet someone I know, I am afraid to go into any shop, and yet I cannot keep to my room all the time. If Papa knew of my state, he would go after Bysshe with pistols, but I cannot see that violence would be of any use, Bysshe will do as he pleases, and while he is still in thrall to Miss Godwin he will not return to me, so much is certain.

What I fear above all is that I may jeopardise the children's right to their inheritance. This is what Eliza has impressed upon me most strongly. And yet, how could any act of mine put their future at risk? I am much perplexed about these matters – but I do know that it is better for them to be in the country than to be breathing the foul air of London.

Thursday, September 19th The weather has turned fine and I have been walking in Hyde Park, past the barracks, and alongside the lake. This morning for half an hour I stopped to watch the geese flying low over the water, screaming as they went; they settled then into a military formation, facing all in the same direction, until one or two flew off again, and the others followed. There is an old man who stands on the bridge to feed the birds, which perch along his arms and fingers, and even on his head and sometimes on his nose. He told me that he is there in all weathers, and although we do not say much I feel that he is a friend.

In the afternoon I sit at the window looking out on the street below, and I try to read or to do my work. I am sewing a suit of clothes but I do not seem to progress very quickly, often I let the work fall from my hands and day-dream, minutes or even hours pass in this way, and when I come back to myself I find that I have been weeping. Mrs Thomas comes each day and asks what I would like for dinner, and she would sit with me if I gave her any encouragement, but I prefer to remain alone with my thoughts. She is puzzled that I receive so few visitors, only Mary Ann and Henry, who has called every day. Yesterday he brought me flowers. As he was leaving I heard Mrs Thomas say to him, 'Such a respectable young lady!' which made my tears flow even faster.

Friday, September 20th Eliza has been to see Mary Ann, she brought a letter from Mrs Nugent, and she expressed her severe disapprobation, she said I was always going off (which is certainly not the case) and no good would come of it, but she would not interfere, I must do as I liked. She made Mary Ann promise to let her know if she should be needed. She said the children are well. Mary Ann brought the letter, also a basket of plums from her garden. I asked her if Eliza seemed very angry. 'I did not think she was angry, more annoyed than angry. She seems to think it is a whim which will pass.'

'If only it were so,' I said. I cannot expect Mary Ann to understand – I cannot face Eliza's anger, and her bitter disapproval. I must stay quietly as I am, counting the days as they pass. *Dear God, let them pass quickly.*

21st September, 1816.

My dear Mrs Nugent,

Thank you for your kind letter, which my sister Eliza has sent on to me, since I am living away from home at present.

I am very sorry to hear you attack Mr Shelley with such passion, though I know you do so because of your great sympathy for me. I myself have forgiven Mr Shelley a hundred times over for the distress he has caused me. I truly believe that 'he knows not what he does', but is the victim of his own kind and generous nature. He is not like other men, his ideas are peculiar to himself, and it is very difficult for the world to understand and judge him properly.

For three years while I lived with Mr Shelley and was in daily conversation with him, I endeavoured to share his ideas and to act upon them. He wished us to devote our lives to the reform of society and the liberation of all oppressed people everywhere in the world. In the end I could not set aside my own needs as he would have liked; we travelled about so much and I thought we should purchase a carriage, which I now think was the beginning of our trouble, and I wish I had not insisted.

I know the world condemns Mr Shelley as an atheist, but I do not think he is an unbeliever. The God he believes in is a God of love. He is a worshipper of Love, he believes that love is the greatest good we know, and that it would be a crime against nature to deny its call. I am sure that he loved me during our happy years together, and I believe that he loves me still. I am sure he *thinks* that he loves Miss Godwin. It is natural to him to idealise those he loves. He thinks better of people than they deserve.

I do not know if I am making any sense – my thoughts are sadly muddled today. I have great worries which I cannot share with you at present but I hope that you will continue to write to me, and if I am not at home to receive your letters (which may be the case for some time), my sister Eliza will see that they are sent on to me. Goodbye, my dearest friend – believe me,

ever, your affectionate Harriet S.

22nd September, 1816.

My dear Mrs Boinville,

You will think I am very remiss for remaining silent after all your kindnesses to me, ever since I have had the happiness of knowing you and your dear family. I must have presented a singular appearance, when I appeared at your door two weeks ago, arriving unannounced, and no doubt dishevelled and unkempt – not the Harriet you always complimented on her fine looks. You were very gracious, as always, and I shall forever be grateful to you for persuading me to stay the night, not to rush off into the darkness, for if I had, I am sure I would not have lived many hours longer, no, I would have put an end to this existence which gives joy to no living human being, least of all to myself, the unhappiest of women. But you prevailed upon me to take rest and comfort. I am still among the living, and I shall try to follow your good advice and remain so.

I write to tell you that I am settled in lodgings. My sister does not know my address, but she knows that I am well, and I am in touch with friends.

If you write to Mary Phillips, at the sign of the Fox, Knightsbridge, she will see that I receive your letters. Please do not worry yourself about me, I am not worth troubling about. Believe me your devoted and

unhappy Harriet S.

Wednesday, September 25th Eliza has been to see Mary Ann again and this time she questioned her closely, asking whether I was in town or in the country, and who the 'friends' were with whom I was staying. Mary Ann says she does not think she can hold out much longer against such an assault. She advises me to take my sister into my confidence. 'What then are sisters for?' she said, but she does not know Eliza as I do, she has the best qualities in the world, but I am making her a sad return for her support and loyalty, and I cannot bear to think of her reproaches. 'Then you must write to her,' said Mary Ann, and I agreed.

All day I have been trying to compose a letter to my sister, and each time I begin my heart fails me, indeed I have most grievously betrayed her trust. But I must try to write.

My dear Sister,

I depend upon your generosity and goodness – you must forgive me. It is necessary for me to live away from home. I am with child, and I cannot bring this new disgrace upon my parents.

You will want to know the circumstances. I am sure you remember that I visited Mrs Boinville at Bracknell a year ago last summer, and again during the winter and spring. You will also remember that when Bysshe and I first went to Dublin, we were befriended by a Major Ryan, who subsequently visited us in London, and offered to help negotiate with my creditors after Charles was born, indeed he paid several visits to Bysshe at that time, to no avail. Major Ryan's married sister also lives in Bracknell, not far from Mrs Boinville, and we became friendly, so friendly that she invited me to live with her, and at that time I felt under such restraint at home (as I am sure you will remember) that I accepted her kind offer. The children were boarding with Rev. Kendall in Shropshire, and I had little reason to remain at Chapel Street. Her brother was a frequent visitor, in short we resumed our friendship, friendship grew into intimacy, intimacy into love, or something resembling it. But in April Major Ryan was called to Dublin on business, and since then I have heard nothing from him –

No, I will tell you the truth. It was last April, Bysshe was in London, his grandfather's estate was in dispute, and Sir Timothy asked that Charles be produced in the Court of Chancery as Bysshe's legitimate heir. All this you know. Bysshe was at that time trying yet again to raise money for Mr Godwin. I wrote to him through Mr Hookham to say that I could let him have some money and that he should come to me at our house in Chapel Street. I named a day when I knew I would be alone. Papa had taken Mama to drink the waters at Cheltenham, and you had gone in to Shropshire, to bring Charles back to London. Bysshe came to me – his aspect was wild, he was beside himself with worry. I said that I would help him if I could, I still loved him and wished him to be happy. I had access through Papa's solicitor to over £200. Bysshe said I was the most generous of women, and he would forever be grateful to me. Then I wept and he tried to comfort me. He assured me that he loved me still, with a pure and brotherly love. I gave him all the money I had, I told him there would be more if he came the next day. He kissed me and said I was a good girl, and that he would return.

When he came the next day I had the money ready for him. He embraced me, and I saw there were tears in his eyes. I rested quietly in his arms. 'Why cannot we always be like this?' I said.

'Because life is cruel, and people sneer at what they cannot understand, they do not trust themselves and so they heap calumny on their enemies.'

He appeared terrified of going out again with the money, and when I asked what the matter was, he trembled and turned pale, and said he was being followed by an agent of his former landlord in Nangtwyllt, who intended to murder him. This sounded to me like his ancient delusion, but I tried as well as I could to calm him, and persuaded him to stay the night. I said he could stay in your room. He agreed and we had some supper brought, and I gave him brandy to restore his spirits, for he was strangely agitated and unwell. He said I was very good to him and still as beautiful as before, and we remained together on the sofa talking quietly until it was late, and then when we went upstairs he stayed with me, as I half expected, for he is still my husband and I shall always love him.

No, I cannot send this letter – I cannot write to Eliza, I cannot tell anyone the truth about any of these things, I must remain silent.

MARY
October 1816, Bath

Tuesday, October 1st What a great relief it is to hold my dear love in my arms once more. These partings must have an end – they are torture to me. Shelley does not mind them as I do, but it is bad for his health to have no settled abode, to eat nothing but bread and raisins, and to worry continually about money. His life is being worn away in endless negotiations with Longdill and Whitton, odious little men with their deeds and reversions. Now Shelley has decided that he must make his Will, and I know it is to protect the children, but Harriet is to have £200 per annum and £6,000 on Shelley's death, with £5,000 for each child, and

Clara is also to have £6,000, which seems excessive to me, though I did not say so. All these things take time and they cannot be settled anywhere but in London. Shelley is more optimistic about raising the money for Papa, which is a weight off my mind. Poor Papa has been behaving very badly – but he cannot help himself, no one will believe him unless he paints the blackest picture. S. says Fanny is in despair and her colour is bad but then Fanny is naturally sallow and is always in despair about one thing or another.

But let me write down the events of the past few days: our visit to Marlow and our search for a permanent home.

September 24th–28th My love was waiting for me at Maidenhead Bridge when the coach arrived, an hour late, a nerve-wracking journey since the road from Bath was deeply pitted and we almost overturned twice. We walked half a mile along the tow-path to the Taplow mills and Boulters Lock, then a mile further along the river, along a most beautiful stretch opposite the Cliveden woods, which come right down to the river's edge. The path led across a field of barley stubble to Cookham, where we purchased buns and currants. We consumed these in the church-yard, and rested for a while under a magnificent yew tree.

Shelley said he thought Clara sounded reasonably happy; he had had a letter from her in London.

'Bath suits her very well,' I said. 'She is amused by the bustle, and the pretensions of the visitors, who do not seem to realise that they only impress one another. There is no real society; only people in search of it.'

'And are you amused by the bustle, my love?'

'I do not go out into it. I leave it to Clare, who keeps me well informed.'

'Well, dearest, we shall soon have a home of our own, and you shall have all the quiet you require, and the companionship of those you love. Bear with Clara for a little while longer. She is trying hard to be independent, but it is all very new to her.'

'You would think she was the first woman ever to conceive. How she goes on about it!'

'Is she well?'

'Oh yes, fit as a fiddle. Eats prodigiously. Talks a stream. She is glowing with health and high spirits.'

'And you, my love? Are you well? The strain isn't tiring for you?'

'Nothing is tiring for me when we are together – it is so simple!' And it happens so rarely, I could have added.

We crossed by ferry to Bourne End, and soon afterwards fell into conversation with a genial old farmer, a Welshman, white-haired but hale and hearty, dressed in cloth cap and leather jerkin and breeches; a fresh-faced young woman hung on his arm and a sheepdog trotted along beside them. He said the local people in this prosperous valley were suffering hardship on a scale never before experienced. Since hostilities ceased a year ago, many people have been thrown out of work, and the lace workers have no orders because of the imports of cheap lace from the Continent. Labourers and farm workers have very little employment, and wander from one village to the next, where they are forced to throw themselves on the mercy of the parish. But the parish will care only for their own people. Shelley questioned him closely about the condition of the poorer classes, and the degree of unrest. He said that only last month there had been several incidents of machine-breaking in Buckinghamshire, not as extensive as those in Leicestershire and Nottingham, but still a cause of alarm for the manufacturers. Shelley said what a pity that peace brought greater hardship to ordinary people than war. But the resumption of trade has brought a flood of cheap foreign goods into England, and local people cannot compete. The old gentleman said it was the machines that caused the most anger; the manufacturers were pressing ahead in spite of the low quality of the work produced, and were indifferent to the plight of the cottagers.

Yet as we walked along the tow-path, with farmland stretching along each bank, and the woods beyond tinged with autumnal yellows, with the fine mansions of the rich occasionally visible in the hills, it was hard to believe that people in this valley could be struggling to feed their families. It is such a calm, prosperous-looking countryside. There were barges on the river laden with timber and malt; we saw flat boats carrying hemp and rags for the paper mills.

When we reached Marlow, at about seven, it had started to rain. We stood by the bridge looking into the murky depths below, and I was suddenly assailed by the strangest thought. I was convinced that I saw a drowned babe, pale and bloated, floating up to the surface, but it was held down and could not rise all the way. I shivered and held more closely to my darling.

Peacock met us at the bridge and we joined his mother for tea in their snug cottage, tucked away behind St Peter Street. They had a fire blazing, and Mrs Peacock had baked meat pies and apple cakes. I was very hungry, and consumed two pieces of pie and three small cakes; Shelley would take only bread and cheese and an apple. Mrs Peacock is the soul of good humour and common sense; she has had to struggle to make ends meet, but does not complain. She too remarked on the dire poverty of the lacemakers, and the signs everywhere in the valley of hardship and distress. Peacock, however, is incapable of serious conversation; he turns everything to puns and quips. He is writing a satirical ballad on the present state of the nation, set in medieval times. Shelley is very fond of him.

The next morning, Peacock went to fetch Mr Madocks and then we all went to see the house that Peacock has found for us. It is on the Henley road, only ten minutes' walk from Peacock's cottage, above the river but within easy reach of it by a charming lane that winds between old brick walls, with orchards to one side and a brewery to the other. It is called Albion House, and it is in a sadly decrepit state, with signs of recent habitation by vagrants. But there is a large garden with an apple orchard, and the fields beyond lead to great beech woods. The rooms are large, and there are at least five bedrooms, or there will be when the walls are made good; room enough for all of us – for we must provide a home for Clare for some time at least. Peacock said he would see that the house was made entirely comfortable, the roof repaired and the walls plastered and papered, and the fireplaces and chimneys cleaned. The rent is quite reasonable, only £30 per annum, and Shelley agreed to take a 21-year lease, which gratified Mr Madocks very much – I suspect that he had lost hope of ever letting such a damp and cheerless property. In his enthusiasm Shelley suggested to Peacock that they might purchase a boat together, and Peacock said he already had one in mind. Mrs Peacock poked her finger through the plaster in two or three places. 'I am afraid, dear children, that there is a distinct smell of mildew,' she said. But on seeing our disappointed looks, she quickly said she was confident that the house could be made dry and comfortable. 'It is a matter of overseeing the workmen. Alas, they are not perfectionists. But they are quite willing to follow directions. Water is the great enemy – it enters through every crack, it seeps up from below, it is a home to moulds and fungi, and it will defeat you unless you are eternally vigilant. But we shall do what we can, and hope for the best.'

I think she will be an excellent neighbour to have, especially when our menfolk go wandering off in their boat.

We stayed four nights with Peacock, walked about the neighbourhood and along the river as far as Medmenham, and talked much of our plans. Shelley spent one day in London; he saw Fanny and came back somewhat relieved about Papa, since Mr Owen is once again serving as a guardian angel. S. then decided to return with me to Bath, and I could not hide my joy at this news. He was not able to settle our debts as he had hoped to do, but he has left matters in Whitton's hands. Meanwhile Peacock will see to repairs at Albion House, Mrs Peacock will select wallpaper and fittings, and we hope to be settled in our own home by Christmas.

FANNY
September 1816, Skinner Street

Saturday, September 28th I am not to see Shelley again. He has taken a house in Marlow and will remain in Bath until it is ready. Meanwhile, he is leaving all financial affairs in the hands of his solicitor, Mr Whitton. We have a short reprieve; Mr Owen has raised a subscription of £200 and Papa is easier.

My aunt has returned from Yorkshire, and is staying with us again for a week. Now it appears that she would like me to come with her to Ireland, the sooner the better, so I can commence my teaching duties at once.

The thought strikes a chill to my heart! I do not think I am suited to teaching young girls, I have nothing of the taskmaster or the disciplinarian in me. Even when I was teaching William his letters, he could twist me round his little finger, and if I tried to be firm, I was the one to end up weeping. I am simply not strong enough. And Ireland is so far! Am I to go across the sea from my dear sister and godson, without once holding them to my breast?

Last night Papa summoned me for a serious discussion. We were alone in his study; the lamp was lit; the fire glowed; my mother's portrait looked down at me benignly.

'Well, Fanny, you have reached an age at which it becomes necessary to decide upon your future. You are twenty-two – I do not think you will marry. I would like to see you settled in useful employment that will render you independent. Your aunt offers you a year's place as Assistant Teacher for twelve girls. It will be hard work, and she offers only £30 wages – but you will have a home with your mother's sister, and you will have the opportunity of meeting a new circle of cultivated people. Society in Dublin is extremely hospitable; there is a great deal of simple informal entertaining. The country people of Ireland, of course, are hardly more than savages.'

I remained silent. I could not explain the reluctance I felt to agree to a proposal which, as Papa described it, sounded so reasonable. I could not say anything except that I did not wish to go – which seemed too childish a thing to say.

I suspected that Papa was contrasting my timidity with my mother's fearlessness when she went as governess to Lady Kingsborough's children, though she was 27 when she went to Ireland. And yet she was miserable, and left her post after only five months. Why should I be happier, with twelve unruly girls instead of three to control? And with Aunt for company instead of Lady Kingsborough, who from my father's account was a lady of the highest cultivation?

I fear that I should die under Aunt Everina's disapproving looks – I cannot bear coldness.

'Must I go, Papa?' I said at last. My voice quivered despite my best efforts to keep it steady.

Papa looked uncomfortable. 'I do not say you *must* go, Fanny. Do not charge me with that. I ask you to make a decision, and I trust that you are sensible enough to act in your own best interest.'

'Well then, I cannot go!' I burst out. 'It cannot be in my best interest to tear myself from my home and from everyone I love, and to go among strangers – for though Aunt is my mother's sister, she does not look upon me as her own flesh and blood, she sees me as nothing more than a useful piece of furniture. She disapproved of my mother and she disapproves of me.'

I suddenly had the most vivid sense that Aunt was crouched just outside the door, listening to us. In terror, I asked Papa where Aunt was.

'Why, downstairs, with Mama,' he said, surprised. 'She is anxious to know your decision, for she plans to leave for Wales in two or three days; she is to visit there with cousins before embarking for Dublin.'

'Tell her I will meet her in Wales – if I am to go at all. I cannot be ready in two or three days.'

It was the first happy thought I had had. If I were to meet Aunt in Wales, could I not go first to Bath, and spend the night with my dear sister? I would happily sleep in a corner of the room, or with my little godson, and how useful I could be to the dear little household, whose members I love better than anyone else in the world. And if matters turned out thus – could I not make myself so useful that I might stay on? Why should I not follow the longings of my heart? A short letter to Aunt at Swansea, and my days as a schoolmistress would be ended before they began.

Papa seemed greatly relieved. 'Am I to take it that you are willing to go?' he said.

I looked up at my mother's portrait, seeking guidance. How frank and warm-hearted she looked. Dearest Mama, give me strength to go on, I prayed. Let me not fail in my duty to myself and to the memory of my dear mother.

'I will go,' I told Papa.

'I am sure it is the right thing, Fanny,' he said, and rose to dismiss me.

But I sat where I was. I was suddenly assailed by a feeling of black despair. I felt that tentacles of ice were spreading through my veins. This is foolishness, I told myself; it will pass. I forced myself to rise, and left the room; but I could not meet Papa's eyes.

Sunday, September 29th A very strange dispute with Mama. Indeed, I cannot tell what is in her head, she behaves so oddly. I was packing up some books to take with me to Ireland, and a suitcase of clothes, when Mama appeared in the doorway, her face red from puffing up the stairs. 'You must pack everything, Frances,' she said. 'We will send your things after you.'

'I do not think that will be necessary,' I said. 'I will take a few books and some items of clothing, which I can carry with me. I do not wish to put you to any expense.'

'The expense will be trifling. But you will want your things with you.'

'Why, I shall be back here in a year; there is no need to remove my books. I am sure I will be able to find books in Dublin.'

'To be perfectly truthful, Frances, it would be better if you did not think of this house as your home; there is no reason to assume that it will be home to any of us a year from now.'

For a moment I felt sorry for Mama; it was not like her to be so gloomy about Papa's prospects. 'Why, I am sure that Papa will come through this latest crisis; and in any case, I can return to you wherever you are.'

Her pale little eyes fastened upon mine with a look of malevolence. 'You refuse to understand me, Frances. Has your father said you are to return here?'

I could not believe I had heard properly. 'We did not discuss the question,' I stammered. 'But I assumed . . .'

'You must assume nothing. I suggest that you speak with your father again.' And she stormed back downstairs.

A few minutes later William appeared, smirking, to summon me to an interview with my aunt. She was seated in state in the dining room, her black bonnet tied under her chin, hands folded grimly in her lap, her polished black boots planted firmly on the carpet. 'Well, Frances,' she began, without inviting me to be seated. 'I am glad to hear that you have agreed to accompany me to Dublin. We leave first thing tomorrow morning, and I expect you to be ready in good time.'

This was a fine change of plan. 'I am sorry, Aunt,' I said, 'but Papa has agreed that I will meet you in Wales. I cannot possibly be ready to leave tomorrow morning.'

'So your father has said, but I am sure it is far more convenient for us to leave together, as soon as possible. I have many things to discuss with you about your duties and your prospects, and I do not see any reason for you to proceed alone, unchaperoned, to Wales, when you could perfectly well accompany me there.'

I do not know where the strength came from, but I stood my ground. 'I have engagements in town which I cannot possibly cancel. If it is not possible for me to meet you in Wales, then I shall have to come to Dublin by myself, later in the year. I shall do whichever you prefer.' I left the room before she could reply. If it is to be war between us, then we might as well draw up the battle lines now.

William followed me upstairs, and when he saw me crying he put his arms around me and said, 'Don't go to Ireland, Fanny, you'll hate it. Aunt is a witch, she'll eat you. Shall I go and tell her you've changed your mind? I'm not afraid of her, not a bit. Do, do let me go and tell her you're staying here.'

This put me to shame, and I dried my eyes and told William not to fret, it would all come right in the end. Then I wrote to my sister and copied out the letter.

29 September, 1816.
My dear Mary,

All is settled: I am to go with Aunt Everina to Dublin, to teach in her school. I shall have twelve girls, nine to fourteen years of age, and shall be tutoring them in French and in mathematics. The salary is only thirty pounds, but I shall be living with Aunt, and my expenses will not be great.

But oh my dear sister, how sorely my heart grieves me at the thought of going across the sea at this time, when I have not even seen you and my little godson since your return from Switzerland. I have proposed to Aunt that I will meet her in Wales, where she will be visiting her cousins, and we shall proceed from there to Dublin. My secret plan is this: I will first take the coach to Bath, where I can once more clasp you to my heart and kiss little Willmouse a hundred times. I can then stay the night with you, and we can exchange all our news and gossip to our hearts' content. Indeed, I could stay with you longer – for as long as you need me. I could take my dear godson for walks, and help you with your sewing and housekeeping, and leave you free to write your story – for Shelley tells me that you have a wonderful work in progress, and it must be hard for you to write when you have a little one under your feet all day long. But these are matters we can talk about when I see you. Write to me by return post, and I shall set forth at once. I do not like to stay in this house a minute longer than necessary.

Your loving sister,
Fanny

MARY
October 1816, Bath

Wednesday, October 2nd My first task is to nurse Shelley back to health. I was extremely alarmed at his state when we left Marlow, and since then he has been agitated and unwell, unable to sleep, incapable of eating anything more substantial than soup or porridge. He complains frequently of pain in his side, for which he takes laudanum. The pain does not seem so great when he keeps regular hours. I shall insist that we have quiet evenings by the fireside, reading aloud or conversing among ourselves – this is surely the best medicine.

Long discussion about Fanny. Clare does not want her to visit us here. She says that even if we swear Fanny to silence, Mama will get the truth out of her in five minutes. I am afraid Clare is right – it is better that Fanny should not know, for the present. Eventually she will have to know – but for Clare's sake we must try to put off her visit.

I think it would not hurt Fanny to spend a year in Ireland. She has always been at home, and they take advantage of her loyalty and affection. In Ireland she would meet new faces, and she would be a person of interest. Even if she were unhappy at first, she would learn something about men and manners, and she would look back on the experience with some degree of satisfaction. It is possible that she might enjoy teaching young girls; teaching is certainly the most useful occupation open to her and far more stimulating than being companion to an elderly widow. I should hate it, I'm sure – but Fanny is patient and understanding, the qualities most necessary to a teacher. It is a pity that she must live with Aunt Everina, one of the most disagreeable women in the world. If Fanny were not fully grown, I am sure Aunt would beat her for weeping, which poor Fanny does at least once a day. It is Aunt's theory that children should be beaten not when they are naughty, but when they show signs of weakness. Beating will make them strong, Aunt says. She is incapable of logical thought; a most unsuitable person to be running a school. But she cannot be the only person in Dublin. All Fanny needs is one sympathetic soul, and she will be able to weep to her heart's content.

I must write to her tactfully to discourage her from coming. She cannot visit us now, the risks are too great.

Thursday, October 3rd Worked all morning on my story. Everything feeds into it – conversation, books, memory, above all the scenes and events of last summer. I begin to understand Papa's behaviour when he is writing a novel, his remoteness, his air of abstraction, his curious mixture of high excitement and irritability.

I could not possibly continue to write without the support and counsel of my beloved. He entered into the character of my hero from the beginning, but now I think he is an even stronger presence in the character of Clerval. I am also shamelessly indebted to Shelley's favourite theory of Love and its origin in the divided egg, as in ancient myth. He is fond of saying that the ideal love is that of brother and sister – we are forever searching for our 'other half', the lost, irreplaceable twin. It is true that one experiences a strange sense of recognition when falling in love, which cannot be explained in rational terms. When I first saw my love, before we exchanged a word, I knew that he was my fate; he recognised me in the same flash. He says that he never had this experience with Harriet; he pitied her, and was attracted in a superficial way by her beauty; he had a strong desire to assist and instruct her. But he never felt that she was his destiny. When he began to find her boring, passion died, as it must when it is no longer fed by a true affinity of mind and spirit.

What is its source – that true affinity of soul? This I know: that it is the most precious single thing that we have, Shelley and I. If we were to lose it, to destroy it – but no, 'let me not think on't'.

I am sure I have put something of us into Elizabeth and Victor, something too of Shelley and his friend Hogg into the friendship between Victor and Henry Clerval.

Alas, my plot requires that I lose several of my characters before the story has properly got under way. But the characters whom I must kill off are uninteresting in themselves; it is their fate that is interesting and pathetic. They will have played their small roles on stage; they must disappear in order to leave space for the epic battle of the central protagonists.

Still, I have become rather fond of Elizabeth. I think I have put something of my mother into her character. Shelley and I were recently reading my mother's letters, and I was much struck by her gentleness and her honesty – great virtues which, alas, do not serve well in the struggle for survival which is life.

Friday, October 4th Great flare-up with la Chiarina. She has written twice to L.B., expressly against instructions. His lordship has written to Shelley in high displeasure, forbidding all further communication on the subject of Clare.

I put it to Clare that she must choose between her child's future and her sentimental attachment to his lordship. L.B. has £10,000 a year; he has agreed to provide an education and a position in life suitable for his heir. Does she really want to sacrifice these advantages? Or does she still harbour a secret dream: that one day a letter will arrive in which his lordship admits his error; he underestimated her hold over him, he wishes to see her again, to take her to his heart . . . If she is thinking along these lines then she is more besotted than I thought, and will do incalculable damage to herself and to others unless she is stopped.

'Write if you must,' I said, 'but tear up the letter. Your best policy is to agree to everything he says, at least until the child is born. Why irritate him further?'

She paces back and forth angrily. 'You do not understand him as I do. He rails against me, but he enjoys being courted. He reads my letters and files them away. If he did not want to read them, he could return them unopened.'

At this I exploded. I am afraid I said things I should not have said. But Clare does not seem to realise that she is putting us to great trouble and inconvenience. She cannot rely for ever on

Shelley's generosity. She cannot forever remain attached to us like a third leg. She does not even cook for herself, and she is hungry all the time.

The result was that she stormed out, and I have not seen her since this morning.

6 p.m. Elise has just come to the door, with that crooked smile on her face. Though she has never said anything improper to either of us, I know she takes a malicious pleasure in our quarrels.

'Mademoiselle is gone,' she said. 'She has taken everything.'

Of course, she has given no address. How childish she is! I doubt that anyone can disappear in Bath for more than a few hours. I suppose Shelley will have to walk the streets searching for her, and tomorrow she will come back meekly, penniless and hungry. It is really the last straw – as if I did not have enough to think about without these tantrums.

CLARE
October 1816, New Bond Street, Bath

Saturday, October 5th Terrific row with Mary, and so I have left Abbey Churchyard, and I am now in lodgings at New Bond Street, in two pleasant rooms on the ground floor of a modest terraced house, looking on to a pretty rose garden. Shelley has promised to have a piano delivered next week. We have arrived at a very sensible arrangement. Shelley will pay the rent, and will provide me with an allowance of two guineas a fortnight until the child is born, and I will have privacy and the consideration due to a lady in my condition. Mary is not to know – though she may wonder how I manage to live. If she asks, I shall say that I have a Protector, who has asked to remain unnamed. Which is indeed the truth.

My first act as a free woman was to subscribe to the Lending Library, and I have six books, *The Empire of the Nairs, Manfrone,* or *The One-handed Monk* by Mrs Radcliffe, Monk Lewis's *Tales*, and three volumes of Dr Burney's *History of Music*. No Rousseau, no translation exercises set for me by certain persons . . .

Mary could not have spoken more plainly. She said she longed for nothing so much as my absence. And so I have taken the hint, and here I am. She is certainly the most tactless person I know. Poor Shelley – he bears with her temper very well, but I predict that he, even he, will find his patience wearing thin one day. She has a truly vile tongue. She is also extremely jealous. She cannot bear not to know where Shelley is every minute of the day; if he is in the same room, she asks every five minutes how he is feeling, what he is thinking, where he is going. How he puts up with it is beyond my understanding. Perhaps he does not listen. I told him that he must come to see me whenever he likes – that is, whenever he needs to breathe freely.

I am sure I shall be much happier on my own. In spite of being so clever, Mary is sometimes very stupid. She was actually thinking of inviting Fanny to visit! I cannot imagine anything more awkward. Mama would be here in a flash – and then, what scenes would follow, what floods of tears, what a deal of screaming and shouting. It does not bear thinking about.

As for writing to Albé, I shall do as I please. I cannot see that it is anyone's business but mine.

Sunday, October 6th Examined myself carefully in the glass – another benefit of living *toute seule*. My breasts are much enlarged, the area around the nipple has darkened to a deep wine colour, and the nipples are hard. I purchased a cream of cocoa butter, coconut oil and lanolin at a little shop in Milsom Street, which is specially made by a chemist in Bristol, and is intended to prevent the nipples from becoming dry and cracked. I also purchased a cocoa butter cream for the skin, and aromatic oil for the bath; in fact I had to make quite a dent in my first fortnight's allowance. But I can already see marks appearing on my thighs. I am determined to keep my skin free of blemishes; I have no intention of becoming old and wrinkled before my 20th birthday.

This afternoon again I felt little Albé move. He seemed to be turning right around. It is the strangest feeling. I thought if I watched long enough I might be able to observe it in the glass, but nothing happened while I watched. Probably he must be caught unawares – like his father. I wonder if he can hear me when I sing. I can hardly wait for the piano to arrive.

FANNY
October 1816, Skinner Street

Thursday, October 3rd Aunt Everina is gone, at last. I await an answer from my sister. Please God she will write soon, and I will fly to her.

Meanwhile, I have been reading and re-reading my mother's last work, a novel which she left unfinished at her death. Papa says she wrote it during the previous twelve months, that is, when I was in my third year. It is called *The Wrongs of Woman*. The heroine is named Maria! How interesting that my mother used her own name for the heroines of her two novels. And yet Maria's life is not at all like my mother's life. She is abducted by agents of her jealous husband and imprisoned in a madhouse; her four-month-old child is seized and she is led to believe that the child has been murdered; and there are many other episodes in the plot which can only be attributed to my mother's powers of invention.

But there are also passages which must have been closely modelled on my mother's experience. I was deeply moved by a long letter of advice which 'Maria' writes to her infant daughter. With joy it suddenly dawned on me that the daughter to whom 'Maria' addresses her letter was none other than myself. My mother seems to have guessed with a mother's tender fore-thought precisely the situation in which I now find myself. I can hear her voice speaking to me over the distance of twenty years.

'Dear child,' she writes. 'I fondly hope to see you possessed of that energy of character which gives dignity to any station' – oh, would that this were true! – 'and with that clear, firm spirit that will enable you to be the mistress of your own actions.'

I ask myself again and again how I can live up to my mother's expectations. I believe that my spirit is firm; I hope that I see my situation clearly; and I wish most ardently to be mistress of my own actions. But I fear that I am wanting in what my mother calls 'energy of character' – and I wonder if it is this energy that gives life to everything else. Without it one drifts, and is the passive thing of circumstance, to be blown this way and that.

Most beautiful to me is the ending of the fragment, which Papa reconstructed from the notes my mother left in her writing desk. Maria has been abandoned by everyone dear to her; she believes her child is dead. She longs for death, and takes laudanum. Then the old nurse who attended her in the madhouse suddenly appears, leading a small child by the hand. The child lives – she was not murdered, but was placed secretly with a poor family in the country. The nurse rescued her and has brought her to be reunited with her mother. 'I snatched her from misery,' cries the nurse, 'and now she is alive again, would you leave her alone in the world?' Maria clasps her lost child to her heart. 'I will live for my child,' she vows, tears streaming down her face, and gradually she is restored to health and happiness.

Oh, my poor dear mother – did you really wish to die? Were you so unhappy? And did you choose to live for your daughter – for your Fanny? I shall remember this always, in my own troubles.

Shelley says that love is all we have; it is the same whether it is our love of mountains, forests and streams, the love of a mother for her child, or the love of a man for a woman. I too believe that love is what gives meaning to life. To love is to be part of the living world; to be loved is the most beautiful of dreams. The loving nature transforms everything it touches, as my mother transformed and ennobled the lives she shared, for such a brief time. I must always remind myself that I once basked in her love, and breathed its atmosphere as an infant. I can remember the feeling of being held, being sung to, the warmth of a mother's embrace. I am sure this is what I remember when I catch the faint scent of lily of the valley, when I hear a few notes of a familiar old song that affects me to tears.

But how terrible to be deprived of that love, to grow to adulthood shadowed by the tragedy of her loss. I believe it is worse for me than for Mary, who remembers nothing.

Friday, October 4th All is now clear to me. There are no more mysteries. Papa's discomfort during our recent interviews, Mama's winks and hints, all, all are explained. In the last hour, each event of the past week, each conversation, has returned upon me with the sharpest clarity. What was dark before is brilliantly illumined, what was obscure has a meaning that is etched upon my soul. I know now that nothing matters. How petty my small worries have been – Shall I go to Dublin? Shall I stay at Skinner Street? Which books shall I take? Which books shall I leave behind? Nothing matters, nothing at all.

I live now from hour to hour, for there are chores to be done, letters to be written. Apart from William, I have seen no one, spoken to no one. Aunt is in Swansea, where she expects my arrival within the fortnight. I may join her there; I may voyage to Ireland. I may travel further, to places unknown to any here, in this vale of sorrow.

At the moment I cannot think beyond today, or tomorrow. I must write again to my sister. I must see her once before I set forth. But let me gather my thoughts together.

Papa, first. He summoned me to his study this morning. This in itself was most unusual, for his mornings are sacred to his work. He was not at his desk, but was seated in his leather easy chair, near the fire. He was dressed in his usual black. 'Sit down, Fanny,' he said, indicating the footstool by his chair.

I did as he bade me, wondering greatly at his manner, his tone was kind and at the same time he appeared nervous and ill at ease.

'I must speak to you frankly,' he said. 'I should have spoken to you long ago about these matters. Indeed, I tried to speak to you about them four years ago, just after your eighteenth birthday. Do you remember coming to me then, and sitting where you are now seated, and talking about your mother's life in Paris, after the Revolution?'

I nodded. I remembered that talk very well, just as Papa described it. 'Yes, Papa. You told me that my mother had seen her dearest friends arrested, one by one, and she listened each morning to the wagons carrying the prisoners to the place of execution. And you told me she had fallen in love with an American writer, and she had been so unhappy when he returned to America that she thought of suicide. And that you met her just after she returned to London, when her mood was at its most despairing, but you gradually restored her spirits, and fell in love with her, and she with you.'

'Well, Fanny, I am glad you remember what I said. But there were things that I did not say, and that I should have said at that time. I intended to tell you the whole truth – but somehow it seemed better to proceed in stages. That was the first stage, and I regret very much that I did not follow it at once with a second and a third stage. I hope you will bear with me, Fanny; I have always tried to act in your best interest. What I have to say now may be hard for you to understand. But I cannot allow you to remain in ignorance.'

I was thoroughly mystified. Papa was so unlike himself, his manner so confused and contradictory, it seemed that it was I who had to reassure him. And yet my heart was pounding hard, with a kind of terror.

'I am strong enough to bear it,' I said. 'Nothing you tell me can damage the image of my mother that I carry in my heart.'

He rose and paced back and forth, his hands clasped behind his back. Then he stood with his back to the fireplace, and tugged at his waistcoat. 'Well, then. Listen to me carefully, and try not to judge too harshly any of the parties concerned. When your mother returned to England she was not alone. She had with her a child, a little girl. The child was hers; its father was the American who had deserted her in her need. He had gone not to America but to London, and she was deluded into thinking she could rejoin him here, and make a life with him. Instead, she discovered that he was living with another woman, and had no intention of accepting his responsibility to her and to their child. In despair, she left the child with its French nurse, with instructions that they were to return to friends in France. She set off towards the river, determined to put an end to her life. It was raining; she walked back and forth on Putney Bridge to soak her skirts, then she leaped into the river. Fortunately she had been observed, and she was rescued by watermen. It was shortly after this terrible event that I met your mother, and fell in love with her.

'The child, Fanny, was yourself. The American, Gilbert Imlay, was your father; he later returned to America, and I do not know what became of him. After your mother and I decided to unite our lives, I formally adopted you as my daughter.'

I listened to this account in mounting horror and disbelief. I think Papa could not have been unaware of my emotions, for he took my hands in his own and tried to comfort me in his awkward way. 'Do not grieve, Fanny,' he said. 'Nothing is changed. The only change is that you know more about yourself than you did formerly. In the end this can only be productive of good.'

But I kept thinking to myself: as a small child I lost a mother; now I have lost a father. Mother gone, father gone, all gone. It was like a nursery refrain, repeating itself over and over in my head. *Where are thy mother and father? say? They are both gone up to the church to pray.*

As if he read my thoughts, he said, 'I have tried to be a father to you. But you are no longer a child; you have the right to know who your parents were. I could not allow you to leave this house, the home of your girlhood, without informing you of the truth.'

I bowed my head. My tears flowed; I did not try to hide them, and for once he did not reprimand me.

Then he took two small leatherbound volumes from his desk and pressed them into my hands. 'I want you to take these books, Fanny. I know you will treasure them.'

Fanny 83

I opened the first volume and read the title: *Memoirs of the Author of a Vindication of the Rights of Woman.*

Papa sat down in his chair. 'Shall I continue?'

I nodded.

'After your mother died, I believed it was my duty to present her as she was, in her true nature, to the world which had so brutally been deprived of one of its chief adornments. Her honesty and courage deserved a truthful memorial. And so I published these memoirs, in which I included her letters and journals, unedited, uncensored, just as she had written them, in her joy and sorrow. It was a cruel mistake. The great world turned on its would-be benefactors in scorn and fury. I was attacked for publishing, your mother for writing, truths which offended convention and threatened the institutions of marriage and the family. To my great and inconsolable grief at her loss was added the bitterness of calumny: my enemies said I had maligned the memory of the woman I loved and revered above all human beings.

'You were three years old, Mary was an infant; you were both a constant worry to me. I became ill with anxiety; I suffered severe chest pain and thought I would die. How was I to provide a home for you? I withdrew as many copies of the offending volumes as I could; I pretended the work had never existed. I kept it concealed from you and Mary. I give you these volumes now with the hope that you will not think too harshly of me for trying to protect you against the world's cruelty. Life is a series of compromises, Fanny. We can only try to steer a prudent course, and hope for the best.'

I sat at his feet in my numb misery for what seemed a long time. We sat together in silence. He did not dismiss me, did not reach impatiently for pen and paper. I think he was moved, on my account. Perhaps he felt remorse for his cowardice in delaying so long to acquaint me with the truth. Yet I do not know that I blame him; I was happy in my ignorance. Now I am no longer ignorant. Indeed, my education is only just beginning.

At last I roused myself. I thanked him for the books and promised to read them. Then I slipped upstairs, grateful that

Mama was nowhere to be seen, and I shut the door behind me, and here I have remained ever since, alone with my thoughts.

4 o'clock. William has just brought me a letter from my sister. My hands were trembling when I opened it and I could hardly read the words the first time through. I read it twice more before I could make sense of it.

3rd October, 1816.

Dearest Fanny,

I am so rushed and bothered that I can hardly find the time to write, but write to you I must. We have just returned from Marlow where we have taken a house on a 21-year lease, and we hope to move there as soon as the house is ready. I cannot tell you how happy I am at the prospect of having a home of our very own, at last – a nest where with our loved ones we can take refuge from the world's storms. Unfortunately there is a great deal to do, the roof needs to be repaired, and there are signs of damp everywhere, which would be very bad for Shelley's chest, so we must have all made snug and comfortable, the fireplaces cleaned, etc., etc. All of this is a great worry, and we must go back and forth to see to the repairs, and supervise the workmen, who find a hundred excuses for delay if someone is not standing over them. As you can imagine, things are generally in a state of upheaval here, so I do not think this would be the best time for you to visit us. When we are settled in Marlow, I hope you will come and stay for a long time, three or four weeks at least.

Why do you not tell Aunt to delay your trip to Ireland for six months? Or if she wishes you to take up your teaching duties at once, you could plan to return to England at Christmas, which we could then spend together, without the worry of uncomfortable lodgings, landladies, etc. My darling little Willmouse longs to see his Aunt Fannikens, and I tell him that we will soon all be together, and he can bounce up and down on you and tease you and torment you to his heart's content. He seems to understand me, and laughs and gurgles as if he agrees entirely.

Fanny 85

Jane has promised to write to you with all her news. Meanwhile she asks me to thank you for the blue velvet mantle and hat, to which she has added an ostrich feather, and in which she parades about the quaint lanes and alleys of Bath, as fine as any grand lady. As soon as Shelley has settled the terms of his inheritance, we will reimburse you for your expenses incurred for this and other purchases. Thank you also for sending Jane's music; once Shelley can arrange for a piano to be sent I am sure she will be happy as a lark.

I think you should insist that Aunt provide a new outfit for your journey; it is very cold and damp in Dublin, and you must not try to make do with old boots and gloves. Shelley said you go out in all weathers, and refuse to dress warmly. Do try to take better care of yourself.

Fanny dear, try not to be so despondent about Papa. I am sure he has no idea of the pain he causes those nearest him. He means well, but is not the most tactful of men.

In haste,
your loving sister Mary

Saturday morning. I intend to follow my sister's advice; I shall purchase a new cloak and hat, and shall have my boots mended before I set out on my journey. Papa has agreed to advance the money from my first year's salary. He says he is anxious for me to take all steps necessary to prepare for my next stage in life.

Saturday evening. It is done. I am calm and well satisfied.

William accompanied me to the dressmaker on Holborn. I selected a warm brown cloth cloak trimmed with brown fur, and lined with white silk.

'Why do you always wear brown, Fanny?' William asked. But the little dressmaker said brown suited me very well. I then left my boots to be mended at Smith's. They will be ready on Monday morning, when I can also call for the cloak and hat.

I sent William ahead when I went into the chemist. The child has been following me like a shadow. Mr Stubbs asked me if I was still having stomach cramp. I said I was much improved, but would like a small bottle of laudanum. I also asked for laudanum for Papa's rheumatism. Both bottles are safely put away in my reticule.

As I came up Snow Hill it was raining and I thought of my mother walking on Putney Bridge in the rain to soak her skirts. I wondered what thoughts passed through her mind as she walked back and forth. Did she think at all of her little girl? Or was her mind filled with one thought only – how best to ensure that the oblivion she so longed for would be final and irrevocable?

When I reached home I asked if I might have supper in my room, and Mama made no objection. She has not spoken to me since my interview with Papa, but goes about with a self-satisfied expression, as if she has finally managed to have things her own way, after a long and difficult battle. Papa is very quiet indeed; for most of the day he has remained in his study, behind closed doors.

The Bristol mail leaves at half past seven from Lud Lane. But I think I shall reserve a place on the Tuesday morning coach, which departs from the Angel at Fleet Market. Then I shall be at Bristol by 8 in the evening, after changing coaches at Bath, and on Wednesday morning I can proceed to Swansea.

For all of Papa's fine words, he does not have money, and so I shall have to pay for my clothes with part of the sum Aunt left to cover the expenses of my journey.

Monday, October 7th Rain again all day. I cannot get the thought of my mother out of my head. How she must have suffered, in her loneliness and solitude, abandoned by the man she loved, humiliated and despised. Was there no one she could turn to in her trouble? From St Paul's, where she was lodging with Mr Johnson, it is a good four miles to Putney Bridge, at least an hour's walk. Papa said the pavements were far worse than they are now, and my mother did not have proper boots. She was seen on the bridge by several passers-by, one of whom must have alerted the watermen below. Most people are kind, if their natural impulses are not stifled by a misguided sense of duty.

I am pleased with my warm new cloak and bonnet, and my boots are almost as good as new. I have the gold watch Shelley brought me from Geneva for my birthday, which I have not yet worn. I was saving it for a special occasion.

I have packed a small case with my mother's books, and a pair of her stockings and stays, and her blue and white striped skirt. I shall take with me this journal of my sorrow.

Tuesday, October 8th This morning I said goodbye to Papa for the last time. He was very kind and solicitous, but I saw him as if through glass. Mama gave me apples for the journey and wished me Godspeed with a small show of affection. William walked with me to Fleet Market, carrying my case, and waited until the coach left. He made funny faces at me through the window, and waved goodbye until we were out of sight.

Bristol, nine in the evening. I could not write on the road for the jolting. We changed horses at Bath. The streets were full of gaily dressed women and men in top hats. I took each woman I saw of medium height, brown hair, and fair colouring to be my sister. Once as we were waiting at the inn for fresh horses, I was almost convinced that I heard Shelley's high-pitched voice, but I could not see him anywhere.

I have composed a letter in my head which I shall now write out and send. I have a place in the Cambrian coach tomorrow for Swansea; after paying for the inn I shall have only a few shillings left.

Tuesday evening.

My dear Mary,

I was in Bath two hours ago, and looked eagerly for a sign of you and Shelley. Once I thought I heard Shelley's voice, but he was nowhere to be seen. A figure that I thought might have been yours turned out as the coach passed to be that of an old woman.

I am now in Bristol. Do not seek for me here; by tomorrow I shall be gone. This is but one stage in my journey. Do you not think the most beautiful lines in Shakespeare are spoken by

Kent, Lear's loyal servant, before he dies of a broken heart: 'I have a journey, sir, shortly to go. My master calls me, I must not say no.'

My mind runs much on journeys. I cannot see any future for me, try hard as I may. It could have been different – but all that is past. I have been a great nuisance to everyone, from my unhappy birth to the present time. Papa injured his health caring for me, I can never make amends to him for his trouble.

Do not think ill of me. I have thought carefully about what I am doing. I have followed your advice and bought a warm cloak, and had my boots mended. Decisions have been made, and I take comfort in my readiness. I have the small gold watch which Shelley brought me from Geneva for my birthday.

May you and your loved ones be all in all to one another, is the last wish of your unhappy sister,

Fanny

MARY
October 1816, Bath

Wednesday, October 9th A most alarming letter from Fanny. Shelley sets off immediately for Bristol. We fear the worst.

Thursday, October 10th Shelley returned last night at 11 – no definite news. He asked at each of the coaching inns, and at last met with a description of a young woman resembling Fanny, but she had departed in the morning, the landlord thought to Swansea. As he was about to leave, S. thought of asking to see the room occupied by the young woman, and when they inspected it they found a case which proved to be Fanny's, marked with her initials. S. brought it home; it had almost nothing in it, only a change of clothes and a few books. This morning Shelley took the coach to Swansea; he will stay as long as necessary.

Sunday, October 13th S. returned with the worst news. As soon as he appeared, his face said all. He embraced me without speaking, and pressed the newspaper cutting in my hand. It was from the *Cambrian*, Saturday, 12th October.

Swansea, Friday 11th October. A melancholy discovery was made in Swansea yesterday. A most respectable looking female arrived at the Mackworth Arms Inn on Wednesday night by the Cambrian coach from Bristol; she took tea and retired to rest, telling the chambermaid she was exceedingly fatigued and would take care of the candle herself. When she failed to appear yesterday morning her chamber door was forced, and she was found dead, with the remains of a bottle of laudanum on the table, and a note, of which the following is a copy:

> I have long determined that the best thing I could do was to put an end to the existence of a being whose birth was unfortunate, and whose life has only been a source of pain to those persons who have hurt their health in endeavouring to promote her welfare. Perhaps to hear of my death will give you pain, but you will soon have the blessing of forgetting that such a creature ever existed as—

The name appears to have been torn off and burnt, but on her stays the letters 'M.W.' are visible. She was dressed in a blue and white striped skirt with a white body, and a brown pelisse, with a fur trimming of a lighter colour, lined with white silk, and a hat of the same. She wore a small French gold watch, and appears about 23 years of age, with long brown hair and dark complexion. She had a reticule containing a red silk pocket handkerchief, a brown berry necklace, and a small leather purse containing a 3s and 5s 6d piece. She told a fellow-passenger that she came to Bath by the coach from London on Tuesday, from whence she proceeded to Bristol, and from thence to Swansea by the Cambrian coach, intending to go to Ireland.

We spent a most melancholy day. I could not weep, but my heart felt like a stone in my breast. Fanny was always at Skinner Street, always to be counted on; it does not seem fair that she should have left us like this, without any warning. Shelley blames himself; he saw Fanny several times in London, and he could see that she was unhappy, but he did not think she would take her life. He thinks we could have done more to help her.

But I cannot see that we could have prevented the catastrophe. She was always prone to melancholy, and she also had very firm ideas about what she would and would not do.

In the afternoon we told Clare, who says she is not as deeply affected as she would have imagined by such an event. She did not love Fanny; but I am surprised that she should be so unfeeling.

The inquest is next week.

Monday, October 14th Letter from Papa – he knows all. Fanny wrote to him from Bristol, and he immediately wrote to Aunt Everina in Swansea, but she had already left for Dublin. Apparently she had not expected Fanny to come, or perhaps she assumed that Fanny would continue to Dublin on her own. Papa set off in pursuit, but had only come as far as Bath when he saw the notice in the *Cambrian*. It does not seem to have occurred to him to come and see us, though he stayed the night at the York House Hotel, only half a mile from the Abbey.

He warns us that we are not to go to Swansea; he wishes above all to avoid publicity. He begs us 'not to take from us the power to exercise our own discretion.' This is meant for Shelley, who certainly will attend the inquest. I cannot believe that Papa will allow his child to be buried unknown, unattended, in a pauper's grave. Yet this is the plain meaning of his letter.

Thursday, October 17th A second letter from Papa in answer to mine. He insists that we do nothing. 'Disturb not the silent dead,' he writes. 'Do nothing to destroy the obscurity she so much desired.' S. is very unhappy about it but I have prevailed upon him not to disobey Papa's instructions.

But oh, how horrible it is to think of being buried without ceremony – even though, as Papa says, Fanny can no longer be hurt or helped by anything we do. Papa has the strongest dread of the public papers; he says it is to protect Mrs C. and William, but it is himself he thinks most about. Fanny wrote to him from Bristol: 'I depart immediately to the spot from which I hope never to remove.' Papa takes this to mean that she did not expect to be discovered. He insists that we respect her last wishes; nothing is to be gained from disregarding them, and much will be risked by exposing the truth. I cannot understand why he is so terrified of the opinions of those he claims to despise.

And so we are to do nothing. We are to act as if nothing has changed, and the gap left in our lives is to close, as if Fanny never lived. This is what she predicted in her last words to us: *You will soon have the blessing of forgetting that such a creature ever existed as—*. How well she knew us – how truly she prophesied in her distress.

Monday, October 21st The inquest was held on Saturday. The verdict: 'found dead'. She will have been buried by now.

I asked Shelley if he knew how the body of an unclaimed, unidentified but respectably dressed young woman, 'found dead', would be dealt with by the authorities, whether there would be any ceremony or care. At least she will not suffer the fate of the suicide – to be buried at the crossroads with a stake through the heart – though Shelley says this barbaric custom has not been observed for many years.

'Do not think about it, my love,' he said. 'It makes no difference to the dead – and as for us, we must try to remember Fanny as she was, and try to forget this misery.'

Wednesday, October 23rd Yet another letter from Papa. He proposes to let it be thought that Fanny is in Ireland, since she was planning to go there as a teacher. He does not ask us to collaborate in this charade, simply to avoid hindering him.

I have now had three letters from my father in two weeks, the first letters he has written to me since I united my life with Shelley two years ago. He does not ask about me, or about my child, his namesake. Does he think of us at all? Does he have feelings like ordinary men? He says that he does; he asks me to imagine his feelings. But I wonder if feelings, habitually suppressed, simply wither and die. His strongest feeling appears to be an aversion to being gossiped about.

Friday, October 25th Shelley's health is somewhat improved, though this blow has been a severe setback. We do not talk much about it, but now and then a silence falls, and I know we are both thinking of her. Though I respect the Xtian rites as little as S. does, I think one of us should have been present at her burial. True, we were following Papa's instructions – but in my heart I know that we have collaborated in an offence against nature. How is her 'perturbed Spirit' to find rest? If there were to be a haunting – but she would not wish it, surely.

I have been unable to work at my story since the fateful day. Whenever I look at the page I seem to see Fanny's poor, wan face gazing reproachfully up at me. Yet Shelley says I am not to blame; I had no choice but to obey my father's wishes.

Today I forced myself to write, and after a few minutes of agonised blankness the sentences came one after the other. There is no going back; my hero is in such an exalted state of guilt, remorse, and terror that he must inevitably bring his doom upon himself. He has been mastered by an *idée fixe*. Nothing matters to him but his single goal: to find and destroy the monster he has himself created. Love, hope, delight – the natural emotions that make life worth living – all are gone from him. He seeks his mortal enemy, his monstrous double; he goes to meet his own death. Each stranger he encounters along the way, each incident, feeds his single vision. His flight takes him further and further north. In the Arctic wastes, in that inhuman frozen and sunless world, he will find his terrible end.

I have done all I can – the story now writes itself. I am only the scribe.

Wednesday, October 30th It is three weeks since Fanny died. I ordered mourning but I have not worn it as yet.

Clara's spinet arrived on Friday from London; she must have asked about it a dozen times in the past week. She is in pleasant lodgings ten minutes' walk from us, a far more convenient arrangement for all of us. Shelley visits her every afternoon, so she does not feel deserted, and we take meals together.

The weather has turned fine again and we have been walking out every evening – this is our silent homage to Fanny, who would have loved the gentle Somerset landscape. We walk across the Old Bridge to Beechen Cliff, and then into the hills and back, an hour each way. Fields and hedges are bathed in a soft autumnal glow, and the stone terraces turn pale gold in the setting sun, crescent upon crescent rising from the Abbey tower. From a distance they are like dolls' houses, surrounding a doll village. Walking arm in arm with my Beloved, I could be happy – if it were not for the shadow of death that hangs over us, the heavy sense of an utterly wasted life.

We have had no further word from Papa. Perhaps we shall be permitted to live quietly while waiting for our lives to take on a more settled character. Clara practises her singing and awaits her confinement; we read and write and monitor the progress of Albion House. We hope to move in by Christmas – but I have learned through experience not to take anything as definite until it actually happens.

HARRIET
October 1816
Elizabeth Street, Hans Place, Knightsbridge

Wednesday, October 9th Today I forced myself to go out at midday. It was not so fine as yesterday or the day before, and I am sure the weather will soon break. I walked to the Park but I felt a strange unwillingness to walk along the lake, and instead I took the path between the alley of chestnut trees towards Hyde Park Corner, and as if all unconscious of the direction I was taking found myself at Chesterfield Gate, only a few minutes from Chapel Street and my father's house. I was well wrapped in my black shawl, and I thought it could not hurt to go closer, so I drew my shawl about me to conceal my face and walked down

Stanhope Street to South Audley Street, and when I reached Grosvenor Chapel I took shelter in the porch and watched our house, with the strangest feelings of joy and sorrow, mixed with great apprehension lest I be discovered. I stayed for a quarter of an hour at least but I saw no signs of life, no one entered or left the house, no face appeared at an upper window. I was very tired and thought I would sit in the Chapel for a few minutes to rest. It was dark and cool, and quiet, and I must have sat for half an hour, perhaps longer. Then suddenly I was overcome by terror at venturing so close to home, and I retraced my steps as quickly as I could, holding my shawl close, until I reached Knightsbridge. I went into a chemist and asked for *sal volatile* because I was feeling faint, and the chemist made me sit for a while with my stays loosened until I had recovered. When I left the chemist it had turned quite cold and windy, and it was growing dark.

To my surprise it was almost six when I reached Hans Place. Mrs Thomas seemed quite concerned when I appeared. She made me lie down, and brought me tea and a currant bun. I am sure she would have stayed, but I thanked her for the tea and asked to be left undisturbed.

Thursday, October 10th Last night I dreamed that I was in the Mount Tavern, on Lower Grosvenor Street. My father was behind the bar, handsome and jovial, serving ale in dark brown jugs and laughing and joking with his friends, and I was behind the bar helping him. He lifted me up onto the polished mahogany bar to show me off to his friends. 'Isn't she a pretty little thing, my Harriet,' he said, then he asked me to dance for the gentlemen, and I danced on the bar, just a few steps and a pirouette, then I curtsied, and they all applauded and said I was as graceful as any princess, and they complimented Papa on his pretty daughter. Then I woke and it took me two or three minutes to remember where I was. I saw the bedstead, the little work table, Mrs Thomas's flowered curtains, and my tears flowed for my enormous belly and my swollen legs and ankles.

At four o'clock Henry came. He brought me pears and a tea-cake from Mary Ann, and asked if I needed anything. He would not stay, but stood in the middle of the room holding his cap, and looking uncomfortable and ill-at-ease in his workman's clothes. 'You must not stay in bed all the time,' he said. 'It cannot be good for you.'

'What does it matter?' I said.

'Nay, then, you mustn't think that way,' he said. 'You must take better care of yourself.'

'You needn't worry about me – my husband always said I was a healthy animal, and so I am.'

He looked even more uncomfortable at that. 'If I had him here, I'd break every bone in his body,' he burst out. I'm sure he would, too.

Sunday, October 13th Though I know Eliza would be very angry with me, I have a great desire to write to Bysshe. He was abroad in the summer – I cannot think he would return to England and make no effort to communicate with me or with his children. Perhaps he has written, and Eliza, for her own reasons, has decided to withhold his letters. Or he may still be abroad. I could send Henry to Mr Hookham, at his Old Bond Street library, to ask whether Bysshe has returned to England – surely he would wish me to know.

It will not hurt to set down a letter to Bysshe, and I can decide later whether or not to copy it out and send it.

My dear Bysshe . . . So far I got when my pen stopped. I have no idea how long I have been sitting thus, but I shall press on.

My dear Bysshe,

I have hesitated for a long time before writing to you, but I feel that I must write, you would not forgive me if I failed to inform you of my present state.

I want you to know that I do not hold you to blame for my unhappy condition; it is no one's fault but my own, unworthy as I am of the love that has been mine in the past and of the high ideals once shared – oh, for too short a time – with the partner of my heart.

I am living alone and friendless, far from my children, my parents, and my sister. My health is good but my spirits are low. I do not know how long I shall be able to sustain this unhappy existence. Regret is my daily companion. My fate is in the hands of that God whose existence you taught me to doubt, that Spirit of Good which animates all life, but which is far withdrawn from me at the present time.

I do not think I am made to inspire love. If there were a single human being who cared for me, to whose existence my life made a difference . . . but let that go. I have been a great disappointment to my father, I have ignored my sister's advice and counsel, I cannot even care for my own children. I am a weak and wandering creature, and I cannot think what is to become of me. But we cannot choose our destiny. You once argued otherwise, and I believed you. I wonder sometimes if you too have been the victim of forces beyond your control. I forgive you for everything, as I hope you will forgive

your unhappy Harriet

PS Do not try to trace me – I have left my father's house by my own choice and I do not wish my present whereabouts to be known.

I felt a little better after I composed this letter. I shall not send it just yet – my circumstances may alter, or my spirits improve, though I do not think it likely. The letter is in my writing desk; in a fortnight I shall decide whether to send it. I have written the date in my diary.

Saturday, October 26th Eliza knows. She has been to see Mary Ann and dragged the truth out of her, all but the address of my lodging house. Eliza says I must go into the country to await my confinement; she knows a family in Devon who will take me.

I have started a letter to her three times, and each time I have torn it up. I must not let her know how low-spirited I am – she would not rest until she found me. But, oh, I dread going out of London. Here at least I see people even if I do not talk with them. There is a feeling of bustle and activity which I can watch though I cannot share in it. I know that if I need Mary Ann or Henry they can be here in ten minutes. But in the country I would be a prisoner of my solitude – I could not even walk out. Never to hear a friendly voice, to be so far from all my dear ones – oh, I cannot think of it.

At four Mrs Thomas brought me a nice mutton chop and boiled potatoes but I could hardly touch the dish. I am sure she noticed my tears. When her girl Polly Jones came to collect the tray she asked me why I had not been out, since it had turned fine. I said I had not noticed.

She admired my ring and asked what the stone was. It is an old ring, I said, it belonged to my grandmother – a large amethyst surrounded by rubies and set in gold. I told her that I did not know if it had much value, but it had sentimental associations for me. Indeed, my poor fingers are so swollen that I could not get it off if I tried.

After she left I felt very heavy and lay in bed. The baby moves about so that I cannot rest for long. I am hungry all the time but as soon as food is brought I feel nauseated. It is impossible to find a comfortable position; I cannot lie too long on my back but I am equally uncomfortable on my side. Worst of all is the lethargy which I feel in all my limbs; my legs are like inert weights, my arms heavy without strength. My body has become very ugly. I have large purplish blotches on my thighs, and my breasts are swollen and ache all the time. I can see in the glass that my face has become fat and puffy; I am sure nobody would call me pretty now.

As for Eliza . . . I dread seeing her. I am not strong enough to fight against her plans. She would immediately take charge, she would pack me off to Devon, she would see that the baby was given to a responsible woman, she would insist that I am not to be trusted. She would arrange things, as she arranged for Charles to be nursed when I was nervous and unwell, and as she arranged for the children to be sent into Shropshire when I was too low in spirits to care for them. And the prospect of 'explaining' – no, I cannot contemplate it. She will turn into an avenging spirit, she will take Bysshe to court, we shall all be ruined – no, it is impossible. If she finds me I am lost.

Sunday, 3rd November, 1816.

Dear Mrs Boinville,
    You have been like a mother to me, I have tried to follow your good counsel. But my strength is gone – I cannot see any future for me. I have no hope. I know you will forgive me – you are so kind, so generous. But you live surrounded by your loved ones, your hearth is cheerful and each day brings new joy. My life is solitary and comfortless, and each morning I waken with a deeper sense of the misery of my situation. I see no way but one.
    Please try to forgive
                        your unhappy Harriet S.

CLARE
October, 1816
New Bond Street, Bath

Friday, October 25th Today my piano arrived. Three men took it up the front steps and carried it through the hall while my landlady watched in consternation. Mr Clarkson came to tune it, and I have gone through the music Fanny sent and have chosen my favourite songs.

Shelley came this afternoon, when Mary was writing her story. She must have three hours of solitude for her work. I cannot pretend that I have an important task that would prevent me from chattering away with Shelley, walking with him about the town, or sitting and gossiping. The truth is that I have no talent, no goal in life; at most, I have a talent for amusing some people and annoying others. But I have no creative gift. I am one of life's copyists, clever at observing men and manners, and taking notes.

If I were to write a novel it would be a story of real men and women, free spirits, who seek to experience everything that life has to offer. I would take my motto from Albé: 'All things are permitted.' Which, for Albé means: 'All things are permitted to me . . . whatever the cost to others.' It is an exhilarating creed, which I cannot fully share. But I believe that one is permitted to be happy, and to enjoy life.

Poor Fanny – she suffered from the sad constriction of her domestic world, in which *nothing* was permitted to her. She was forever the servant of other people's desires. We all assumed that she was only too happy to make small purchases, to run errands, to procure books and music for us. The only thing she ever asked us for in return was a copy of Albé's poems. It is a pity that neither Mary nor I had time to do this small favour for her. When I first learned of her death, I did not feel it as a great shock. True, we were never friends. But I am sorry now that I teased her, and laughed at her sentimental enthusiasms and her agonies of conscience.

Perhaps I should write a story of my own, after all. I would take as my heroine (for every story must have a heroine) a young woman with certain marked resemblances to the authoress. Let us say she lives under an assumed name, and is carrying the child of her secret lover, the chief poet of the day. She lives alone, but she has friends close at hand, one friend in particular. I would write the story of her past happiness and her present grief (for her lover has abandoned her), and I would trace the adventures of her valiant spirit struggling against the pettiness of a rigid, conventional, hidebound society of colonels and solicitors and their wives and daughters. My novel would be set in a town like Bath, where these people congregate, and look down their noses at anyone who does not conform to their notion of respectable behaviour. My heroine would die in childbirth . . . but the novel would not end with her death. No, life would continue, people would carry on with their affairs, one story might have an end but another would begin. On, on with the dance.

I am sure it would be more interesting to read a true story, the memoirs of a real flesh-and-blood woman, than a novel in which the characters are invented out of whole cloth and you can see the catastrophe coming from the opening page. Would it not be amusing to read the journal of a person who was not famous or distinguished, someone quite ordinary, a little woman like myself, for instance?

Monday, October 28th Shelley appeared today after lunch, extremely distraught, with the wild look he has when trouble looms. He had had a letter from his friend Peacock containing alarming news. He must go to London, he said, but he could not let Mary know the reason. I finally prevailed upon him to let me read Peacock's letter, which I have copied out.

My dear Shelley,

I was in town last Tuesday, and, walking through Hyde Park in the early afternoon, it seemed to me that I saw the beauteous Harriet. That is, I saw a young woman who resembled her in height and colouring, but she was across the lake from me, on the path bordering Kensington Gardens, and I could not be positive that it was indeed Harriet. And yet I could almost swear that it was. She was alone, elegantly dressed as always. She was walking slowly and with effort along the edge of the lake, and she seemed to be in pain. Then she sat for a while on a bench, with a most dejected air, I thought, and when she rose and retraced her steps, walking back towards Knightsbridge, I could see that she was with child.

I thought of overtaking her, which would not have been difficult as she was walking very slowly, stopping now and then to rest. But I suspected that she might not like to see me or anyone associated with her former life.

I knew I must write to tell you. I took the bold step of inquiring of our friend Hookham, who said that he had been given to understand that Harriet was not living at home, and that the children are with friends in the country. No doubt he will be able to tell you more.

Your house is coming along. The workmen have not yet finished repairs to the roof, and as we have had so much rain lately they are much impeded in their labours. But I have no doubt that all will be set right in time for you to celebrate Christmas in Marlow, in true pagan fashion.

'I am sure it *was* Harriet,' Shelley said. 'Peacock would not make a mistake. I must try to find her.'

This was certainly an interesting development. But I was puzzled that Shelley would still feel responsible for Harriet.

'She is like a child,' he said. 'If her father and her sister have abandoned her, she might become desperate.'

'Why do you think they have abandoned her? She may have been for a walk in the Park, but that does not mean she has been abandoned by her friends.'

'You do not know what they are like – they are people without any feelings. They would not hesitate to turn her out, if it suited them. The father is a tyrant and the sister is a monster – she has always twisted Harriet around her little finger, but if Harriet were to defy her she would be implacable. I shall go up to London and find out what I can from Hookham.'

'But if she is really with child, perhaps she has a protector?'

He did not make the obvious retort, though I am sure we both thought it. It appears to be a general rule that a woman is more likely to have a 'protector' before she is with child than after. I have a protector in Shelley, but he is not the father of my child. I am fortunate in some ways, I suppose.

'If she has a "protector", as you put it, then I shall be much easier. But Mary must not know. I cannot talk about Harriet with her; it distresses her, and she will not listen.'

'She would like you to put all thought of Harriet away from you. She would like to erase Harriet.'

'Harriet will not allow herself to be erased. I left her for the best of reasons, and I feel no remorse. I have no regrets whatsoever. But Harriet felt it as a great wrong. I cannot make her any true amends, but I cannot leave her to perish. She loved me – she would call it love, knowing nothing better – she trusted me, she is the mother of my children.'

This is the first time that Shelley has spoken to me of matters he wishes to conceal from Mary. I could not help a secret feeling of triumph. 'Do you still love Harriet?' I asked.

'I never loved her as I love Mary. I pity her, and it pains me that someone with whom I lived in the most intimate connection should be suffering.'

He did not add 'and that she holds me responsible for her suffering,' but I saw his meaning.

'But you always say that we must be responsible for ourselves,' I said. 'We make choices and we must live with the consequences. That is, if we are to have any self-respect.'

He kissed my cheek. 'You are a dear, brave girl,' he said. 'You have always been ready to take the most tremendous risks. But Harriet is not like you. She is weak and confused, easily led, easily manipulated, and she does not understand what has happened to her. She was only a schoolgirl when we married; she had no experience of life. She looks back on our three years together as a period of unalloyed happiness – which I assure you is not a true picture, not at all. She cannot understand why I left her; secretly she still believes I will return.'

'But would it not create false hopes if you were to see her now?'

'I shall not try to see her. I shall simply try to find out what I can. I'll go up to London tomorrow – I shall tell Mary that it is about the estate.'

His eyes had that alarming brilliance they sometimes have after he's taken laudanum.

'It is a terrible thing, Clara, but nothing ever has a clean ending; actions taken with the best intentions can produce a misery beyond belief . . . I don't think I am to blame, but neither is Harriet to blame, she cannot have had any notion of the events that lay in store for her. On the whole, she behaved well, with a generosity I had no right to expect from her . . . But her family are monstrous; they are avenging demons, especially her sister, who is cold, mercenary, priggish, manipulative – all the things Harriet is not. If she is alone, if they have abandoned her, I doubt that she could survive on her own. She has never been independent, she has always needed someone to advise her.

I know she was unhappy living at her father's house, but she would not have chosen to live alone, she would have gone to friends. Fortunately, she has her own income; she would not actually be in want. But if she is alone, she will sink into melancholy. She used to talk romantically of suicide, and I have no doubt that if she were low in spirits, over a long period, she would be capable of taking her life. She's a sentimental creature, affectionate, with a great need of affection from others. She was sure of my love, and it was easy for me to allow her to remain undeceived, since I continued to feel affection for her; indeed, it was she who rejected me, at first. But I had no idea what true passion was, I was a child myself. I took the gilt and tinsel for the real thing. What fools we are, Clara.'

We sat for a few minutes in contemplation of this great truth.

'But come, you must not think sad thoughts.' He took my hand.

'My thoughts are usually quite cheerful,' I said. 'I try to be cheerful for the sake of the little one. He shall have enough to think about when he is out in the world.' I put my hands on either side of my belly. Then I felt him move. 'Oh, you must feel him,' I cried, and held Shelley's hand to the moving creature. What white hands S. has – like a girl's.

'He's quite a wriggler.'

'He's going to be a hungry one, too; my breasts are swollen and twice their normal size.'

'You must be sure to use salve on your nipples.'

'I'm using Mr Nelson's cream.' I think I blushed.

He put his arms about me and rested his head on my breast. 'Ah, Clara, you must advise me,' he said.

I ran my fingers through his tangled hair. It was rather pleasant, holding his long, slim, boyish body close to me. I could not help thinking that Mary would be mightily annoyed at the sight. Yet I felt no desire, simply affection, and a melancholy pleasure in taking and giving comfort.

He is the best of men, kind, unselfish, infinitely sensitive to the needs of others, utterly careless of himself. I am fortunate indeed to have such a friend.

Wednesday, October 30th Shelley has decided to delay his trip to London. Instead he has written to Hookham to ask what he knows of Harriet's condition and her whereabouts. He is unwilling to upset Mary without cause. He will wait to hear from Hookham before pursuing the matter further.

This suits me very well, since it has poured with rain since the weekend, and it is very pleasant for me to have Shelley's company in the long, dull afternoons. We sit by the fire and play at chess, and are very cosy. At four, Mrs Andrews brings a tray of tea and toast and jellies or currant buns, and then S. returns to Abbey Churchyard, and I read or sew, or write in my Journal. I am reading *Clarissa*, which I find most entertaining. She is my namesake, but how unlike me she is in her virtue and simplicity. On the other hand, Lovelace, who is truly 'loveless', bears the most striking resemblance to Albé. I wonder if he has read the book! Lovelace is charming to men and women alike, he is a rake who laughs at conscience, love, reputation. Even Clarissa is charmed, deluded into thinking that she alone can reform him. But he must have his way with her; repulsed, thwarted, his pride at last is touched, and he descends to fraud and force – O Shame! He has won her and lost her for ever, and has lost his soul into the bargain. He is truly Satanic – which I do not think is true of my dear Albé, for all his faults.

Thursday, October 31st I have copied out for Shelley the poem he composed on our trip to Mont Blanc last summer. How far away that happy time seems! How different our circumstances and our surroundings! There we were in the bosom of nature at her grandest and most sublime and solitary – the great expanse of water, the towering mountain peaks beyond, immense forests and waterfalls – here we have the bustle of a provincial English town, that for some reason considers itself to be the centre of the universe, awash with little shops and market stalls, and ladies promenading arm in arm, gossiping about children and servants, planning their costume for the next ball. Yet Shelley says that only three miles away the women who formerly knit the lace used to trim fine gowns are begging in the road, for the industry has been destroyed, women and children are being driven from parish to parish, and no one will take responsibility for housing them.

Shelley says the war was financed by loans from the banks and the landed proprietors, and it is the interest on this enormous debt which is crippling the nation. The taxes levied to pay the interest have hurt the small manufacturers most; as they are driven out of business the cottagers lose their employment and cannot pay their rent, and so must throw themselves on the mercy of the parish. But the parish will care only for families long resident in the county, and now there is an army of the homeless and the dispossessed on the road.

Of course, we do not see this in Bath, where one would think the whole of England is prospering and entertaining themselves nightly at gay dinners, fancy-dress balls and fêtes. But Shelley says that when he goes up to London he sees men, and women too, lying on straw in doorways or sleeping in the parks wrapped only in horse blankets. He says new breeds of popular leaders are arising who prey upon the discontent and misery of the masses, and threaten to plunge the country into chaos.

'There are times when I hope they will succeed, for it seems that nothing but the prospect of violent revolution will rouse this government to take measures to relieve the distress of the people. They refuse to see what is obvious to everyone else: if they do not listen to the peaceful voices for reform they will not be able to stop the zealots, and the nation will once again be the scene of a bloody civil war.'

I love to watch Shelley as he talks – his pale face becomes flushed with earnestness and his brilliant eyes shoot fire as he blasts the rich and the powerful, his voice thrills with the eloquence of his words and the ardour of his heart. I believe no one of his class cares as he does for the sufferings of the poor. He cannot pass a beggar without emptying his purse, and I have known him to bring a poor little gypsy child home with him, to feed and clothe it and question it seriously about its parents and brothers and sisters. Poor Mary has much ado to find out where it came from, and return it to its parents, or, more likely, to its abandoned mother, who would be only too glad to have some kind gentleman take the brat off her hands.

This afternoon I played a Scarlatti sonata and then sang 'Batti, batti' for Shelley. He sat opposite me on the sofa and when I finished there were tears in his eyes. He left early, I think because he was moved – perhaps he was thinking of Fanny.

Saturday, November 2nd Shelley came early today, much agitated. Yet another letter from Godwin, written in the coldest tone, and demanding money, which S. does not have. 'I cannot understand the man. He has driven one daughter to her death, does he wish to destroy his remaining daughter? If she catches sight of his handwriting, Mary starts to tremble – she thinks each time that he will unbend, at last there will be a word of comfort or affection. But no, his theme is money, money, money, and he does not mention her name, does not ask about his grandson – he is inhuman. Does he think it is easy for us to live like pariahs, outcasts from human society?'

'I feel responsible,' I said. 'It is on my account that you must live like outcasts – yet if it were for me to decide, I would not care, I would parade my state for all the world to see.'

'It is not only on your account,' he said. 'Wherever my name is known, I am the object of abhorrence. I am the outcast, not you, certainly not Mary. Mary suffers only from being linked with me. I am the occasion of untold injury to those I love, and I cannot see that it will ever be different.'

I had not known him so despairing before. 'I thought you did not care for the world's opinion.'

'That was true five years ago. But my life has changed. I have not changed – I still desire only to serve humanity, to oppose the misery and vice which I see everywhere around me. But I cannot serve humanity if my loved ones, who depend on me, are the object of execration simply because they share my name and my fate. It is intolerable, Clara. It is as if a curse hangs over me, and I can do nothing to escape it.'

He has heard nothing from Hookham. He seems to have forgotten his plan to go to London to discover Harriet's where-abouts. He is being harassed to death for a debt of £1000 to Thomas Charters, the coachmaker, all on Harriet's account, for she insisted on a carriage when they were living in Wales three years ago, and the extravagance (as it must have seemed even then) was never paid for, other circumstances intervening. Poor Shelley cannot possibly pay for it now, and is trying to raise money on a post-obit. Perhaps it is for this reason that the worry about Harriet has receded somewhat from his mind.

Saturday, November 9th I am now two months short of my time. Little Albé kicks and punches me as if he is demanding to be released from his prison. I feel amazingly well, I am eating for two, and I have the energy of ten. Life is extremely interesting – whether it is the passing scene, the cosy chats with Shelley by my fireside, or his lordship within making his presence felt. I sleep as soundly as a bell, and dreamlessly – though I have been visited two or three times by a gentle youth who kisses my forehead and chafes my hands, and whispers that he loves me and will care for the child and for me, I am not to worry or fret about the future. In my dream he looks exactly like Albé, even to his dishevelled shirt and his lace wrist ruffles; his voice is Albé's, but he is so kind, so affectionate, that I cannot believe it is Albé when I wake. I think I have confused the outward man with the spirit of my dear friend S., my best and truest friend in the world.

HARRIET
November 1816, Hans Place

Friday, November 8th My troubles grow apace. This morning, at ten o'clock, Polly had only time to whisper that my sister was come, when Eliza appeared in the doorway, arms akimbo, her face purple with anger.

'Well, Harriet, it is a fine thing you have done to us,' she began.

I begged her to be seated, and asked Polly to bring tea.

'I have not come to pay a social call,' she thundered on. 'I have come to take you from here and to conduct you to a place where you can await your time in safety.'

'Please, Eliza, my dear, dear sister,' I implored her, 'do not be so angry with me. I did not mean to cause you trouble.'

She sat down at last and removed her bonnet. 'You never mean to cause trouble, Harriet. It is always someone else who is causing the trouble. It has been so since you were little. But I did not expect that I should have to lie in wait at a public house, and spy on the landlord's daughter and the handyman to discover where my sister is lodging.'

'Ah, it is not what I wanted, Eliza. I could not think what to do. My first care was to spare you and Papa.'

'I cannot imagine what was in your mind. To take lodgings half an hour's walk from your father's house – and no doubt you have been strolling in the Park, and chattering away with the shopkeepers in Knightsbridge – really, Harriet, your thoughtlessness is a cause of wonder. I have had to pretend to Papa that you were in the country with friends, each week I have invented letters from you. Papa has been led to believe that you are enjoying dances and dinners in gay company – and at any time during the past two months one of his tavern friends could have seen you promenading in town— '

'That is most unfair of you, Eliza,' I protested. 'I have hardly been out of my rooms, and when I go abroad I am careful to conceal my face, indeed you do not give me credit for any sense at all.' I could not restrain my tears. Fortunately, Polly appeared with a tray of tea and cakes, and Eliza consented to take some refreshment.

Suddenly I felt a pang low down and, most alarmed, I held both hands to my belly and sat very still. Eliza asked what it was, and I said it was nothing, but I could not be sure.

'This will not do, Harriet. On Sunday I will be here at six in the morning. I shall go with you to some good people in Devon, and they will attend you as long as necessary. I must impress upon you the absolute need for secrecy. Your children have almost forgotten their mother. They have no father – but Charles is heir to his fortune, in law, and we cannot allow any hint of impropriety on your part to endanger his claim. Do you understand me?'

I nodded in dumb misery. Her words were so hard, so cruel – I could not believe I deserved to be treated so. Can it really be true that my children have forgotten me? My darling Ianthe – my poor little Charles – abandoned to the care of strangers.

I am sure my sister read my thought. 'The children are well,' she said, and her tone was less frosty. 'Do not worry your pretty head about them. All will continue well, if you do as I say. You should not have left me, it showed poor judgement. You see I do not ask you any questions, it would not serve any purpose. But from this time you must allow me to make all decisions.'

I said I was grateful for her concern.

'Mr Hookham came to see us; he said he had had an urgent letter from Shelley demanding to know your whereabouts, and asking whether the children were with you. I told him the children were boarding in Shropshire for their health, and that you were visiting friends in the country, but he seemed to think you might be in town. Apparently you were seen by the lake, and this was reported to Shelley. I hope you realise that it is absolutely essential that Shelley knows nothing about this. I shall put off Mr. Hookham as long as I can, of course.'

'Yes, you must try to put him off,' I said.

'I am glad to see that you can be sensible, after all. You will be ready for me on Sunday, it will not take long for you to pack your things.'

'I shall be ready,' I said. She tied her bonnet, drew on her gloves, and kissed me on the cheek; then she was gone, and I have been sitting here since, much as she left me.

So Shelley has at last inquired about me and about his children. I wonder if he needs money again. Too late, too late. He must never be told, I can now see it plainly, if I did not understand it so well before.

It is good that Eliza did not ask me any questions, for I do not know what I might have said. My poor head is so muddled – I do not know that I could swear to the truth if my life depended on it.

That he came to me last April I know; he needed money and I promised to give him what I could. That he stayed in my father's house is true; he feared arrest for his debts, and in his terror had one of his fits and took laudanum for it, which meant he could not travel abroad.

But that he called me his 'silly goose' and said he loved me and had always loved me may have been my fantasy. It is what I wished him to say, and longed for him to say, but I fear this is a dream only.

That he came into my bed must be true, for here I am, large as a hippopotamus, and as ugly, and the one thing I can be sure of is that my time draws near and there is nobody on earth who cares for me. I have offended my sister and deceived my father, my children do not need me, and I am alone in my trouble.

Saturday, November 9th The mist is pressing close. I have been in bed for most of the day, with the curtains drawn. I have not had any new pains since yesterday, for which I am grateful. When Polly came to make the fire, I asked to have dinner brought early.

My mind is running on the strangest things. I keep remembering the weeks we spent in Dublin, and Shelley throwing his pamphlet from the balcony of our Sackville Street lodgings into the street below. What a comical sight he was, with his wild hair standing out in all directions, and his shirt open at the neck, and the respectable Dublin folk looking up at him in puzzled alarm. I thought my sides would split from laughing.

That was when Major Ryan came to dinner and paid court to me. Shelley said he was in love with me and asked me to be kind to him because he was a Republican and hoped to free his suffering people from the English yoke. At that time I would have done anything for Bysshe; it was only when he asked me to make love to his friend Mr Hogg that I demurred – I found him so ugly, his hands were always moist and his breath smelled of onions.

I must write to my sister, then all will be done. She will be very angry with me, but I can smile now at the thought. Then I shall dress in my warmest clothes, for Polly said it has turned bitter cold, and rain is expected by nightfall. It will be dark by five o'clock.

I am surprised that I feel so calm. The fancy struck me that I am going to meet my bridegroom, the father of my unborn child. This is a pleasing thought, which I shall keep with me.

Polly has just brought dinner, a mutton stew, which I do not think I can touch. I will try to drink some brandy.

But it grows late. I must write now to Eliza.

Saturday evening

My dearest and much-beloved Sister,

When you read this letter I shall be no more an inhabitant of this miserable world. Do not regret the loss of one who could never be anything but a source of vexation and misery to you and all belonging to me. Too wretched to exert myself, lowered in the opinion of everyone, why should I drag on a miserable existence embittered by past recollections and not one ray of hope to rest on for the future? The remembrance of all your kindness which I have so unworthily repaid has often made my heart ache. I know that you will forgive me because it is not in your nature to be unkind or severe to any. Would that I had never left you; O, that I had always taken your advice, I might have lived long and happy, but weak and unsteady have rushed onto my own destruction.

I have not written to Bysshe, oh no, what would it avail, my wishes or my prayers would not be attended to by him and yet – should he see this perhaps he might grant my last request, to let Ianthe remain with you always. Dear lovely child, with you she will enjoy much happiness, with him none. My dear Bysshe, let me conjure you by the remembrance of our days of happiness to grant my last wish: do not take your innocent child from Eliza who has been a mother to her more than I have, who has watched over her with such unceasing care. Do not refuse my last request – I never could refuse you and if you had never left me I might have lived but as it is, I freely forgive you and may you enjoy that happiness which you have deprived me of. There is your beautiful boy. Oh! be careful of him, as you form his infant mind so you will reap the fruits hereafter.

Now comes the sad task of saying farewell – oh, I must be quick. God keep and watch over you all. You dear Bysshe and you dear Eliza. May all happiness attend you both is the last wish of her who loved you more than all others. My children, I dare not trust myself there. They are too young to regret me and you will be kind to them for their own sakes more than for mine. My parents, do not regret me. I was unworthy of your love and care. Be happy, all of you. So shall my spirit find rest and forgiveness. God keep you all is the last prayer of the unfortunate Harriet S—

There, it is written. I shall only add a note about my few possessions.

To you my dear sister I leave all my things as they more properly belong to you than anyone and you will preserve them for Ianthe. God bless you both.

I shall leave the letter unsealed on my night table, where Eliza will find it tomorrow morning. And now, to get dressed, and leave this place for ever.

CLARE
December, 1816, Bath

Saturday, December 14th Terrific uproar – Shelley has been sent for by Hookham, who writes that Harriet has been found drowned in the Serpentine. This happened last Tuesday, but it seems that she disappeared from her lodgings more than a month ago, and has been lying at the bottom of the lake ever since. Her corpse must have been caught in the undergrowth – it would have been unrecognisable were it not for the ring she always wore.

It is a terrible fate – poor S. is beside himself at the horror of it. He is staying in Hampstead with his new friend Leigh Hunt, the *Examiner* editor, who is providing what comfort he can, and Hunt promises to keep us fully informed of all developments.

It appears from the inquest that Harriet was in the last stages of pregnancy. Who the father might be no one can guess. Apparently she left her father's house in September and took lodgings in Knightsbridge, under the name Harriet Smith. Her landlady testified that she had paid by the month in advance, was a 'most respectable' young lady but had few visitors. She appeared in the family way, and was during the two months that she lodged there 'in a very despondent and gloomy way'. The servant said that six weeks ago, on a Saturday, she had asked to have dinner brought early, and when the girl returned to her room at five, she was gone, and had not been seen since. The body was identified by a plumber who lodged nearby at the Fox and Bull public house; he knew the family, and had accompanied Harriet when she first went to her lodgings. He testified that she had been married five years but lived apart from her husband, and that she had laboured under lowness of spirits for the past several months.

The verdict was 'found dead in the Serpentine'. I must confess I felt a chill of terror at the thought of this event coming so soon after Fanny's death, the unclaimed body, the inquest, the verdict 'found dead', etc., etc.

Tuesday, December 17th One unexpected consequence of these shocking events is that Shelley was invited to dine with Godwin, which he did, accompanied by Hunt, since his nerves were so bad he would not go by himself. Godwin told S. that Harriet had descended the steps of prostitution and was living with a groom named Smith, who subsequently abandoned her. I cannot believe there is any truth in this – it sounds like one of Mama's stories. Godwin also said he had evidence that Harriet was unfaithful to Shelley before he left her, two and half years ago; this is most certainly untrue, and it is very naughty of them to spread such tales about the dead.

It now seems that Harriet wrote a very strange letter to Mrs Boinville shortly before she died, which caused Mrs B. to hurry immediately to London to try to prevent the catastrophe. But she could discover only that Harriet had disappeared from her lodgings, and so she returned to Bracknell. She has refused to have any communication with Shelley.

Friday, December 20th Now Shelley has sent for Mary to join him in Hampstead; while they remain in town I shall stay with Elise and Will at Abbey Churchyard. Godwin has urged them to marry as soon as possible for reasons to do with S.'s estate and the inheritance.

Shelley has been to see Eliza, who showed him a letter Harriet left for her, full of love and forgiveness and self-remorse. Apparently Eliza received this letter the day after Harriet left her lodgings. A week later, fearing the worst, she had the Serpentine dragged, with no result. In her letter, Harriet asks that Shelley allow the little girl to remain with Eliza. But S. is determined to have both children, he has asked Eliza to produce them forthwith, and he fully expects to return here with them. This may be a shock to Will, who is accustomed to coming first in all things. I wonder if Mary is altogether happy at the prospect of acquiring an extensive family all at once. Let us hope they do not resemble their unhappy Mama too closely, in feature or, more particularly, in intellect.

Monday, December 30th Shelley and Mary are to be joined today in the solemn Xtian rite of matrimony. The licence has been purchased, and Godwin's consent obtained under oath, since the bride is a minor. There is to be a wedding breakfast before going to the church, and a dinner and supper afterwards. How sorry I am to miss these festivities! On Wednesday they return here, without the children, who have yet to be produced by the monstrous Eliza. S. fears the Westbrooks are plotting new and strange devices to keep them away from their father, who they claim is an atheist and revolutionary, and therefore unfit to take custody of his children. S.'s greatest fear is that they may try to have the children made wards of Chancery. This seems most improbable, but in any case he can do nothing further in London, and so returns to Bath – for which I give thanks, since I doubt that my new lord and master will wait much longer before making his appearance on this great scene.

THREE
Spring 1817
Albion House, Marlow

Now has descended a serener hour,
And with inconstant fortune, friends return . . .
                    Shelley, *Laon and Cythna*

MARY
March 1817, Albion House, Marlow

Tuesday, March 18th On this day I begin a new Journal in our first true home. I am enchanted with Albion House; from the outside it appears deceptively small, hardly more than a cottage, with its pretty rose trellis and stucco windows, but inside the rooms are very grand and commodious. Shelley ordered the furniture, with Hunt's advice, while they were attending the Chancery case last month, and evidently no cost was spared – for we have a fine mahogany dining table that will seat twelve (only six matching chairs, however), and sofas, sideboards, and lamps in the latest fashion; there are striped silk curtains in the chief rooms, and rich Indian carpets. Mrs Peacock has done her part to perfection; I was in no heart to consult with her after the terrible events of the autumn, but she seems to have guessed perfectly at my taste. The bedrooms have feather beds and sprigged muslin curtains, plain oak wardrobes and chests, and brightly patterned rugs from the Wycombe workshops. Mr Madocks, our agent, is a carpenter by trade, and he has fitted beechwood shelves in the library, and installed new cupboards in the kitchen and larder.

I am writing this in my upstairs study, which is papered in a pleasant design of palm trees, in pale green and gold; here I intend to complete my Novel.

Indeed it is hard to recognise our house as we saw it only a few months ago, when it seemed so dark and inhospitable. Now it is dry and warm throughout, the fires draw, and for the first time we have enough space for all of us, as well as room to entertain our friends. Shelley is unpacking cases of books in the library, a large handsome room which looks out on to the spacious lawns and gardens. We have also taken a lease on the adjacent meadows, four acres in all, so we are surrounded by green fields, extending to the ancient beech woods and the hills beyond. Will is rosy-

cheeked and has taken his first steps. And I am again with child
– I feel new life stirring within me – I am now certain of it.

Best of all, since our marriage my father has looked kindly
upon me, as if the past three years of bitter recriminations and
estrangement have been obliterated from his memory. I had not
realised how deeply hurt I was by his coldness and disapproval.
Suddenly I feel cheerful, as if an immense weight had been lifted
from my chest. During the week we spent in London, he talked
with Shelley with his old frankness on the topics they both hold
sacred: justice, and freedom, and the necessity we all labour
under to increase our knowledge and to perfect our lives. I sat
quietly, listening to the high enthusiasm of one and the calm,
measured reflections of the other, and my heart was overflowing
with love for both.

If we can build on this foundation, how happy we may be!

Thursday, March 20th How can I describe my passion for my
Beloved? I cannot step back to see it clearly – I cannot hold it to
mind, so inseparably is it part of me.

Yet I have my child, my studies, my Novel. I write to Papa, I
make lists of linen, kitchen supplies, I arrange for dinner to be
prepared, I talk with Elise, I tell Will his bedtime story. But
everything I do, each task, each small labour, is an extension of
my love. The self that writes, thinks, breathes, is the self formed
and constituted by my love for Shelley. If he were to die – or if he
were to cease to love me – I too would die, the being I am would
no longer exist.

He whom I love more than life, whose thoughts I read as
surely as if they were my own, says that he too cannot conceive
of life without me, without my love.

But I know there is a difference. It is true that he loves me.
But he is also happy alone, or with others. More important, he is
entirely himself whether he is with me or apart from me. He is
the whole person, who includes me in his life; I am like the vine
that clings, the vessel that waits to be filled.

Yet this is not the whole truth either. It is not I but my
happiness that is entirely bound up with him.

Tuesday, March 25th After our months of enforced seclusion, we are quite a society, and have every prospect of becoming more so. Peacock calls every day, often with his mama, whom I like more and more. She is Peacock's saving grace; without her he would be all froth and whimsy. They are great tea-drinkers, and usually bring us an astonishing supply of tea-cakes, seed-cakes, and fruit pies. Then the Hunts have promised to visit at the end of April, and Papa is to come this weekend, and we expect Shelley's friend Hogg daily – he has become our chief legal adviser, and is once again indispensable to Shelley. Elise does not sniff too audibly at the prospect of company; I suspect that she is secretly pleased. We have a girl from the village to clean, and a woman to cook, and a gardener, Harry, who is also a handy-man – in short, something approaching to a household. Clare and the babe will be installed at the end of next week, and, all being well, we should soon have Shelley's children with us. I look forward to this prospect, for his sake; he has a most powerful longing to educate them, and is determined to pry them loose from the grasp of the despicable Westbrooks.

There are two nurseries, both large, clean, and bright, and the garden has everything to delight a child. Shelley has attached a swing to the great cedar; it is meant for Will, of course, but has been occupied chiefly by his papa. Early in the morning, the boy brings milk, butter and new-laid eggs from the Old Farm, and we have a fine local cheese and a good supply of local produce. Mrs Peacock has taken charge of the larder, and ignoring my feeble protests, she has laid in salted meats, bacon and cured pork, and we can order fowl from the farm. The local fish is plentiful, and Peacock keeps us well supplied with trout. Shelley plans to keep to a vegetable diet, but we shall have meat for those who wish it – it is only Shelley who can live like a sparrow on a crust of bread, raisins and nuts.

Wednesday, April 2nd Papa has been to stay for five days. This is the first time that he has visited me as a guest in my own house. I did not think it would ever happen. But now that we are friends once again, his manners are entirely simple and natural. He complimented me on the house, the garden, the meadows, the distant beech woods, as if all had been made to order for us. He seems truly pleased at our good fortune. But I could not forget that he does not have a home of his own, and this grieves me. He has not paid rent for the past ten years, and lives in constant fear of being dispossessed and thrown into debtors' prison.

We had an earnest conference, just the two of us, sitting at ease in my little study, with the fire blazing merrily away, and the oil lamp providing a warm glow.

'I am pleased with you, Mary,' he said. 'I hope you know that I take pride in your marriage.'

'I'm very glad of it, Papa,' I said.

'You have always been my favourite. I believe you have inherited my best qualities, and have been spared the worst. I have always been convinced that there is a strong mental kinship between us.'

'I certainly hope so, Papa.'

'You have what is commonly called a masculine mind. That is, a capacity for organised thought, for logical argument, for dispassionate analysis. Your mother's intellect was of a very different order; she was a creature of sensibility. This was her great virtue as a writer; but it was also a disadvantage. Her argument followed her enthusiasm, and she did not convince those who did not already agree with her. It is just as well that you do not take after her.'

I was half-inclined to protest; it is true that I am my father's daughter, yet I believe I also have something of my mother in me.

As if he read my thoughts, he added, 'One thing you have inherited from your mother. You have her stubbornness – or, should I say, her wilfulness.' He sighed, and dabbed at his eyes with his handkerchief. 'These past three years have been very difficult for me, Mary. I was very ill; I thought I would die.'

My feelings would not allow me to speak. It is true that he has aged; his hair is thinner and entirely grey, and his face is deeply lined.

'I trust, dear girl, that we can put those years behind us.'

'Oh, yes,' I said. 'Let us think only of the future.'

'I will not conceal from you that I am glad to see you well settled. Shelley will have an income while his father lives of £2,000 per annum. When Sir Timothy dies you will be a rich woman. No, do not protest – I say these things with your best interests at heart. We must face facts. You have a child; you are expecting another. There are Shelley's children by Harriet to consider. You cannot always live from hand to mouth; you have seen the consequences of living without an income. It is a cruel thing, to be plagued by debts large and small, to have bills coming due and no funds with which to pay them, to be scrambling always for a few pounds here, a few pounds there, to be indebted to friends for loans which can never be repaid, to have those friends drop away because they are too embarrassed to sit with you at table. It hurts me to speak to you of these things.'

'I know, Papa. I wish Shelley could do more for you.'

'He does not seem to understand his financial situation at all. He refuses to take advice. If he passes a beggar on the road he instantly empties his pocket. If it were up to him, he would give everything away. He refuses to see that the great wealth he is heir to entails great responsibilities.'

At this he rose and paced back and forth, extremely agitated.

'Dear Papa—'

'Please do not try to defend him. You are both children when it comes to money. I have tried to explain matters clearly. I have asked him to see Newton, I have made half a dozen proposals, any one of which would answer, but he must do things his own way. I have nothing more to say on the subject.'

I longed to talk to him of Fanny, but I knew that I must wait for him to introduce her name. We were so close to speaking of her – it would have been so easy to say 'poor Fanny', or 'how I wish Fanny could be here'. But he did not mention her, and in a strange way it was as if she did not exist, had never existed, except perhaps as the small child of our mother's writings, who was to be told stories, and encouraged to run and play freely.

Yet one day we must talk of these things – they will not go away of themselves. Fanny still comes to me in dreams, pale and thin, her dark eyes like saucers, and I know she means to reproach me, but she says nothing, nothing at all, it is I who do the talking. I scold her for taking so little care of herself, for refusing to eat properly, for dressing too lightly for the cold, for wearing thin shoes instead of stout boots. She does nothing to defend herself, but regards me mournfully, and bows her head, and then the others arrive all at once, Papa and Clare and Shelley, and she hastily ties on her cape and her brown bonnet and fades into the distance, her eyes bent upon me, and I wake with a feeling of utter misery and blankness.

Saturday, April 5th The Chancery case is going to drag on for ever. Lord Eldon has ruled that the hearings are to be resumed in his private chambers, and the Westbrooks have retained Sir Samuel Romilly, who is a very clever lawyer. I fear that our man Longdill is not in his class.

Shelley returned to London with Papa, and will remain until Wednesday; Hunt has been in court with him every day, and writes me full details. Hunt is, as always, cheerful and optimistic, and has offered to keep the children at his Hampstead cottage until we are ready to receive them; he says, what are two more added to his four? (I am not sure Mrs Hunt would agree.) Shelley is overwhelmed by his kindness and his unfailing attentiveness. It is as if he has no other claim upon his time than to attend S. to Westminster and to provide tea and comfort on their return. Yet the Hunts have no money; they can stay in Hampstead only until their landlord returns from abroad, probably in the summer, and where they are then to live, or how, is a mystery. Hunt says they will manage somehow or other, and of course Shelley is helping out. Meanwhile the children are still in Shropshire, and it is not at all certain that the Westbrooks will be required to produce them before the Court has ruled. This may take weeks if not months.

How tedious it all is! But the Westbrooks will stop at nothing, they are motivated solely by revenge. They have petitioned to have the children made wards of Chancery, and they obtained an injunction denying Shelley access to the children until this has been decided. Old Westbrook has settled an annuity on each child to show that S. has failed to provide for them; he must have done this immediately after Harriet's death. Hogg is the only lawyer S. can speak to with complete frankness, and he advises us that it would be unthinkable for the court to deny a father custody of his natural children; it would set a most dangerous precedent. In the absence of proven insanity – which even the Westbrooks have not the nerve to suggest – they would have to demonstrate S.'s 'moral unfitness' to be a father.

But implausible though it may be, their case is very worrying. Their chief evidence is a copy of *Queen Mab*, which, they say, is an attack on Xtianity and Xtian institutions including marriage; this, they claim, lies behind Shelley's 'abandonment' of his wife and his connection with me.

What defence can S. make to these charges? He cannot deny that he is the Author of *Queen Mab*, nor that the book challenges the 'truths' of Xtian revelation. It is all there in black and white: 'There is no God,' repeated three times! But his lawyers say he must present this work as a product of youthful error, and it is true that it sold no more than twenty copies.

As to S.'s 'abandonment' of Harriet, the Westbrooks have produced letters contradicting Shelley's position, which is that they separated by mutual consent. Yet Harriet was informed; everything was openly discussed. She agreed in principle, though she may have changed her mind afterwards. But the lawyers say these events must be presented as the folly of youth, the consequence of an overmastering passion, etc. The situation is now altered; Harriet is dead, we are married and settled, and can offer a home to the children.

But Shelley cannot bear to be attacked in this way, and I fear the effect of a prolonged court case on my Beloved's health and sanity. It is so unfair – there is nothing in his writing or his behaviour that has not been dictated by the highest principles. Was he to chain himself to a living death to conform to what the world calls the 'sacred bond' of marriage? He would have sickened and died, or put an end to his misery with laudanum. Harriet knew this; she did not insist. It is her odious sister who thinks to revenge herself in this way on Shelley.

Tomorrow Clare arrives with little Alba and her nurse. I have given them two rooms on the north side, under the attic, at the opposite end of the house from my little study. The rooms overlook the garden, and Clare can be as private as she likes.

Then on Wednesday my dearest one returns, to stay until he is summoned yet again by Lord Eldon. He will bring Hogg down with him for a few days' visit, and we can then plan our strategy.

Sunday, April 6th I should have known. 'How dark it is!' and then 'How damp it is!' And then, 'I cannot possibly have the little Darling in a room that faces north.'

'Do you want her to be over the road, with all the noise and dirt?'

'It is just as well for her to get used to the sound of horses and carts, she will sleep the better for it.'

And so we have switched the rooms around, and we have fires burning day and night, and tea at all hours. Evidently we are finished with all attempts at a vegetable diet, for Milly, the little nurse, is partial to boiled beef and cabbage, and Clare must have beef tea to regain her strength, and roasted marrow bones, in short a diet that requires continual scurrying about on somebody's part to obtain the unobtainable.

Unfortunately this tremendous bustle coincides, for me, with the onset of an exaggerated sensitivity to all sounds and odours. I am nauseated by all smells rising from the kitchen, in particular boiled cabbage, fried or boiled eggs, fish cooked in any shape or form, pork of any description, fresh or smoked. At the same time, I am constantly hungry, and long for something light and delicious and entirely odourless – strawberries and fresh cream, ripe melon, preserved figs . . .

It did not take long for Clare to put two and two together. She immediately began fussing over me.

'You must be sure to rest for an hour in the morning and an hour in the afternoon,' she said. 'It is an excellent idea to take a glass of wine with dinner, but you should avoid drinking tea. Tea will make you feel bloated; it is better to take a glass of warm water.'

'I find that tea has no unpleasant effects whatever,' I said. 'I must write in the morning, and again in the afternoon. I cannot rest all day long.'

Why must everything be such a battle? Then she exclaimed with glee: 'You must have conceived when you were staying in Skinner Street!'

'Really, Clara, it is no concern of yours where this child was conceived. It is pure speculation.'

'Very well, then, let us speculate. You drank champagne at the wedding breakfast – for there was a wedding breakfast, you told me so yourself. You attended the solemn ceremony at St Mildred's Church. You returned to the house, Mama resumed her labours in the shop, Papa withdrew into his study and fell asleep over a book, you and Shelley went upstairs to rest . . . *et voilà!*'

I could not help smiling at this picture.

'There – I've guessed it!' she said, and threw her arms around me. I could not remain annoyed – she is such a child. And so, as usual, we kissed and made up.

I wonder if it is only an old wives' tale that attributes conception to the nature and quality of the act of love and its surrounding influences.

The act of love was memorable – I could not get it out of my thoughts for days afterwards. My whole body continued to feel languorous, almost drugged, with a sweet, voluptuous sense of oneness with my Beloved. I could still hear his voice whispering in my ear, crooning, hypnotic, compelling my senses to fasten on to the rhythm of his body in mine, moving, rising, falling, rising, falling. It must be the most primitive rhythm in the world, like the mother's heartbeat, the rocking of the cradle, the ebb and flow of the sea. And so it continued, on and on, until I was far away, my mind utterly emptied and at peace, my entire being surrendered to his, surrounding his, murmuring his words, moving with him, and there seemed no reason ever to cease being one body, one motion, one breath, until the rhythm quickened and became urgent and with a high-pitched cry he released his life into mine and our child was conceived.

This happened on the 30th of December, 1816, in my father's bed, in which I was born on the 30th of August 1797 and in which my mother died little more than a week later, on the 10th of September.

Thursday, April 10th At last my love has returned. He arrived at ten o'clock last night, exhausted from the strains of the past week; he and Hogg were six hours on the London coach, held up by the rain and poor roads. We talked until two in the morning. What is to be done? The Westbrooks have no thought for the children – they are only concerned to ruin Shelley. If they had the children's interests at heart, they would rejoice to see them in the care of a father who stands to inherit £6,000 a year. S. says they are truly diabolical – it is impossible to know who is more vindictive, the father or the sister.

We must now have some time together, just the two of us. I insisted that S. must adopt a strict regimen of rest and relaxation. Long walks, a healthful diet, and congenial society may restore him to health. He slept in my arms all night, like a child at the breast.

In the midst of his troubles, he remembered to bring me Mawe's 'Gardening Calendar', which I have been studying with the greatest interest. I asked Harry if we could plant artichokes and asparagus, but he said he 'doubted they would do'. The soil is too chalky; we could have peas, and beans, and carrots, leeks and radishes, lettuce and spinach, cauliflower, and broccoli, and rhubarb – these would do very well. (These familiar names came out slowly, and were enumerated on his fingers for emphasis.) Harry, who is as brown and gnarled as the apple trees in the orchard, is extremely dour, calls me 'missus', and seems to have few words – chiefly monosyllables and grunts. I did not think it was the right moment to raise the subject of cucumbers and melons, as these would require a fairly extensive discussion. He said we should cut down the great cedar and the cypress trees, as they block the light, but I could not bear to cut down such handsome trees, they are like living beings. He agreed reluctantly to let me have a corner for a herb garden, but the dung has just been spread, and I must wait until the ground is ready.

Friday, April 11th What a strange creature Hogg is. I know he is devoted to Shelley. But they are as different as two friends can be, who have been the closest of companions since the age of eighteen. They form a striking contrast, Hogg being short, plump, and coarse-featured, with shiny black hair that grows low upon his forehead, and a thick glossy moustache of which he is inordinately proud. As far as I can tell, he has no convictions of his own, but embraces Shelley's principles simply out of loyalty and a desire to please. I believe he is at bottom utterly cynical. For all his supposed rebelliousness, he is following the path laid out for him by his barrister father, and will no doubt become a rich and successful lawyer.

Yet I am sure his loyalty is sincere – he would lay down his life for Shelley.

Today he declined to accompany Shelley and Clare on a visit to Bisham, and instead followed me about as I did my domestic chores. He questioned me closely about Papa, interrogating me about his early life and opinions, and his present mode of existence. I could not tell whether he was seeking information as a lawyer, a student of social manners, or a disciple of *Political Justice*. I finally became exasperated with him and spoke to him sharply. If he wished to know more about Papa, I said, Shelley would provide an introduction, and he could question Papa directly.

To my astonishment, he laughed, and said: 'You're very beautiful when you are angry – your lovely brown eyes flash and you have the most severe expression imaginable.'

It occurred to me that the entire conversation was an exercise in provoking me. If so, he succeeded all too well. I was extremely annoyed, and told him so.

'You don't frighten me,' he said. 'Shelley has told me all about you. It shall be my privilege to study your moods – even if I have to suffer your displeasure for it.'

'Is this your usual procedure?' I said.

'Naturally I would prefer it if you co-operated with me.'

'And why should I co-operate in such an absurd exercise?'

'Because, my dear Mary, we both love and cherish Shelley above all other human beings. If we are to serve him well, it is necessary for us to know each other, and to love each other.'

He put this so convincingly, and sounded so sincere, that I was ashamed of my earlier sharpness, and gave him my hand on it. 'Very well, on that ground, and that ground only, I consent.'

'But then we are best of friends, and shall remain so. I shall get to know you, and you shall come to know me. I am sure I have the harder task – you are a woman of genius – no, you must not protest – you inherit the gifts of two of the great minds of the age. And I am one of Nature's fools – I am simple in my affections, sincere in my enthusiasms. You shall find it the easiest thing in the world to know me.'

There was enough truth in this to disarm my natural suspicion and reserve. After all, he is right – the first person in his thoughts as in mine is our beloved Shelley. Together we can try to protect him from his tendency to injure himself and those he loves best.

Hogg is now gone up to Scotland, but he will stop here before returning to his chambers in town, and we shall then resume our conversation.

Sunday, April 13th Shelley has written a most wonderful pamphlet on the first issue of the day: the making of a new Constitution. He begins by declaring that the nation is governed and taxed by a Parliament which represents less than one-thousandth of the population. It is widely accepted that this is unfair and unjust; half a million people have already signed petitions for the reform of Parliament. S.'s proposal is simple but radical: to discover by a poll of the *entire* population whether it is their will that they continue to be governed in this undemocratic manner. He suggests that the country be divided into 300 areas, each to contain an equal number of inhabitants, and that 300 persons be commissioned to put the question to each inhabitant directly: whether or no they desire their representation in Parliament to be reformed.

The virtue of this plan is that it separates the question of reform from its contents, about which there is much disagreement. It is not at all clear whether it would be better to advocate universal manhood suffrage or household suffrage, whether the public interest would be served best by annual Parliaments; whether the upper House should be abolished and the monarchy replaced by a Republic. Shelley says there is so much division on each of these issues among the friends of reform that their strength is dissipated in squabbling among themselves, and the entire movement is dismissed as ineffectual.

We argued these matters at length with Peacock, who is now writing an amusing satire on the present system of representation. Shelley believes that a Republic is best calculated to promote the happiness and welfare of the nation; but Peacock is convinced that a Republic would soon collapse into anarchy, with demagogues and fanatics leading a popular party. He says, besides, that the common people are too attached to the signs and symbols of monarchy to relinquish them easily; the peculiar English habit of holding their 'betters' at once in deference and contempt is deeply ingrained. They both agree that it would be premature to advocate universal suffrage, which is commonly taken to mean universal male suffrage – though I disagree on this point with my Beloved, who believes ardently that women should be included in any reform, however moderate. I am afraid I am not a champion of my sex in this regard; the vast majority of women are too ignorant, too timid, too conventional to choose wisely if they were granted the suffrage. They are easily swayed by appeals to stability and order and would be a force for reaction. No doubt with education these things will change.

Peacock advised S. to disassociate himself firmly in his pamphlet from those who advocate violent revolution. He went one step further, and suggested that the Author promise to engage in no further activities to overturn the popular mandate, should it prove to endorse the existing system. At this point Shelley demurred, but I added my voice to Peacock's and I think we have persuaded him.

The pamphlet is to be printed and delivered to booksellers as soon as possible. The Author styles himself 'The Hermit of Marlow'.

With characteristic generosity, S. pledges to contribute £100 to the cost of his proposal. This is a nice gesture, and would in fact put us to some difficulty, but I do not think it likely to happen.

Tuesday, April 15th In a week, the Hunts are to come – Hunt and Marianne, the four little ones, and Marianne's sister Miss Kent. This will be a very pleasant addition to our little society. I wonder how long they think of staying. They must give up their Hampstead cottage, and it is not easy to find lodgings for a large family in town. Hunt is vague about his plans – he says that he lives in the present moment, and is content to leave the future to chance. This means that we are likely to have their company well into the summer. So much the better, for there are days when I find Peacock's whimsical humour trying; then too it will be good for Clare to have musical companionship. I cannot write if I am aware of her restless presence at the other end of the house, and I am not altogether happy about her eagerness to accompany Shelley on his walks, which often last from morning until dinner-time. This means that Alba is left to the nurse, and, by default, to Elise, who has made it clear that she has more than enough to do caring for Will. Perhaps music will provide an inducement to stay closer to home. Clare is not as domestic a creature as I am, and requires constant diversion if she is to be content.

CLARE
April 1817, Marlow

Monday, April 7th How happy I am, how fortunate – this is my last thought on retiring, my first thought on waking. The morning sun pours into my room, I look out onto the bustling road, with farmers driving their carts to market, and the young village girls in woollen shawls and pattens going down to work at the mills, and my Darling nestles close to my heart, safe and secure. I want one thing only to complete my happiness – and since I cannot have it, I am content with things as they are.

Albion House looks like a quaint cottage – the front windows have curious Gothic frames, and there are stucco ornaments above the door and along the roof. But it sprawls in every direction, with extensions to the back, so that inside it is very grand, at least in comparison to what we have been used to. I cannot tell whether it is meant to look more simple and unpretentious than it really is, or more ancient and venerable. The library is large enough for a ballroom – though I do not think Mary is planning this style of entertainment. I must suggest it to her; I imagine Mrs Peacock would be delighted to organise it. We could hire a band of country fiddlers, we could invite our gardener, and Mr Madocks the agent, and Elise could invite every fifth person she sees in town.

Meanwhile the fireplaces draw, the larder is stocked with hearty fare, and I see no reason why we cannot all live happy here – at least for the next few months, or until our fate contrives to move us on.

We have been so unsettled that I have neglected my Journal sadly. Three months ago, in Bath, on the 12th of January, I was delivered of a fine healthy girl. We call her Alba, for Dawn, also for her absent father Albé, whom she resembles in her blue-green eyes, the scornful curl of her lip, and her imperious will. Everyone says she is a beauty. She certainly has temperament, and when I catch her tiny finger in mine she breaks into a radiant smile. In short, she is Baby, and my very own delight and joy.

My confinement – well, the less said the better. It passed, and it is over. I remember Mama saying that if women ever told the truth about having babies the race would die out.

I then had to make the hardest decision of my life – not to suckle my Darling myself. But I bowed to Mary's arguments, put with her usual force and clarity; hard though it is, it seems that I must not be known as the mother of my child. By good luck, we secured a country girl as a nurse, Milly by name, whom I intend to educate. She barely knows her letters, but we shall start our lessons as soon as she has more time – for Alba seems to require the attention of at least two grown persons, 24 hours a day. Milly has left her two little ones with her mother, and I agreed that she is to visit them every second Sunday – I will have to manage somehow without her. We have also secured an ass, who gives enough milk for both children, and who is now tethered to an apple tree in the orchard.

A few days after the birth, when I had regained my strength, we had a solemn conference about the future. Mary said that her home was mine for as long as I liked. This was very gracious of her, I thought. But she and Shelley both feel that the best hope for Alba's future rests with his lordship, who has agreed to pay for her maintenance and education, which is to be suited to her station in life – that is, to his station in life. I hope and pray that Albé returns to England; otherwise we may have to take the little one to Italy.

'Now, Clara,' said Mary, in her most schoolmistressy fashion. 'This means you must not allow yourself to become too attached to the child. You will be known as her aunt; your relationship should be warm but distant.' I thought it best not to argue the point.

Shelley had already written to Albé to inform him of the birth of his daughter, and the safe recovery of mother and child. 'I must ask you to promise not to write to him, my dear. I know it is painful to you – but you will not want to prejudice the child's future.'

'I assure you I will do nothing to place her future at risk.'

'Dear girl, I knew you would be sensible.'

But Mary would not leave it at that. 'Promise that you won't write to him, Clary.'

'I have given you my word.' She could not press it further.

But oh, what a farce it is. I have no doubt that the physical presence of this enchanting child would alter all things in his eyes. It is simply a matter of time – and I must be patient.

Friday, April 11th Shelley and I have been exploring the country-side, while Mary writes away at her story. Yesterday I left the little one sleeping, and walked with Shelley to Little Marlow, about two miles distant, then down a quaint cobbled lane past the church and the ruins of a nunnery and old farm buildings to a footpath that leads across the fields to Bourne End, then back along the river. It was an unusually mild day, the sun was warm and there were yellow flowers in the hedges. The river meadows were still flooded from the recent rains; we saw ducks and geese, and Shelley thought he spotted a heron.

Today Peacock joined us – we sailed Shelley's boat across to Bisham Church and climbed up into the woods that extend along an escarpment high above the river. There were cowslips on the hill, and violets peeping through the undergrowth. Peacock pointed out some wood anemones, which I picked to press in my book, but they seem to have fallen out. Peacock is a great enthusiast of the Thames valley, and has promised to show us all places of interest within a sixteen-mile radius. He proposes to do this by foot, weather permitting. He is a great walker, and it is fortunate that I have sturdy boots and an appetite for pedestrianism. I would like to know the names of all the trees, the birds, and the wildflowers. Peacock says there are at least thirty different kinds of tits and finches in the woods, and a great variety of water-fowl in the river meadows.

Next time I plan to take a sketch book with me, and I shall be more methodical in my collecting.

As we approached the cottage I could hear the little one crying – what a strong, lusty voice she has at three months! But naturally, the sound tears at a mother's heart, and I rushed into the house and swept her into my arms. Milly assured me that she had slept soundly for most of the time that I was gone – poor darling, she must have sensed that I was returning at that very moment.

Tuesday, April 15th Despite my best efforts, I have been required to attend an interview with Mama at Skinner Street. Godwin insisted to Mary that I come, and though I pleaded various excuses – the real one being that I am most reluctant to leave the little Precious overnight – no excuse would do. And so on Sunday I took the mail from Maidenhead and arrived in London at six in the morning, having slept a little on the way, but I was hardly in the mood for being scolded. Mama was good enough to offer me tea and bread and butter before launching her attack.

'Well, Jane, I hope you will take Mary's example and find yourself a husband with a thousand a year, heir to 3,000 acres and a title. After all that has passed, her father is highly pleased with her. But I cannot say the same for you – in truth, Jane, you are a perpetual worry to me.'

Mama has become very fat, and when she has any exertion at all goes quite red in the face. She was deeply flushed now, with the effort of speaking frankly to me. I could only laugh, which incensed her further.

'And, pray, what do you find so funny?'

I could not help thinking that if Mama was impressed by Shelley's baronetcy, what would she say to his lordship as a son-in-law?

'I have no intention of marrying, Mama,' I said. 'You may set your mind at rest on that score.'

'What is to become of you, Jane? If you continue to live with Mary and Shelley, people will reach their own conclusions. Wherever he goes, Shelley attracts gossip, and it cannot be good for you to be talked about in the High Street of a small town where everyone knows everyone else's business.'

This is sound advice from a prudent mother. I doubt that Mama would like to be questioned too closely about her wanderings in

France and Spain some twenty years ago. The identity of my own papa remains to this day a closely guarded secret, and it is just as well that I have not the faintest interest in discovering who or what he may have been.

'People can say what they like. I am not going to rule my life by what people may or may not say.'

'Bravo, my girl. You shall do as you please – very well. You say you will not marry. Do you propose to attach yourself permanently to Shelley's household? Are you entirely convinced that it suits the second Mrs Shelley to have her attractive, vivacious sister – for you are an attractive girl, Jane – hanging about at all times? I fancy she might like to have her new husband to herself, at least now and then.'

'I cannot imagine who has been gossiping to you about our affairs. I assure you that I am a member of the household by Mary's invitation, and I will remain in the house only as long as I am welcome.'

'And if it should appear that you are no longer welcome, how, may I ask, do you propose to support yourself? Have you a plan for earning your living?'

This was rapidly turning into a most unpleasant conversation. I restrained myself from walking out in a temper.

'I am not entirely without resources. I know French and Spanish, I am learning Italian, and I am sure I could earn my way as a governess or schoolteacher.' (Hateful thought!) 'I am also taking singing lessons from a music master in Wycombe, who thinks highly of my voice.' (This was sheer improvisation – though Hunt told Shelley that Signor Corri lives in Wycombe, and might be persuaded to give lessons.)

'Do you think of going on the stage?' (said with high sarcasm).

I burst out: 'You have always underestimated me! You have no faith at all in my abilities. Mary was always the clever one. Well, so she is. But I also can make my way – you need not worry on my account.'

'Very well, Jane, I shall not concern myself about you. But I warn you now: you are not to come to me in six months' time, asking for help because you have no home and no money. I cannot offer

you a home, and I certainly cannot give you money. *Au contraire.*
We could not have paid William's school fees if Mr Lamb had not
come to the rescue. The shop survives from month to month – it
is a continual struggle. The burden falls on me, as I am sure you
are aware, nor do I get any credit for managing our affairs. Oh no,
nothing but complaints from that quarter.'

This I certainly did not want to hear. Fortunately, at that very
moment William Jr. appeared, grinning and smirking, to say that
Papa wished to see me in his study when we were finished. 'Jane,
Jane, has a new name,' he sang in falsetto.

'What is the matter with that boy?' I said indignantly. 'Why
isn't he at school?'

Mama ignored me, her nose in the air. He is just like her, a spy
and tattle-tale.

'Shall I go up to him?' I said.

'Do as you please. I have nothing more to say to you.'

I stormed upstairs. Really, what is the point of trying to
conciliate such people? Godwin was waiting for me, seated
behind his desk, under the portrait of Mary's saintly mother. He
stuck his thumbs in his waistcoat, which is decorated with the
same stains it had three years ago.

'Well, Jane, I trust you are all well in Marlow?'

'Very well, thank you.'

'Ahem . . . I do not wish to add to anything your mother may
have said. I support her entirely in her views about your future
prospects. All I wish to say is that I trust you will do nothing to
. . . ahem . . . disturb the peace and . . . ahem . . . serenity of
Shelley's little household. They have come safely through a very
difficult time . . . I would compare their union to a frail bark,
tossed on stormy seas, which has at last reached harbour. I trust
you follow my meaning.'

I was so angry that I could hardly speak. 'I cannot understand
why you all think so little of me. *I* am not going to disturb their
peace. *I* am not going to destroy the happiness of my dearest
friends. How can you even imagine such a thing? Am I so cruel,
so inconsiderate? Could I be so ungrateful?' Then – to my shame
– I burst into tears.

At this, Godwin frowned severely and took up his book. After a few minutes, he said sternly, 'Have you finished?'

I nodded. I was still shaking with rage, and was extremely annoyed with myself.

'Well, then. I was going to suggest that you might like to go to our friends the Danvilles in Somerset as a governess. I believe your mother may already have made this proposal to you. They have three girls, very quick and well-behaved, all under nine years of age, and they would like them to study languages, music and drawing. I am prepared to recommend you for the post – I would do so with full confidence.'

'Mama proposed nothing of the kind. I do not contemplate going anywhere as a governess, at present. I am engaged in a course of study of the Italian language. I am reading Tasso with Shelley.'

'That, my dear Jane, is precisely the problem. Your friendship with Shelley looks very odd to the rest of the world. They assume that friendship between a warm-blooded young man and an attractive young woman can mean one thing only. I do not say that I agree with them. But I want you to be aware of the risks you are taking. There are others to think of besides yourself.'

'I am thinking of them. I have no intention of disappearing into the depths of Somerset because you and Mama are worried about the gossip of fools who know nothing about true friendship and honour and loyalty. I am surprised that you would listen to such people.'

He sighed. 'I told your mother there was no point in talking to you. You are as stubborn as the others.'

'I have my own life,' I said. 'I am no longer a child, to be told what to do.'

His face was turned away from me – a 'noble head', Shelley called it – the thin grey hairs neatly combed across the high domed forehead, eyes hooded, large nose pocked and fleshy, thin lips pressed together, large square chin jutting forward. His head is very large for his body; he looks quite normal when he is seated, but his legs are very short and when he stands he is only a little over five feet tall. I wondered how this man could have inspired love in the female breast, and wild admiration in a host of young men, including Shelley. I find him pitiable – timid, conventional, vain, and pompous.

I stayed to lunch, which was as unpleasant as might be expected. In my honour, Mama had stewed a most revolting mess of pork bones and cabbage, peas and potatoes, gluey and congealing in the dish. William Jr. fidgeted, rolling pellets of bread and flicking them in my direction.

'Is Shelley still taking a vegetable diet?' Mama asked.

'Meals are not as important to us as they are to other people,' I said. 'We walk a great deal. It is a much healthier life than it is in London, where you can hardly breathe the air, it is so full of smoke and dirt.'

Mama asked if I would stay the night, but I said I had booked a place on the evening coach, *and must return to my home*. I am sure my expression defied them to contradict me – but no one dared.

At last I was released, and I walked about for the rest of the afternoon. The air was damp, the skies grey, the shop windows dusty and streaked, the pavement muddy underfoot. But the Strand was full of bustle and activity. I went into a linen drapers and a haberdasher, and was extremely tempted by a charming pink lace cap for the Darling. Fortunately, I did not have the guinea to buy it, or even a shilling to spare. Then I walked in Temple Gardens, and threw crumbs to the lazy fat carp in the Fountain pool, which seemed not to appeal to them at all, though the crumbs eventually disappeared. I do think that of all creatures fish are the least interesting – I cannot understand the masculine passion for angling, which Peacock, for one, praises as if it is a high art. Solemn pink-faced gentlemen drifted past in their black gowns and wigs, their mouths working, memorising briefs or rehearsing pleas, or simply digesting the remains of their dinner. I had to laugh, they reminded me so much of the carp circling about in the pool. I thought of surprising Hogg at his attic perch at 1 Garden Court, but then I remembered that he was in Scotland. It would have been worth it, just to see his expression on having a Woman appear in his rooms! I saw a few

primroses sprinkled about under the great plane trees in Fountain Court but they are city flowers, carefully tended, delicate, and ready to droop, utterly unlike the profusion of healthy native blooms in our country lanes.

And now I am back at home with my Precious, a piano has appeared in the drawing room as if by magic (in reality through the good offices of Hunt) and I have no intention of removing from this spot until called by Fate or Necessity.

Wednesday, April 16th Mary and I have lived together since we were three years of age. Yet I do not think two human beings could differ more thoroughly in their habits of mind.

Now that we have such a busy household, it is rare for the two of us to be alone together. But we found ourselves sitting together in the library this afternoon – Shelley and Peacock had gone to Maidenhead, Elise and Milly were busy with the little ones, and Mary suddenly broached the forbidden subject.

M.: Do you ever think of Fanny?

C.: Not often.

M.: I do not think of her often – yet the pain is as fresh as when it happened. I do not think I shall ever get over it.

(I was tempted to say: It makes no difference to poor Fanny whether or not you get over it.)

M.: Why do you think she did it?

C.: She was unhappy. She had nothing to live for.

M.: I am convinced that she felt that we had abandoned her. That is the thought that haunts me – I cannot put it out of my mind.

C.: We did abandon her, if you want to put it that way. What else could we have done?

M.: You are cold, Clare – you do not feel things as I do.

C.: I try to see things clearly. I refuse to lie to myself about my feelings. Perhaps you are right, my feelings are not as refined as yours.

M.: I cannot help thinking that we sacrificed her to protect ourselves.

C.:   If you insist on thinking of her as a sacrifice, you may do so. I refuse to take the blame for her death. It was Fanny's choice, her decision. She had a longing for death, she was always talking about it. We could not have prevented her.

M.:   I could have offered her a home. Now that we have a home, it is too late.

C.:   Mama thinks she took her life because she was in love with Shelley.

M.:   What nonsense! That woman is impossible – she does nothing except make trouble.

C.:   I don't think it is nonsense. Why should Fanny not have been in love with Shelley? He was always very kind to her, he sent her presents and read poetry to her. It would not have been a reason to take her life, of course.

I was tempted to ask Mary if she ever felt haunted by the ghost of poor Harriet. But we do not talk about the Unnameable one, we do not ask searching questions about why she decided on a cold, rainy night last November to leap into the Serpentine River and end her troubles. We do not regard her as a sacrifice, she was simply a nuisance, an inconvenience. Why do we not mention her name? Because it would upset certain people to hear it mentioned. It was all a terrible mistake, a series of avoidable errors.

Hypocrisy, thy name is Woman.

Thursday, April 17th No word as yet from his lordship. Shelley wrote in January – is it possible that the letter has not yet reached Venice? I know Albé too well to think he could remain unmoved – his greatest lament is that he has been unfairly deprived of his daughter by the late lamented Lady B. His vanity is at stake – he cannot bear the thought of dying without leaving a trace of his features impressed on some small hapless creature. And the Darling, to our amusement, looks exactly like her father. If I had not been present at the birth, and fully conscious through every unspeakable minute of it, I would wonder about our blood relationship – for there is not the slightest physical resemblance between us.

Shelley too is surprised that we have not heard from Albé, for there is much to discuss. 'Alba' is charming, but the child must have a Christian name, and her father must be consulted about this. We could christen her 'Clara', but as Mary said, tactlessly, 'Clara' might not be her father's first choice.

Surely we must try to discover his views on this and other matters. I have a strong desire to write myself – it is a mother's duty. I am perfectly capable of writing a dignified letter; my language shall be restrained and chaste. I shall give news of Mary (whom Albé respects) and Shelley, and perhaps provide a glimpse of our daily life – our walks and conversation, our frugal diet, our studies and simple amusements – it is a picture to divert a reprobate like his lordship. There shall be no reproaches, no allusion to the past; no, we must look forward, for we have years ahead of us, an entire lifetime.

Saturday, April 19th The mild weather continues, indeed it is almost unseasonably warm, and the fields and hedges are full of soft new greens and yellows. This morning, while Alba slept, Shelley and I sailed across to Bisham and climbed up to our favourite spot in the woods, high above the river, to read and write for an hour or two. At Shelley's suggestion we have been reading history (Pliny and Tacitus) and philosophy (Locke, and Godwin, Godwin, Godwin). These historians and philosophers, without exception, appear to consider Humanity to be synonymous with Man. I find this a source of chagrin, and have expressed myself forcibly on the subject to Shelley. In the presence of these great thinkers I feel overlooked, a person of no consequence, a mere woman, appendage to Man. I can share in his glorious history, I can participate in his thought, I can stand amazed at his artistic productions, but I am not expected to contribute. To the men who constitute the great onward stream of history and thought, my existence is a matter of supreme indifference. True, I have a function in the scheme of things: to cook, sew, and provide support for men weary after their labours in the service of war and politics. And if I prefer to devote my hours to study, other females can always be found to provide the comforts of home and bed. But I feel obliged to protest, not least on behalf of my Darling.

Mary does not feel indignant as I do. She is above such petty annoyance and resentment. This is because Shelley insists that her qualities of mind far surpass his own. She cannot really believe this to be the case – but she is flattered by his opinion, which he maintains even when he is suffering from her reluctance to join him for a morning of idle walking or boating. This she considers a waste of precious time needed for study or writing. I am quite happy to join him, of course, since I have no 'work' of any consequence, or so Mary assumes. And why she should resent the cheerful hours thus whiled away is beyond my understanding. But I do believe our high-minded Mary is as inconsistent as lower creatures like myself.

The truth is that Shelley sees Mary through a fond mist compounded of his wild passion for her and his infatuation with Godwin and the revered shade of M.W. Mary is extremely clever, but she is not one of Nature's heroines. She can be petty and spiteful like anyone else, and she is an expert at sulking. Then she utterly loses that fair, serene beauty that S. sees in her at all times; she becomes positively ugly, her thin brows meet in a frown, her lips grow pursed and mean, her fine light-brown hair lies tangled and matted, and she is more like a mouse or a mole than an eagle. Poor Shelley is so free himself of the small vices of envy and resentment that he cannot even recognise them in his beloved.

To return to the subject of male egotism, and the tendency of our great thinkers to include only half the race in their speculations on human nature. I must admit that I felt no resentment at Albé's low opinion of women. I think this is because he was so open in his contempt. It is the hypocrisy of the philosopher who claims to believe in equality and women's rights, while thinking of women (if at all) as a sort of one-legged male, hobbling in the rear, falling ever further behind, that is so irritating. And then, Albé was as contemptuous of the generality of men as he was of women, with very few exceptions. Then again, I never had any doubt that he himself possessed the true quality of genius. I felt fortunate to be admitted to his company, even for so short a time.

Shelley too has genius – it is what makes him so strange and unpredictable, so unlike the mass of mankind. His imagination is unrestrained by facts and practicalities; he sees everything in a grander dimension, stretching back to the beginnings of time, and forward to the end of time. Yet he is also capable of the most astonishing kindness and thoughtfulness. It is a pity that he is so worn down by cares – money worries, and anxiety about the Lord Chancellor, and Harriet's children. It is so unfair for him, of all people, to be accused of criminal behaviour – he who is above all devoted to justice and truth.

His friends Peacock and Hogg are lesser beings, pale shadows of the true flame. Mary says Peacock is cold; I would say dry – a sexless man. Mary is still annoyed at him because he had a kind word to say for Harriet; she will sometimes stay in her room if he stops to dinner. Hogg she seems to find amusing, but I cannot bear his possessive attitude towards Shelley; he is as jealous and as demanding of his attention as a lover.

Oddly enough, Peacock and Hogg seem to have struck up a friendship. They both profess enthusiasm for the walk to London and back (a mere 32 miles each way), and they enjoy throwing classical references at each other. Hogg prefers to stay with Peacock when he comes to Marlow, I think because Mrs Peacock provides substantial meals as well as alcoholic refreshment. Neither gentleman has been converted to the vegetable diet.

Jealousy, I think, is the ugliest of passions. Thank heaven it is not a thing I suffer from. I never thought that Albé would not smile on others, either before or after my brief time as favourite. Though I am denied his presence – it may be for ever – I am not jealous of his lovers. It would be as pointless as feeling jealous of his thousands of readers.

Peacock resembles me in this. He looks on the world with detached curiosity, takes what amuses him, attaches himself where he is attracted, and expects little in return. He is cheerful with his friends, but not averse to solitude, and enjoys the company of his thoughts.

Hogg, in contrast, is jealous (of whom, I need not say) and insists on his rights. He must always come first in Shelley's affections – in consequence, he is a great mischief-maker.

Tuesday, April 22nd The Hunts have arrived, and are installed in the rooms opposite mine, with the children joining Will in the nursery. What a bustle and to-do, with boxes of books and music everywhere, trunks of clothes, toys, and bedding, plants and objets d'art, and children running up the stairs, and falling down the stairs, sent out to the garden to play, called in from the garden for tea, sent out into the garden again to play. For a wonder, everyone is cheerful, which is because Hunt is the easiest guest imaginable; he lets everything happen around him and is good-humoured about each contretemps, indeed one would think he is the genial host rather than the embarrassed guest. Although both Hunt and Mrs Hunt are older by ten years than Shelley, it is plain that they are children, and we must be the grown-ups. For once Mary and I are in complete agreement: they are the nicest people, we are delighted to have them as companions, and we are all the best of friends.

Hunt is fair and slender, with a mop of curly brown hair and the pleasantest expression, except when he is worried about money; then he suddenly pulls at his hair with both hands like a little boy, and says: 'What on earth are we to do? I have no idea how we are ever going to manage!' But then he sits down at the piano and all cares are forgotten. He knows all the popular ballads, and all the arias from Mozart's operas, indeed he knows more about music than anyone I have ever met. Mrs Hunt, or Marianne, as I must call her, is very beautiful, with long silky black hair that falls below her waist. She is frail, somewhat nervous and anxious, sporadically offering to help and then being distracted by the children, or by life. They are both wonderfully absent-minded, always losing things or misplacing them, including the children; at least one child is always left behind. It is like a chorus: 'Have you seen Thornton? Is Alice there? O where is that Jemmy? Are we all here?'

Marianne's sister Bessy is the one who manages them all; she insists that Marianne must rest, she takes charge of Hunt and the children, counts their stockings, sees to meals. They go everywhere together, and when Hunt walks out he likes to have Marianne on one arm and Bessy on the other, and he refers to them as his wives or his sisters, depending on his whim.

We have had much conversation, and it is very good to be thrust once again into the real world. I have been so occupied with my own interesting affairs that I had not realised the extent to which our ancient freedoms have been destroyed, just in the past two months since Parliament has been sitting. Habeas corpus has been suspended, and all meetings of more than fifty persons must be authorised by the magistrates, who refuse to entertain a request from any group that has the faintest whiff of subversion about it. This is all because a stone was thrown at the carriage of the Prince Regent as it was approaching Westminster for the opening of Parliament; it broke a window and narrowly missed the royal pate, and this is the excuse the government have used to arrest all their enemies and throw them in prison. (Though Hunt says this has not actually happened yet.) He says the Liverpool ministry is the worst in memory – they have destroyed the freedom and independence of the common people while protecting the freedom of the rich to become richer, and of the powerful to grow more powerful. Throughout the manufacturing centres, men who once owned their own smallholdings have been reduced to wage-slaves, dependent on the masters for employment. The Government's god is Adam Smith, they have elevated *laissez-faire* into an immutable principle, regardless of its destructive effects on the common people, and if an appeal is made to the Government to intervene on grounds of compassion, they point to Malthus, and the necessity of reducing population by war or famine – a regrettable side-effect of The Way Things Are and Must Be.

I said I did not understand how *laissez-faire* authorised laws to prevent combinations, public meetings, and publication of views critical of the government of the day. But Hunt laughed and said I was a naïve child and must think further on it.

Of course we have been taking Hunt's paper, but it is very different having the editor himself in our midst, chattering away about flowers and goddesses one minute and speculating the next minute about whether the Government is likely to last the year, or to be overturned by reform or revolution. Shelley is a great believer in reform, but I myself do not see that reform would be any use; as long as the poor people of this country must work to keep the rich living in the style to which they feel entitled, I do not see that it matters much who has the suffrage, it will only be a choice between the landowners or the manufacturers holding power. I do not like to say this, of course. Hunt alternates writing political articles for his paper with his brother John. He also writes on the theatre and other entertainment, and he occasionally contributes a poem; he signs his pieces with a hand, the finger pointing to the truth.

I wonder if I might write an occasional piece for his journal, under a pseudonym; or perhaps I could do some translating for him. This is how the great M.W. supported herself when she first lived in London, before she met Godwin. I must remember to pursue this interesting possibility.

MARY
April 1817, Marlow

Tuesday, April 15th Today I finished my Novel. It is a most satisfying feeling to have carried a literary project from conception, through labour, to birth. I began my story on the 24th of July, 1816, and composed the last sentence nine months later, almost to the day. Though the genesis of my story lay in a dream which still visits me from time to time – the horrific apparition of a monstrous birth – it was my Beloved who recognised its significance, and insisted that I bring the whole to fruition. So in a sense the story owes its life to our intercourse – like everything else in my present existence.

Still, I take pleasure in the knowledge that the story is truly my own invention, though many sources have fed it. Without the example of my father's novels, I doubt that I would have had the courage to proceed to three volumes. I told him so, and I could see that he was flattered and pleased. I have used my Journal as a source of the landscape and scenery through which my accursed pair pursue each other; I have drawn the broad lake, and the mighty Jura and its surrounding peaks, in sight of which I began my story. My companions during those memorable weeks have entered into my characters, though this has not been deliberate on my part. But I have not excised these details when I have recognised them – let them stay as private memorials to a vanished time.

When I think back to our little villa on the lake, how far off it seems! How changed we are from those carefree summer weeks! How much has been lost – and yet we are happy, and appear to be settled. But at times the thought oppresses me: we cannot build our happiness on the sufferings of others. A curse hangs over us, which it will take all our courage and ingenuity to outwit.

These unusually mild spring days are a great restorative, however. Suddenly there are daffodils scattered about on the garden lawn, and there are celandines blooming in the hedges. I still have much work to do; I must correct my manuscript, which will take at least two weeks, and I will need another two weeks to transcribe it. But I must take time away from my desk to go on the river with my Beloved, if the fine weather holds. We can take Will, and it will be a treat for Elise, who has had no holiday at all since we've been here. This means that Clare must walk, or stay behind. But she has had more than her share of Shelley's company recently. She can practise her music while we are out; the piano arrived last week, and is a very handsome one. I was astonished to learn that it cost 75 gns, which of course we do not have. But Shelley and Hunt have both signed notes for it, which will not come due for three years, by which time Sir Timothy — but who knows, these old gentlemen seem to go on for ever. Meanwhile we have arranged for Clare to have music lessons with Signor Corri – that too will be on account. But then everything is on account, it is the way we must live, for the present. Shelley has arranged to purchase blankets for the poor, on account, and to distribute alms each Saturday, on account. But we cannot allow people to starve. Many of the local villagers are employed at the Marlow mills or the brewery, but the surrounding districts are suffering great hardships, especially among the lacemakers, once the chief industry here. Shelley has been going about to the cottages, and hears harrowing tales of distress. Apparently the lacemakers suffer from an affliction of the spine, from bending over their netting frames from the age of seven or eight, when they are first trained to the work; this means they cannot bear children, for their womb is tilted and the pelvic bones do not grow properly. Their eyesight is also impaired by the close work, and blindness is not uncommon among girls in their twenties. But Shelley said they mind the lack of employment more than this. Certainly we must do what we can to relieve their misery.

Sunday, April 20th Disturbing conversation after tea with Shelley, Peacock, and Clare. The subject: whether love suffers or gains from being shared.

My Beloved argues earnestly that it is in the nature of love to overflow beyond its object; it has nothing exclusive in its claim. The intercourse of the sexes is the highest expression of love, no different in kind from the love of nature, of beauty, of virtue. Love cannot be measured, cannot be contained; it can only give of itself.

Clare joins in enthusiastically. Why should my love for X be less because I love Y as well? Do I divide and apportion my love for my friends? for my children? for my parents? Why then insist on exclusiveness in love between a man and a woman? Monogamy does not exist in nature, it is a social arrangement based on a false principle. The marriage vow sanctified by a hypocritical Church is cant; nobody takes it seriously, certainly not the men and women who solemnly swear to love one another for the rest of their days.

S.: 'It is a device. It is intended to protect property. Marriage regards the woman as property, and ensures the right of inheritance. To this right we owe the inequalities of our society, and their perpetuation from one generation to the next. But love has nothing to do with property; it does not seek to own anything, or to establish rights in its object. Love is a free gift from one human being to another. It enhances and ennobles everything it touches; all the world share in its benefits.'

Peacock nods solemnly. 'It is a rising tide, a flood. Love is a great impersonal force, and we humans are mere victims or spectators. For myself, I prefer to be a spectator, and to keep my feet dry. But I admire all of you lovers – it is the most enchanting thing in the world to share in the overflow of love, in its music, poetry, food and drink and conversation, and then to go home to my dear mother and her calm, quiet house and her well-stocked kitchen, where ecstasy seldom enters in and good sense prevails.'

I cannot bring myself to say a word. All my instincts rebel against the thought of sharing my love with another. And yet I know that Shelley is utterly sincere in his belief. He would have been happy to share Harriet with Hogg, he has told me as much; he truly believes that the circle of love embraces all of us, as brothers and sisters, and that the sexual connection is simply one more expression of relationship, the most intimate and therefore the most precious. I too believe that it is wrong to set chains upon love between the sexes; that would be to poison feeling at its source. But I could not cheerfully live in the way that my Beloved envisages, in his ardour for his friends.

Last night I suggested that Shelley sleep on the sofa in my study, next door to our bedroom. The past few nights, I have been waking several times to pass water, and he wakens with me and cannot fall back to sleep. He has been quite unwell; it is essential that he have an uninterrupted night's sleep. I left the door ajar, and he promised to call if he needed me. This will be a temporary arrangement, I trust.

The truth is that as the baby grows and moves about I sleep better alone. Best of all is when Will trundles in, rubbing his sleepy eyes, and climbs into bed and curls up in my arms, sweet darling. I have been neglecting him sadly.

Wednesday, April 23rd The Hunts arrived on Monday, and everything is topsy-turvy. The children are everywhere, and the library and drawing room are full of boxes, trunks, books, and strange objects, statues and urns and china shepherdesses and chess sets. Shelley is as happy as a child to be offering hospitality to his dear friends, and I suppose we shall manage. Poor Elise was in high dudgeon; she has been displaced from the nursery and must stay in the attic, but I assured her it would only be for a short time. Will is enthralled by the children, he follows Thornton about like a little soldier following his captain, and for his sake alone I am delighted that they are here. Mrs Hunt – Marianne – is very frail; she is expecting again and spends most of her time in bed, but her sister Miss Kent is a paragon of energy. She quietly turns chaos into order, and I shall leave everything to her. I explained to her that we do not plan meals with any regularity, and to my relief she offered to take charge of the kitchen. When I said that we try to keep to a vegetable diet, and do not use sugar because of the slave trade, she laughed, and said she would see that everyone had enough to eat, and a sufficient variety to allow each person to follow his own preference in matters of diet.

Hunt brought with him Lord Eldon's provisional judgement, which is even worse than we feared. He has yielded every point to the Westbrooks; he takes it as proven that Shelley is an atheist and therefore unfit to educate his children. But the legal mind loves to make fine distinctions, and so he argues, if I follow his thought, that it is not because of his principles alone, or because of his conduct alone, that Shelley is to be deprived of his children, but rather because his conduct is in accord with his principles.

One would think this might be an argument in his favour – but apparently Shelley is doubly damned, for thinking and for acting. Triply damned, for defending both his principles and his conduct. In other words, if a man had no principles, and acted viciously, but admitted his fault, the Court would not interfere with his natural right to custody of his children. This seems so perverse that I must set down the precise words employed by this guardian of Society.

This is a case in which the father's principles cannot be misunderstood: in which his conduct, which I cannot but consider as highly immoral, has been established as the effect of those principles; conduct which he represents to himself and others not as conduct to be considered as immoral, but to be recommended and observed in practice.

I consider this, therefore, as a case in which a father has demonstrated that he deems it to be a matter of duty which his principles impose upon him, to recommend to those whose opinions and habits he may take upon himself to form, that conduct, in the most important relations of life, as *moral* and *virtuous* which the law calls upon me to consider as *immoral* and *vicious*.

This refers to S.'s views of marriage as a bond sanctioned by love, not by the Church, and also his refusal to accept articles of Xtian dogma such as the divinity of Christ and the immortality of the soul.

But the cruellest part is the conclusion:

I cannot, therefore, think that I should be justified in delivering over these children for their education exclusively to what is called the care to which Mr Shelley wishes it to be entrusted.

Hunt says it is the first time to his knowledge that a father has been denied custody of his children because of his religious beliefs. But the case is not settled, it has simply been postponed. We must now propose a plan for the children's education to submit to the Master of the Court; the Westbrooks too are asked to submit a plan. Meanwhile Shelley is still denied access to the children; indeed, we do not know where they are. The Westbrooks have shut up their house on Chapel Street, and left instructions to give no address.

Shelley has been plunged into despair by this latest blow. He is convinced that if the Westbrooks succeed in their case they will bring criminal charges against him.

'What charges could they bring?' Hunt asked.

'Blasphemy and seditious libel.'

'It is not impossible,' Hunt said thoughtfully. 'I suppose you know that Lord Sidmouth has sent a circular from the Home Office to magistrates throughout the country, drawing attention to their new powers to arrest persons suspected of disseminating what they call seditious libel.'

Then he confessed that he had altered a line in Shelley's poem, written in Geneva, which was printed in Hunt's paper under the name 'Elfin Knight'. Shelley had attacked as 'frail spells' 'the name of God, and ghosts and Heaven'. Hunt was worried that this might appear blasphemous to the censor, and changed the line to 'the names of Demon, Ghost, and Heaven', which he thought sufficiently innocuous.

'But the evil lies in the name of God,' Shelley said. 'It is in the name of God that governments justify war and oppression, the hounding of their enemies and the stamping out of truth, all the tyrannical steps they take to ensure that they remain in power.'

'My dear Shelley, I agree with you entirely, but if I am to continue to publish, I cannot take a stand on every word, I must make small sacrifices in order to protect the journal as a source of information for the reading public. We are living in dangerous times. It would be a mistake to underestimate the lengths to which this ministry is prepared to go. They are determined to suppress all dissent; they have put spies in all the London Hampden clubs, they are refusing to allow meetings even for charity events.'

Fantastic as it seems, if Shelley were to be convicted of 'seditious libel', which his attack on monarchy in *Queen Mab* would be sufficient to prove, he could be sentenced to imprisonment or even to transportation. As he said, if the Court regards him as a monster who is not to be trusted with his own children, why should he not be locked away in prison? Why should he be left at liberty to corrupt the young and spread his *immoral* and *vicious* beliefs abroad? (These were his words – I tremble as I write them down.)

Hunt tried to be reassuring, but we both became extremely agitated on considering these possibilities. It is impossible to guess what the Westbrooks will attempt, and how far they will be successful in Court. What is certain is that they are Shelley's sworn enemies, and will stop at nothing to take their revenge.

'Try not to take alarm, my dear young friends,' Hunt said. 'The law's delay, in this case, is to your advantage; nothing can be attempted against you while judgement is postponed. Lord Eldon, although he holds the views of his class, is a man of intelligence and cultivation; he will not want to give the children into the care of a retired tavern-keeper and his illiterate daughter. What you must do is draw up a plan of education for the children, in which your own opinions play no part. Indeed, it will be best if you have nothing to do with this plan, except to fix your signature to it.'

We both could see the sense to this, and we have agreed to ask Hogg to draw up a proposal which is free of all offence.

I have re-read Lord Eldon's decision, and to my surprise I thought I detected a grudging respect for Shelley in the Chancellor's remarks. Evidently he has read the Notes to *Queen Mab* with care; he has taken the trouble to study the character and thinking of this sworn enemy of society. Of course, he believes Shelley to be in error; the Chancellor is, after all, pledged to uphold and defend the class of which he is a product. But in recognising the consistency of S.'s belief and conduct he acknowledges his sincerity. I looked again at his final remarks, which we passed over in our alarm. There he accepts two possibilities: first, that the young man whose beliefs and conduct he deplores may be persuaded, with time, to change his views; and second, that he, the Lord Chancellor, may be mistaken – in which case he is prepared to change his decision.

This is a remarkable concession for a man who is so utterly convinced of the 'truths' he upholds.

Or it may be that Hunt is right, and it is a matter of class allegiance in the end. Our best hope is that Lord Eldon will be extremely reluctant to award against a man of property in favour of a tavern-keeper.

When Hogg next comes I shall suggest that the two of us draw up a plan for the children's education. Shelley must be spared this demeaning task. When I see him dancing our darling blue-eyed babe on his knee for hours, or happily playing hide and seek with him in the garden, I burn with anger at the evil institutions of this country and their ermine-robed agents, who dare to decide that such a man is unworthy to educate his own children.

Friday, April 25th I think I have detected the secret of Marianne's languor. To my astonishment, I discovered that she is wearing stays, in her third month of pregnancy. It is not surprising that she finds it hard to breathe, and cannot digest her food, and lies about most of the day in a darkened room. I ventured to speak to her about it.

'But my dear Mary,' she said, 'I cannot go about in a state of undress. It is all very well for you and Clare to dispense with stays; you are both young and energetic. Clare does not seem to care what she looks like, and you live in the country where you do not see people, and it does not matter how you go about. But if I wore nothing but a loose gown I would age ten years in a matter of weeks. The children wear me out so, and I feel swollen and ugly, and, oh dear—' here she burst into tears.

I waited until she had dried her eyes, and said, 'If you would just leave them off for a day—' but she stopped me.

'No, dearest Mary, do not say another word, I really cannot bear it.'

I had to desist. But it is absurd for her to allow her vanity to injure her health. I thought of speaking to Miss Kent about it, but I do not like to embarrass my friends – for I can see that although their living arrangement suits Hunt very well, it is a source of some uneasiness to Marianne.

Saturday, April 26th I have been out on the boat only twice since finishing my Novel, both times in the late afternoon, for a sail to Bisham and back. I have had to devote the mornings to transcribing my Novel; otherwise the pages remain on my desk, and I fancy that my characters reproach me with neglect. But the days have been fine, and it is necessary for Shelley to take air and exercise; otherwise he is overwhelmed by anger at the obloquy directed at him, and his fear that worse is to come. Hunt is far more inclined to stop at home than to walk or go on the river; he says he loves best of all to potter about the garden. But at the first sign that S. is ready to leave the house, Clare leaps up and offers to accompany him, insisting that it is time for Alba to take her nap, and Peacock usually joins them. So I may write undisturbed for several hours, during which time, miraculously, the marketing is done and dinner prepared, thanks to Miss Kent. Meanwhile Hunt has taken a corner of the garden for his reading and writing, and the children play about him without bothering him in the least. Milly tends to Alba (who hardly naps at all), and Elise tends to Will, or sits on the garden seat writing letters, and we really seem to be a community of friends, such as Shelley has in his happier moments always envisaged. I pray that our contentment may last – that we be allowed to protect ourselves and our innocent children from the harm that threatens from a cruel and envious world.

Miss Kent, I have discovered, has a passion for gardening. She has become great friends with Harry, whom she has won over by deferring to his judgement in all matters. As I followed them about, I realised that he is neither deaf nor slow, only extremely stubborn – but he treats her with respect, almost like an equal. Today she gave me a little tour of what she called our 'pleasure-ground', explaining the plants and their relation to one another, from the hyacinths and tulips just beginning to appear along the borders, to the charming variety of the shrubbery.

We looked over the kitchen garden together, and she said she saw no reason why we could not have an asparagus bed; it would take two or three seasons to establish itself, however. She was not so sure about artichokes, and she was positively discouraging about melons, figs, and peaches – she said we do not have sufficient sunlight. Our great advantage is water. The soil is full of chalk, and requires great dressings of dung if it is to prove fertile.

I begin to see that it is not enough to enjoy fruits and flowers in their season; one must be forever vigilant against weeds and pests. It is not a matter, as I had supposed, of co-operating with a beneficent Nature; on the contrary, gardening is an endless battle, in which the chief weapon is the knife. Left to itself, the garden grows wild; the strongest grow rampant and drive out the weak. It is always the coarsest plants, the burdocks and nettles, which establish their roots most deeply and propagate most vigorously; if water is scarce they drink it all, they crowd into what little sunlight appears, and there is no hope at all for the tender shoots and fragile root systems of the more delicate plants.

I fancy this is an allegory of our lives, and an image of English society at the present time.

Wednesday, April 30th Our evenings have been transformed. After supper we have music, Hunt plays the piano and Clare and Marianne sing – for to our surprise Marianne comes to life in the evening, emerging from her room as soon as Bessy has packed the children off to bed, looking fresh-faced and happy, her long black hair brushed and shining. Then we stay up late talking on all kinds of odd topics, dreams, superstitions, curious Eastern religious practices. Hunt is a fund of stories about every figure of consequence in letters or politics, and so we gossip and exchange tales. Bessy quietly slips away, then reappears with a bowl of negus and glasses for everyone. Clare falls asleep in front of the fire, and will not be moved. I know that if I do not go to bed I shall not be able to transcribe my Novel the next morning, so at ten I go upstairs, and an hour later Shelley follows – though neither of us can fall asleep because we are so over-stimulated.

Then I have the most vivid dreams. Last night I dreamt that I was climbing up a mountain behind Papa, and when I reached the top he had vanished, though I looked for him everywhere. At last I came to a lonely cottage, and I pushed open the door and discovered a body lying on a narrow bed against the wall, covered with a white sheet, and I knew with absolute certainty that it was my father. So great was my terror that I woke at that moment and called Shelley, who rushed in from the study and held me. He stayed till morning, and I must have slept a little.

Pregnancy makes one so self-absorbed – all I seem to care about is having enough sleep. But if I have less than seven hours' sleep I am irritable all day, and cannot bear to have anyone about me, especially *la C.* Thank heaven for the Hunts, the easiest, most delightful guests in the world – if they were not here I am sure that Clare and I would quarrel about every small thing, and life would become insupportable. Bessy has promised to return in July to help me put up jellies, if we have a good crop of soft fruit.

Sunday, May 4th Hogg has come and gone – a most useful visit. We worked out a plan for the children, which he will submit to the Master of the Court. I persuaded Shelley to leave it entirely to us, which I think he was secretly pleased to do. He has a terror of the Court which goes beyond the particular circumstances; he now has a mortal fear of being arrested on unspecified charges, held without bail and thrown into prison, and he is convinced that if this were to happen, he would die in prison. He says he does not fear for himself, but he cannot bear the thought of leaving me alone and unprotected. This is not a fantasy; since our talk with Hunt it has been his constant thought. Hogg says that the Government is not interested in poets and pamphleteers unless they make a habit of attending the secret meetings of the Yorkshire mill hands. But Cobbett has fled to America (though Hunt says this is because of unpaid taxes on his 'Twopenny' trash), and Hunt himself was sent to prison five years ago for writing that the Prince Regent was fat – so perhaps S.'s fear is not so far-fetched, after all. Truly, I think we cannot be too careful, since we cannot predict what our enemies may attempt.

Hogg proposed that we should nominate acquaintances of his as the children's guardians. Dr Thomas Hume and his wife Caroline, of Hanwell, near Ealing, are respectable Xtians, of a liberal persuasion; they have five children of their own. He has discussed the case with them, and came prepared with a whole sheaf of suggestions, including separate plans for Charles and Ianthe; both children to be raised in the Xtian faith, their reading to include the classics of ancient and modern literature but to exclude novels, and our older writers and the plays of Shakespeare to be read in versions suitable for the young. The boy to study Greek and Latin, ancient and modern history, and to be prepared for one of the better public schools; the girl to be educated at home in history, geography, music, French, drawing, and the domestic crafts. I felt my mother's spirit hovering about me as I collaborated in this farcical attempt to placate the Law which is the guardian of respectable society and its institutions. As an offering to my mother – for I could feel her clear, melancholy gaze bent upon me as we conferred – I suggested that we include a sentence about the need for both children to take physical exercise in the open air. But Hogg said this would add nothing, and might prejudice the case. So we left it.

Then he asked me if I had thought further about our last conversation.

I said I had no recollection of our last conversation.

'I feared as much.' He pulled at his black moustache. 'My dear girl – you must realise that Shelley is like a brother to me, closer than any brother could be. We met when we were just eighteen. Did he ever tell you the story of our meeting?'

'He has mentioned it.'

'Shall I tell you? Shall I share with you an event that changed my life? It was the Michaelmas term of my second year at Oxford. I was seated next to a freshman at dinner, we fell into conversation, and I invited him to come to my rooms for tea. He was a slim, tall, beardless youth full of nervous energy, talked very fast, walked very fast – his long hair was wild, his eyes were bright and glittering, he was very absent-minded, seemed to have no need for food or drink, though he drank tea with me, and perhaps ate a biscuit. Then, in the middle of a sentence, he fell fast asleep on the hearth-rug before my fire, where he remained for about four hours. Suddenly he shook himself awake, resumed his sentence, and discoursed brilliantly on metaphysics, the natural sciences, German literature, politics, theology . . . We talked through the night and into the next morning, resumed the conversation at night, and have continued it ever since. We became inseparable companions; we met two or three times a day, in his rooms or in mine, and spent all our spare time together. In fact, we were often taken for each other – and, as you know, we do not look alike.'

This is certainly true. Hogg is short and solid, inclining to fat; his black hair is carefully combed across his forehead, he has a flourishing moustache, his mouth is sensuous; he already has a serious, methodical, almost stately manner about him, like a barrister-in-training. There is very little of the impetuous Oxford youth left in him, at least to my mind; while Shelley can hardly have changed at all.

'Alas, our brief stay at Oxford ended in ignominy. As I am sure you know, we composed together a short pamphlet disposing of all conventional arguments for the existence of a Deity who is presumed to have created Man in order to damn him for ever. Shelley published it; we sent it to several college officials and a few bishops. To the discomfiture of Shelley's good father and my own, we were both expelled from the University, and left the next morning, glorying in our defiance.

'I was in love with Shelley's sister, Elisabeth. Did he never tell you? He wrote letters for me, I copied them out. I only saw her once, through a window. He was always very fond of his sisters. He met Harriet Westbrook when he was visiting his sisters at their boarding school in Clapham; she was a pupil there. She was a beautiful, unhappy girl who hung on his every word. He rescued her from her school-prison and they ran off to Edinburgh, where I joined them. I kept Harriet company when he went in search of various relatives, hoping to raise money for them to live on. She was a sweet, innocent young thing, very sentimental. She loved nothing better than reading novels aloud. They went to Ireland, to rouse the peasantry to rebel against their English landlords; nothing came of it. They went to Wales to save the sea-coast, which was being washed away. I followed them there, but they had gone, leaving no address. You must know that our visionary friend cannot be pinned down for very long; he is a creature of impulse, with a knack of disappearing. He cannot stay anywhere for more than a week. Then he flies off, pursuing his vision, pursued by his creditors. Don't be angry with me, Mary dearest' – for I was listening to this tale in absolute astonishment – 'This cannot come as a surprise to you. And nobody, not even your good self, can love him better than I do.

'The truth is that he needs to be restrained from his own impetuous, ardent nature by those who love him. He needs to have obstacles put in his way, not by his enemies but by his friends. You see, his politics – by which I mean his vision of a society which is governed by truth and justice, in which all men and women are free and equal, and pay homage only to the god of Love – his politics, I say, are entirely in his head. He has no idea of what the People are like – for, to tell the truth, the People are an ignorant, violent rabble. Our idealistic friend dreams of leading a Revolution in which no shots will be fired. He has never seen our popular Radical leaders in action. I am not talking of a gentleman like Sir Francis Burdett, but of men like Henry Hunt or Cobbett, who enjoy nothing more than inciting a crowd of idle, drunken London labourers to storm through the West End, looting and burning. If Shelley had been present at the scenes which followed last winter's meetings at Spa Fields, he would have been horrified.

'But I can see you wondering why I am telling you these things. It is because I believe you are not only intelligent and beautiful, but sensible. Like me, you have a practical side; young as you are you seem to me to be a woman of the world.'

And with this he took my hand most earnestly, and held it while he continued speaking. 'Shall we be friends, dearest girl? Shall we be allies? Will you permit me to love the best beloved of my dearest friend? Will you admit me to your heart?'

I hardly knew what to say. He took my silence for consent, and joyfully embraced me. 'There – it's done! Now you will trust me, confide in me, call on me when you need me – and I shall not disappoint you, I will be there for you, always.'

This was surely the strangest interview I have ever had with anyone. I do not think I said more than two words in the course of it. But it is plain that something has occurred between us – and for Shelley's sake, I must give it welcome.

FOUR
Summer 1817
Albion House

Love is like understanding, that grows bright,
Gazing on many truths . . .

Shelley, *Epipsychidion*

CLARE
June 1817, Albion House

Friday, June 13th, 1817.
My dear Lord Byron,
   I hope with all my heart that you are well, and enjoying your residence in Venice, the most beautiful city in the world.
   I thought you would like to have news of our lives here, and in particular of your little girl, who is the image of her papa. She has his blue-green eyes, and his perfect oval face, and her black hair has fallen out and is now replaced by a lovely shade of auburn. We call her Alba, for Dawn. She is an enchanting child, with a radiant smile, and we all dote on her, especially little Will, who is her favourite. Yesterday we had a party to celebrate her six-months' birthday. We all gathered on the lawn for tea and cakes – Shelley and Mary and Will, Leigh Hunt whom I think you know, Mrs Hunt, her sister Miss Kent, and the four Hunt children, who have been staying with us for several weeks, our good Swiss nurse Elise, whom you will remember, and a young girl from Somerset, who helps me with Alba, and whom I am hoping to educate. Shelley's friend Peacock was here too, and his mother. In short we were quite an assembly, and the little Darling seemed to know that she was the centre of attention and to take it as her right. I thought of you, and wondered whether you would enjoy being present at this scene – our pleasures here are so simple, and you have been accustomed to much grander ceremony. But I think you would have been pleased.

I am not at all sure about sending this letter – it does not say anything that I wish to say. I fear it will simply annoy him. Indeed, I became quite depressed on re-reading it. Why should he want to hear news of us? He seems so remote – his life is so different from ours, surrounded as he is by Venetian countesses,

carabinieri, gondoliers, masked ladies of the night, and the pea-
cocks, dancing bears, and assorted creatures of his usual entourage. How can I write to him about drinking tea and eating cakes
on a garden lawn in Buckinghamshire?

Well, I shall send it anyway. I just added a short note:

The political news here is as bad as it could be. After the riots
last winter, habeas corpus was suspended, and all meetings of
more than fifty persons are banned, for any purpose whatever.
The Government lives in terror of the masses rising against it,
armed with pikes and staffs, and led by the most violent rabble-
rousers. But the countryside is quiet, at least in our corner of
England. People suffer the most appalling poverty with a kind of
stoical despair, and no hope of ever changing their condition.

Dearest friend, please be assured of my continued esteem and
affection. I hope for all good things for you always.

As ever, your
Clara

Done. The letter is sealed and sent to Venice. I have not told a
soul – I cannot see that it matters. I feel better for sending it, and
perhaps it will have the desired effect. For either his lordship
must return to England, or we must to Italy. For the little Darling
is irresistible – as soon as he sees her, and clasps her to his heart,
he will soften – not only to her, but to her long-suffering,
uncomplaining mama.

Monday, June 16th Hunt has been called to London, amid much
excitement. Last Monday night, 200 hand-workers and labourers
from the Derby Peak villages marched on Nottingham, and
several hundred textile workers marched on Huddersfield – they
had been led to believe there would be simultaneous uprisings in
London, Birmingham, and throughout the West Riding. In both
places the men were met by the militia, who had been fore-
warned, and the leaders were arrested. Now it appears that it was
all a plot by Government spies. The *Leeds Mercury*, which Hunt

says is the greatest Whig paper in the country, has exposed the villainy of a hired thug named Oliver who has been going about the workingmen's clubs for the past three months, inciting the men to take violent action, and co-ordinating a national insurrection for the 9th of June. Now Hunt is to reprint the articles verbatim in his paper for Sunday, and they are to agitate for an immediate Government inquiry.

The two Hunt ladies and the four Imps are left with us; they are to join Hunt as soon as he has found a home for them, probably with his brother John in Paddington. As a farewell gift, he left us two life-size plaster casts of Apollo and Venus, which he rescued from the woods near Medmenham, chipped and missing a few vital parts. He requisitioned a farmer's cart to deliver them, and Marianne is now scraping them clean. They are to grace the library, as a memento of our friendship and its two patron deities, the god of poetry and the goddess of love. They are quite badly damaged, but Marianne is confident that she will be able to repair the cracks.

Mary has sent off her story about the love-starved monster to John Murray, at Shelley's suggestion. I could not help a twinge of pique at this news. But it would certainly be a great coup to be published by Albé's publisher. Although her labours are now finished, she is as busy as ever, sewing infant clothes, and superintending everybody. Also, although she denies it, I think she is dyspeptic much of the time. She is certainly growing quite large, and she complains of pains in her legs and ankles, which are swollen to twice their normal size.

For these reasons or others, she keeps postponing the excursions she said she was longing to take, and so Peacock and I continue to accompany Shelley on his jaunts in this delicious countryside, now in full summer bloom, leaving Mary to her cosy domestic world. The three of us are the best of playfellows, happy in one another's company, whether we are conversing merrily on a dozen subjects, or absorbed in our own thoughts. Peacock has a quizzical, curious approach to life that I find most engaging. He has a genius for lifting Shelley's spirits, which are often cast down; the chief cause, I fear, is close to home. When

Mary frowns, Shelley droops. Her moodiness goes straight to his heart, and he becomes utterly forlorn, like a lost child. Yet, as I know to my cost, she has always had her 'black clouds' and probably they have nothing to do with him.

Shelley is well into the third canto of his Poem on the French Revolution, which is to be an Epic in twelve cantos. His hero is a heroine, modelled on none other than his beloved Mary. He believes that the French Revolution failed when the women were forced to take second place. When the women of Paris marched on Versailles, their triumph should have been the signal for the liberation of all mankind. But the National Assembly refused to admit women to full citizenship, direction was lost, and the fanatics took over – men who were out of touch with the common people, and cared only for their own power. Thus the Revolution was doomed. This is all to be part of his Poem.

Today we left Shelley writing in his favourite grove, high above Bisham, and walked down to the river, where Peacock proposed to fish for an hour or two. His angling consists of wedging the rod firmly into the side of the bank, baiting the hook, and allowing the line to drift, while lying at his ease on the grass a short distance away, eating cold fowl and drinking ale and conversing. The refreshments were provided by Peacock's mama; Shelley had taken only a loaf of bread and some apples, which we left with him.

I asked Peacock what he thought of Shelley's epic design.

'I think it is far more sensible for our friend to write a poem about revolution than to try to lead one himself. His imagination does not descend to particulars. He has a great love of abstract ideas like truth and freedom, but a very limited acquaintance with real men and women. If he truly wished to reform society, he would be agitating in the workingmen's clubs of the great manufacturing towns. Now that manufacturing work has dried up, the men are angry and ready to take arms; they cannot return to the farms, because there is no work for them on the land, and they are ripe for action. This is why the Government spies found such fertile ground for their agitation.

'But he is happier sitting under a tree, or lying in his boat, under the willows, his notebook in hand. He has a vision of a young man like himself, a poet, favoured in his birth and education, who has eagerly drunk in Utopian visions of freedom and justice, from ancient Greece to the present. This eager youth – let us give him a romantic name like Lionel, or Laon, or Julian – sets forth with a female companion, young, beautiful, equally ardent – let us call her Cynthia, or Rosalind, or Mary – to lead a revolution. Obviously, this has to be a revolution in which tyrants are persuaded to recognise their errors and resign their power, and the oppressed shake off their chains and forgive their former masters, and everyone lives happily ever after.

'I tell you, leaders are not made of such gentle stuff. To be a leader requires a ruthless and practical nature, and a reckless lack of self-concern. Revolution is an admirable career for a single man who does not care whether he lives or dies, but it does not suit family life. A man like our friend, with a wife and young children, is not free to offer his services in the cause of Freedom. I think Shelley understands this, or he would not distribute blankets and alms every Saturday to the poor of the district. This is in the tradition of the squires of the last century, who chose to relieve poverty rather than change the system of things. Shelley has never even attended a meeting of a Hampden club; it did not occur to him to go to Spa Fields for the great meetings last year, though he was in London at the time. He is a dreamer, not a revolutionary. Political change depends upon the sustained action, over a period of time, of organised groups of men; it is not achieved by isolated individuals. Our poet prefers reading about society to entering it. He is a scholar of revolution, not an agitator.'

'But he cares about nothing so much as reforming the system of things,' I said. 'I do not agree with you at all; I think he is utterly reckless of himself, and plunges into dangerous activity without giving any thought to consequences. The only reason he does not go up to the Northern mill towns is that he knows he would be the worst Luddite of them all; he would probably shoot the factory owners on sight. He is actually a very good shot.'

'Well, you may be right, Clara mia. Certainly I share his anger at the system of things, and I despise the present Government of this country. They care only for the rich; they have a mortal fear that the people will rise and take their revenge for years of exploitation and misery, and they will do anything to prevent that from happening. My only quarrel with Shelley is that I would like him to be more realistic, while no doubt he would prefer me to be more passionate. But my powers are those of a shrewd observer and an enemy of Cant – and I dislike Cant equally whether it comes from those in power or from the dreamers who wish to remake society to their own scheme of perfection.'

We shared the cold fowl, which was excellent. I think Mary might have a word with our cook, whose kitchen skill reaches only to boiling whatever goes into the pot until it disintegrates. This makes no difference to Shelley, who would just as soon eat his carrots raw, and the Hunt children devour whatever is put in front of them, but Elise and I suffer.

'Do you ever catch anything?' I asked. We had been sitting for over an hour, and there was no sign of a bite.

'Sometimes perch, and John Dory, and occasionally an eel. The bait has probably gone.' He seemed disinclined to investigate, but instead lay full length on the grass, his hands crossed behind his head, and gazed meditatively at the clouds scudding across the sky.

'You see, the countryside is so beautiful, and the simple pleasures of country life so satisfying, that it is hard to work at revolution, especially in the summer. This is a climate in which anything will grow. If every cottage had its own vegetable plot, and a few domestic fowl, people could be almost entirely self-sufficient. It is such a prosperous land, it is almost impossible to credit the miserable conditions in which the poor live, many of them on the edge of starvation. Yes, even in a charming town like Marlow. But it is impossible to imagine the poor of Buckinghamshire rising up in their thousands and marching on Westminster. Take the two of us, for instance. We lie on the bank, watching the river – it flows on so peacefully, with its slow barges, and its graceful swans and its pleasure-boats. It seems a perfect image of Nature and Society working hand in hand. It is difficult for us to conceive of a period of storm, in which the river rises and foams and overflows its banks, flooding meadows and houses and entire villages – though, as we know, this has happened in the past and will happen again.'

'I suppose revolutions are always made in cities,' I said. 'I cannot bear London, after living in the country – it is so noisy, and dirty, and the press of people is completely exhausting. It is much pleasanter to be here, among friends.'

'Do you think you will stay in Marlow?'

'I should think so.' I could feel myself flushing. 'I have no plans to leave, at present.'

'I'm glad to hear it, very glad.' He sprang to his feet, and offered me his hand. He collected his fishing gear and the remains of our picnic, and we went back to find the Wanderer, who had written several more stanzas in the manner of Spenser. He read them to us while Peacock sailed us back to the opposite shore. Shelley explained that the poem has a full complement of epic machinery, a struggle between supernatural forces, a voyage to the underworld, battles, dreams, episodes, and a love story, in which the act of love is truthfully presented for the first time in poetry. I cannot imagine that the poem will be understood by the simple folk whom Shelley is hoping to arouse to a knowledge of their oppressed condition.

Wednesday, June 18th What a scribbling lot we are! Shelley says Mary is certain to find a publisher for her story – though the Authoress goes about with a tragic face because her manuscript has been declined by Murray, and has hardly a civil word for anyone apart from the amiable Hunt ladies. Peacock is writing a satire upon rotten boroughs, with an orang-utan as hero, and a romantic heroine who is modelled, he has told me in confidence, on our fair Mary. Shelley's pamphlet on reform has sold only thirteen copies but he takes this in good heart and is well occupied with his poem on the French Revolution, having despaired of Albé, who, he says, is the only poet now living capable of doing justice to this great theme. Hunt was composing essays for his magazine on whatever came into his head (or so he claimed) the entire time he was here. And Bessy, when she is not organising and ministering to the four children, is writing a manual upon gardening.

I still feel tempted from time to time to begin my own novel, though it is much changed from the thoughts I had in Bath, several eons ago. I am inclined to take as my hero a nobleman of ancient family and great fortune, proud, sensitive, tragically flawed by a strain of pride which leads him inexorably towards his own destruction. Knowing himself superior to the mass of mankind, he is contemptuous of his fellows, driven by a demon within to test his powers against every danger known to man. But no sooner does he conquer one trial than he wearies of his success, and restlessly moves on, seeking new diversions, new tests of endurance. Eventually he becomes the saviour of his country . . .

For my heroine, I think now of using the proud Maid Marian – intelligent, beautiful, as arrogant as my hero. But, unlike my hero, she is susceptible to the worst of all diseases, the viper Jealousy.

The Authoress would play only a minor part in her own story; she is a sensible little woman, black-haired and olive-skinned, clever, modest, frank, who enjoys life and keeps her private passions well concealed, except for the occasional explosion. An enthusiastic traveller, she is an amused observer of the gay or great world, fond of her friends, devoted to her little Darling, indifferent to the gossip of small minds. Her chief fault is a tendency to say what she thinks, in exactly the form in which the thought springs to her mind – though why this might offend her friends she cannot understand, since frankness is universally claimed to be a virtue, and dissimulation a fault.

Then there is the Authoress's friend and brother, a gentle poet, a dreamer and a visionary, with a passion for reforming the world, who is happiest when he is drifting in his boat along the river, or seated in his high perch in the woods, his notebook in hand.

So much for the characters in my story; this seems a very promising beginning, if I say so myself.

Friday, June 20th Peacock continues to astonish me. Today, as we were sitting in the garden, watching Alba and Will playing on the lawn, he said suddenly, without preamble: 'You and I should marry, Clare. We are two of a kind, and would suit very well together.'

I could not help laughing at the thought. 'Are you asking me to marry you?'

'I am not ready to marry; I could not support an independent establishment unless I gave up my present mode of life and sought employment in town. It suits me to live as I do, at present. But I am thirty-five years old; I must think seriously of the benefits of family life. If my circumstances were to change, I might very well ask you to marry me. We would be like two bachelors together, no quarrelling, no jealousy; we would cultivate an ideal comradeship, based on mutual respect and affection.'

'Does your notion of marriage exclude any thought of romance, or passion?'

'I would not exclude romance or passion, but I do not think these provide a sound basis for marriage. If passion grew from affection I would not discourage it – but I regard it as a luxury, not a necessity. Indeed, I am not at all sure that passion would be desirable; in my experience, it tends to distort judgement, and to take highly destructive forms. Do you not agree?'

'To be truthful, I cannot imagine marriage without love. I hope I do not disappoint you.'

'You have time to think about it – you may change your mind in a year or two.'

'I see you are not in a great hurry.'

'Marriage is not something I would want to rush into.'

He is such an odd-looking man, with his long thin neck, and his round head, and his brown curls, and his small damp hands. Some women might find him attractive, no doubt. But for all his excellent qualities he is more like a book than a man. I wonder what he would be like as a lover. Considerate, thoughtful, possibly even tender – but passionate? Never in a hundred years. I think I am too young and too hot-blooded, still, to give up all thought of passion. To be in a continual state of physical revulsion from the partner of one's life – what a terrible fate that would be!

Wednesday, June 25th I cannot understand why Mary refuses to join us in our exploration of this divine countryside. I am tempted to speak to her about it, though I know she would be offended with me. She says she is afraid to go far from home, but that is just an excuse. She positively revels in her self-sacrifice, and it is most unfair; poor Shelley feels continually rebuffed.

And since Hunt has left us our entertainment is sadly diminished; we are a house of women, with a surfeit of women's talk and women's occupations. For the past two days we have all been kept indoors by the rain. Mary and Marianne compare symptoms and take turns complaining of bladder problems, constipation, and swollen ankles; the children are in and out and underfoot all day, Bessy bustles officiously about between the garden and the kitchen, Elise writes long letters home, Milly talks baby-talk to Alba and Will, and there is hardly time to read a book or think a serious thought.

Shelley seemed utterly forlorn this morning, incapable of reading or writing, and so when the mist lying low over the river began to lift I suggested that we wrap up warmly and take the boat to Medmenham.

There was a fresh breeze on the river, and as we approached Medmenham the sun came out. We moored the boat near the great trees that screen the 'ruined abbey' from curious eyes. This is where the 'hell-fire club', politicians, poets, and rakes of the last century, met for orgies, according to Peacock; our Apollo and Venus were rescued from the nearby woods, discarded when the revellers moved on to witches and necromancers. It is one of Shelley's favourite spots, but instead of walking about he lay at my feet on the boat cushions, with his eyes shut. I tried to persuade him to recite from his Poem, which usually improves his spirits, but he declined.

'I have no heart for it, Clara. I cannot tell why, but I feel premonitions of disaster. "Thou wouldst not think how ill all's here about my heart – but it is no matter." Will you sing to me, Clara mia?'

'What shall I sing?'

'Something melancholy – a love song. Sing the Willow song from Othello.'

I leaned back and sang:

'The poor soul sat sighing by a sycamore tree,
    Sing all a green willow –
I called my love false love; but what said he then?
    Sing willow, willow, willow;
If I court more women, you'll couch with more men –'

Here I stopped, for my eyes had filled with tears.

'What is it, dearest?' He sat up and took my hand.

I could only shake my head, and the tears came faster. There is nothing like the sympathy of a dear friend to encourage tears to flow – there was almost something pleasurable in letting myself go in this way.

'Are you thinking of our friend in Venice?'

I nodded. 'I cannot believe that I am not to see him again.' With that, my voice broke, and he put his arms about me.

'You needn't say anything more. I told you a long time ago that you must not rely on him. But Newstead has been put up for sale – he will have to return to England to settle his affairs. If he decides not to return, if he stays in Italy – why, we shall have to make other arrangements. Leave it to me – you know I have your best interest at heart, always. Now, my own Clara, my own girl . . .' He stroked my hair as he spoke, and kissed my forehead. 'You will be good, won't you?'

I returned his embrace, and he dried my eyes with his handkerchief. 'I shall be good,' I promised. What a dear man he is – and how sad it is that he is not appreciated as he should be by the only person who really matters to him.

Friday, June 27th Marianne has finished the statues. They are scraped and glued together again, and painted a lovely antique cream, and they stand on either side of the fireplace in the library, the one room in which the children are not allowed to play. They are our household gods, large as life; Apollo, god of light, music and poetry; Venus, goddess of love and beauty. It is a pity that the outside world intrudes on us now and then, with its worship of Mammon, and all the evils Mammon brings in his train. Tomorrow, for instance, Shelley will again receive his pensioners, whose numbers grow each week; they are the innocent victims of the worshippers of Mammon, who flourish even in the pleasant groves of Buckinghamshire, where they grow fat on the sufferings of the poor. After she finished the statues, Marianne sewed Shelley's name in large letters on the blankets he has set aside for the poor, since, she said, they will only sell them if they are not labelled.

The statues are finished just in time, for Hunt has summoned his entourage to Lisson Grove, where they are all to live with his brother John. Marianne did a silhouette of each of us for a parting gift. She is very clever with her fingers – she can make the most wonderful creations out of a bit of paper and string. It is a pity that she suffers from giddy spells; these seem to coincide with the sudden appearance of one or more of the children, and they are allayed by a few sips of brandy. Children can certainly be a great nuisance, though our two little ones have had nothing but joy from their companions. We shall miss them greatly, and I cannot say that I am looking forward to our reduced numbers.

Still, Peacock is in constant attendance, and Hogg, now that he is back in London, spends his weekends with us. He has become Mary's shadow. Wherever she is, whatever she is doing, whether she has her work, or is reading a book, he materialises by her side. I find this most amusing, and I dare say I know a bit more about our ever-attentive friend than Mary does. Shelley confessed to me that he tried to persuade the complaisant Harriet to share her favours with Hogg, soon after they were married, on the theory that love can only gain from being shared. Now Shelley is encouraging his boyhood friend in these tender emotions for Mary; they are a proof of his theory, and, he believes, will restore Mary to him entirely through a kind of participated love. He takes every occasion to leave the young couple alone, and urges them to stroll about the garden together, or to ramble in the woods. Mary is a little uncomfortable at this turn of events; she is flattered but uneasy, and though she has been indoctrinated in the theory for many months, she cannot be sure that Shelley's enthusiasm for his friend's passionate attachment does not have an ulterior motive.

For it is clear to all of us that Hogg is IN LOVE! Even Peacock has commented on it; he is sadly disappointed in the barrister-to-be, and shakes his head over yet another example of male folly. It is true that there is nothing so comical as the spectacle of a friend in love, especially where his love cannot possibly be returned.

MARY
July 1817, Albion House

Monday, July 21st My story has been turned down by Shelley's publisher Ollier. This is a hard blow; I had no real hopes of Murray, but Ollier I thought was our good friend. I cannot help feeling discouraged, though perhaps I was foolish to expect the world to take notice of my amateurish efforts. I have asked Papa if he would read the manuscript; he was pleased, I think, and I shall take his advice.

All is not lost – Ollier would like to publish our travel journals, which we sent to Peacock at the time in the form of letters, and I have promised to transcribe them. Peacock has kept everything in good order, and I have already started on the task.

The letters bring back the keenest memories of our summer in Geneva, exactly one year ago. I am assailed by melancholy as I copy them. Often I cannot tell which of us wrote the original, we shared our thoughts so closely, and took it in turn to record our observations. My Beloved has not changed, but I am a different person now – I feel that I have aged at least ten years. I am no longer a shy young girl, but a *matron* (ugly word!), soon to be a mother again. Then I was so greatly in awe of L.B. that I would sit for hours in his company without saying a word, gazing at him with uncritical admiration. Now I take issue with everyone, have no patience with speculative nonsense, no matter who is speaking, and my opinion of men has undergone considerable change. I see weakness where I believed there was strength, and I have become very sensitive to the male ego, its vanity and exaggerated self-esteem. No doubt women also have their vanity, but it does not cover such a large area.

My pregnancy adds to my sense that I have aged – for I am heavy and slow, and discommoded by a variety of annoying complaints. Will was an extension of the two of us, easily incorporated into our lives; now we are a family, and it is a more awesome thing. I feel a strong sense of responsibility – though I am the only one to feel this, and that makes it harder. But it is clear to me that we must be settled in a real home, one that we can remain in for the foreseeable future – we cannot wander about like nomads or gypsies, as formerly. I also worry about money, for each month we are deeper in debt, and Shelley seems to find this perfectly normal; he is resigned to waiting for Sir Timothy to die, which may not happen for another twenty or thirty years; indeed it is quite likely that he shall outlive us all. Until then, we are to live by juggling our debts, renegotiating post-obits, and selling the family silver from time to time, a situation I find most unsatisfactory. I see no reason why my writing should not become a source of revenue for us; popular novels sell very well, and although Papa's experience is discouraging, I mean to try what I can.

Then there is the ever-present problem of Clare. Elise tells me that the village gossips are convinced that Alba is Shelley's child; and of course they know she is not my child. We must decide on her future, and we still have had no sign from L.B. The Misses Thorpe in Wycombe would take charge of her for

£70 per year, and I have asked Shelley to raise this possibility with Clare. It seems a rather large sum, since Hogg's friends the Humes have offered to maintain both of Shelley's children for £100 a year. Still, Wycombe would be close enough to visit, and far enough to discourage gossip. Clare could settle nearby; she could offer lessons in languages, or in music, and I am sure she could make her way. I do not want her to feel unwelcome, but we cannot continue indefinitely as we are.

Saturday, July 26th This weekend Hogg brought us a confidential copy of the Master's report, which, to our dismay, recommends that the children be placed in the care of the Shropshire clergy-man the Westbrooks have proposed. Shelley is to have visiting rights once a month, as is Sir Timothy – a novel idea, since the old gentleman has never expressed the slightest interest in any of his grandchildren. Hogg suggests that we appeal the decision directly to the Lord Chancellor, on the grounds that the children have been hidden away, the Westbrooks have failed to respond to all communications, and the children have been denied access to their father while their fate is being decided.

I see hope in this initiative, though Shelley is so discouraged that he appears to have lost all interest in regaining his rights as a father. He is worried solely about Will – gazes at him with tears in his eyes, as if the darling is going to be spirited off at any moment. This is nonsense, and I have told him so. But he becomes wild with terror at the thought. He is convinced that he is being followed by agents of the Westbrooks; he is afraid to leave the house by himself, he will not think of going to London, even to see Papa, who is anxious to consult him about a new business venture. He talks continually of being arrested and thrown into prison.

'They will try to take Will from us, that is their plan,' he said. 'They regard me as morally unfit – in their eyes I am a danger to civilised society. It is all in *Queen Mab*. I predict the end of Xtianity, and the collapse of monarchy – and that is proof that I am mad. Perhaps I am mad; I will surely become so, if my enemies have their way.'

I tried to calm his fears. He had made a fire in the library – it has turned cold again, and the mornings are dark and damp. He flung himself on the hearth-rug, between Apollo and Venus; I was seated in the easy chair by the fire. 'Try to be patient,' I said. 'Hogg thinks they have not had time to consider our proposal properly. He has been told informally that they are willing to reconsider, for neither the Master nor Lord Eldon trusts the Westbrooks, whom they regard as vulgar upstarts; they know they are contemptible.'

I persuaded him to sit by me, with his head in my lap. I laid my hand against his forehead. 'You have a fever, my love.'

'It is a fever or chills – one or the other. Do not take your hand away, Mary dear – it soothes me. I cannot rid myself of the thought that they are sending someone to arrest me.'

I was alarmed at his state; he will make himself ill if he gives in to these fantasies.

'Why do they hate me so? I am not to blame for the terrible things that have happened.'

'No one is to blame,' I said.

Then I had the strangest sensation – I felt that I was absorbing his fever and anxiety through my fingertips, and that as he was growing cool and somewhat calmer I was becoming feverish and agitated, and I suddenly feared for the child in my womb. I took my hand away and recoiled from him in alarm.

'What is it, my love? Are you leaving me? Stay with me, I beg you—'

I cast about wildly for an excuse. 'No – it is just that I suddenly remembered, I promised Will that I would take him some seed-cakes—'

He released me reluctantly. I promised to return, and went off, greatly agitated. What are we to do if he gives in to these irrational fears?

He then had one of his amazing sudden recoveries, and took it into his head to go on the rounds of the poor cottagers with Mrs Peacock. He said he could not bear the contrast between the abject misery of their lives and the comforts with which we are surrounded. But this represents a great danger to his health and

I remonstrated with him as strongly as I dared, for these places are breeding grounds of infection.

He was still feverish at night, but he refused to come to bed. First he played at chess with Peacock, then he went through the Master's report yet again with Hogg, then, after they left, he asked Clare to sing, and insisted on having her entire repertoire, which, thank goodness, is still fairly limited, consisting mainly of 'Donne l'Amore' and 'Auld Robin Gray'. I begged him to come upstairs with me, but he said he was too wakeful, and would prevent me from sleeping. At last I heard his steps on the stairs but he went into the study. I could not fall asleep, and called him. He came into my room, and since I must lie on my side he lay behind me, and held me close, with his hand on my breast. I found myself weeping, for no reason I could discover, but I did not let him know. His body felt cool, and after a while we both fell asleep, and lay so until morning.

Monday, July 28th We have read the latest *Examiners*, which Hogg brought with him from London. Thirty-five of the Pentridge men have been charged with High Treason. The trial is put off until October, Hogg says because the Government know they would not get convictions now. One of the men, Brandreth, accidentally killed a farm servant on the night of the uprising, the others did nothing except march with staves, calling at farms along the way to ask people to join them. Most of them are framework-knitters; there are also colliers and farm labourers. Since the revelations about the spy Oliver, juries in Glasgow and Huddersfield have refused to convict, and the men arrested in Sheffield in February have had their charges dropped. And so perhaps there is hope for these men, who, as Shelley says, had real grievances, and were denied any means of relief short of rising up against their masters.

Wednesday, July 30th Hogg is seriously wooing me – it is quite ridiculous, but I can say nothing to discourage him. My large, ungainly state only seems to increase his passion. He is continually offering to support me, his arm is always about me, and however firmly I attempt to disengage myself, no sooner have I removed one hand than the other is in place. He is so solicitous and attentive to my comfort that I must give up the struggle, and allow him to be my knight-errant, as he styles himself. He has taken to leaving little notes for me, signed 'Alexy', after the hero of his novel. This novel is a very curious production; it was written soon after the young atheists were expelled from Oxford, and the hero, Prince Alexy Haimatoff, is a composite figure based on the two friends. The plot is drawn from Lord Byron's Oriental tales, and bears no relation to the life either of the Author or of his friend. The book was privately printed, and received no notice at the time except for an enthusiastic review published in an Oxford newspaper, written by Shelley himself.

I still find that I cannot be as natural and loving to Hogg as Shelley would like. He strikes me as vain and shallow; his enthusiasms are harmless enough but do not proceed from settled conviction. He veers between the pomposity of the would-be barrister and a boyishness that is rather endearing, and makes one forgive his occasional tactlessness. But the strongest element in his character is his genuine and heartfelt admiration for Shelley, and this is the sole origin of the bond between us.

Fortunately he stays with Peacock, so that I do not have him lying on a rug outside my bedroom door at night (as he recently threatened to do), nor do I have to converse with him at breakfast. The world seems to divide into those who are bright and cheerful first thing in the morning, and those who cannot utter a civil word until they have had their first cup of tea. Hogg, like Clare, is in the former camp; I am most definitely in the latter.

As it is, Hogg does not appear until eleven, long after Shelley and Clare have gone off, notebooks in hand – for Clare too is in the throes of composition. She says she is writing a novel in which we are all to appear under fictitious names, and we all humour her in this fancy, though I doubt that she will write more than two pages before going on to something else.

When he appears, Hogg is invariably hungry, and solicits my company for a second breakfast. Then he enquires about our plans for the day. I have no plans, I say; I must transcribe the

Journals, and consult Harry about the vegetable garden (or, rather, defer to his judgement) and see to dinner (for which we now depend entirely on our own produce), and read to Will. Hogg agrees to everything as if it was exactly what he intended to do himself, and I must admit that he makes himself useful, helping me in my various tasks. Tonight he goes back to London and will submit our appeal to Lord Eldon, then he returns to Marlow for Shelley's birthday, and proposes to stay until the Michaelmas sitting, which begins October 1st. I am not sure that I want his company for such a long period, but I have not the heart to tell him so.

Monday, 4th August Today Shelley was 25. Hunt and Marianne sent birthday greetings, also a parcel containing 3 yards of cambric muslin, silk thread, needles and scissors, but not the brooch, which was to be my present – I meant it to contain a lock of my hair and Will's, intertwined.

Clare and Peacock went off to Maidenhead to meet Hogg, and I spent the morning with my Beloved, walking about the garden, which is filled with the exquisite scents of midsummer. We talked about the difference between Hunt and Cobbett (Shelley said Hunt is too mild, and writes chiefly for his friends, while Cobbett is often right, but his bombastic tone alienates all moderate persons), and the prospects for the Pentridge men, who, Hunt writes, are being kept in irons, on a diet of bread and water. I still do not understand how they could be charged with High Treason for marching from Pentridge to Nottingham. They did not break any frames, they did not cause a riot, they were being paid 4s a week for working 16 hours a day and they could not feed themselves or their wives and children. How is this Treason?

'It is Treason,' S. said, 'because they met together, which is a criminal offence, and conspired together to march on Westminster, not to present their grievances, since this is now prevented by law, but to overthrow the Government and establish a republic. 'And if you ask how a few hundred framework-knitters armed with nothing but pikes and a few shotguns could hope to overthrow the Government, you must know that the crime lay not in the act but the intention.'

We also talked on more personal matters.

'You see my hair has turned grey with care,' S. said. 'My pensioners think it is on their account – they have given strict instructions that I am not to worry about them. But it has nothing to do with them, if I am old before my time.'

'It does not seem possible that we have lived together for three years,' I said.

'Are you disappointed with me, Mary dearest?' He spoke so earnestly that I hesitated before replying.

'I am entirely happy with you – I cannot imagine my life without your love. The only cause I have for alarm – my only cause of unhappiness – is your ill-health. When you are in pain, when you talk of dying, then it is as if the bright sky clouds over, my mind grows dark, and I feel utterly lost.'

'I must be well for your sake – I shall be well for your sake. You know I do not care for myself.'

For the first time he told me the story of his new Poem, which is almost finished. I was astonished by the brilliance of its conception. The subject is the French Revolution, the high hopes which attended the overthrow of the *ancien régime* and the setting up of a Republic, and the defeat of those hopes first by the zealots among the revolutionaries, then by Napoleon and his imperial ambitions, and finally by the Holy Alliance of reactionary European monarchies, England, France, Austria, and Russia. S. says this is a paradigm for revolution in every age. The moral is that liberty survives each temporary defeat, since her home is in the imagination, and only there. (This is a very beautiful thought, but over-optimistic, I fear.) To disguise his theme, he has set his scene in Constantinople rather than Paris. His hero and heroine are idealists and visionaries, a brother and sister separated in childhood, but later re-united, at which time they become lovers. This is very daring, though not as uncommon in life as people might imagine. United in their hatred of oppression, they vow together to liberate a humanity which is suffering and in chains. After a series of adventures and narrow escapes from enemies of all description, the heroine, Cythna, leads a women's crusade which compels the Tyrant of Islam to surrender his throne. Shelley asked me to read aloud Cythna's Song of Liberation, which begins: 'Can man be free, if Woman be a slave?' This, S. explained, is the great theme of the epic, which is written in homage to my mother, who serves as the model for Cythna.

'But she is also meant to represent you, Mary dear.'

'Oh, I could not lead a rebellion of women,' I protested. 'Or any kind of rebellion. I would not be capable of it.'

'Dearest girl, you do not know what you would be capable of, if your circumstances were to change.'

'I think I know myself, perhaps better than you do. I am very good at reading and writing – I have a small but genuine gift for both. In a company of strange women, whether they were women of my own kind or oriental slaves, I would become utterly silent. I would want only to disappear. If you want a leader of women, you must go to Bessy Kent, or perhaps Mrs Peacock. There is your practical reformer, who does good in the world without making any fuss at all.'

I could see that he was hurt by my remarks. But how could anyone expect me to lead a revolution, surrounded as I am by children, and approaching my confinement? I have enough to do to keep our little household afloat. There is nothing so damaging to fine ideals of Liberty as a domestic life – though Shelley maintains that the example of our own intimate circle of friends will somehow exert a beneficent influence on the rest of the world. I think we are fortunate to have one another, and should not expect any good beyond this to come of our friendship.

In the evening our friends returned, bearing gifts – books, and pots of herbs for the garden, and 1 lb of black and 2 lbs of green tea, and the latest *Examiner*, also Cobbett's *Political Register*, sent from America. Best of all, we have good news from Hogg, who had an interview with the Master in which he obtained a promise that the report would be delayed until our proposal could be reconsidered. The Master agreed that it was wrong for the

Westbrooks to conceal the children's whereabouts, and promised to pursue the matter. So for the moment we have done all we can.

Mrs Peacock produced a most delicious spice cake, and we had strawberries from the garden, with thick cream from the farm. William and Alba played on the rug, and fell asleep as soon as they were taken up to bed, and we followed not long after. S. stayed with me, and we both slept – this is now the chief thing, for health of body and mind.

Wednesday, August 6th The weather has remained fine, and Shelley has been taking his boat out and composing his Poem all morning. This makes him happy and cheerful, though it also induces a state of high excitement, which is often a danger sign. Yesterday he complained of his old kidney pain, and took laudanum. In the evening, after Peacock and Hogg left, he fell into a deep sleep in front of the fire, and then suddenly leaped up, trembling and shivering, and cried in a strange, high-pitched voice, 'It is not my fault – it is not to be attributed to me!' He looked about him wildly – Clare and I tried to calm him, but he seemed neither to see nor to hear us. I held him close but he continued to shiver. Clary brought him a glass of camomile tea, and we persuaded him to take a little. Then at last we managed to get him upstairs, half carrying him, and into my bed, where we both stayed with him, putting compresses on his forehead and chafing his hands and feet.

Towards morning he slept for a few hours, and he seemed more like himself when he woke. He took some tea and bread soaked in milk. He no longer complained of kidney pains, thank heaven. He seemed to have no recollection of his wild talk of the night before. In all, he was very good, and did as I advised without a murmur.

This afternoon I had a long talk with Hogg about Shelley's state of mind. We were sitting in the garden, screened from the house by the high yew hedge. Hogg said that Shelley has always been subject to these strange fits – he becomes more and more agitated either about the state of the world or an abstract philosophical idea, or a particular enemy who has become the focus of his hatred and fear, like the Lord Chancellor, or Sidmouth or Castlereagh, or Harriet's sister Eliza. Then he collapses with exhaustion, and is reduced to childlike dependence on his companions. And just as suddenly he comes to himself, and is perfectly cheerful. Laudanum seems to exaggerate each of these phases, but it cannot be the cause, which, Hogg says, lies in S.'s peculiar constitution.

'What are we to do?' I said. I could not conceal my despair.

'I am afraid there is nothing we *can* do. It is the penalty paid by genius – we can only watch over him, and help him to come back to earth.'

'But what if he does not come back?' and here my voice trembled and broke.

'My dearest girl – you are so good, and so sensible – but it is no use, he will go where he must, and take his own course. He is not like us, you know this as well as I do. He has been touched by divinity, and he must suffer his fate.'

'It is very hard now, just as we seem to be settled. I do not think I am strong enough to bear it.' At this I could not help weeping. He put his arms about me, and held me to his breast.

'Your hair is so fine,' he murmured. 'It is like spun silk.'

I dried my eyes and gently disengaged myself. 'Thank you, dear friend – you are a great comfort to me.'

'May I ask a favour?'

'Of course.'

'Would you permit me to have a lock of your hair?'

'My dear Jefferson—'

'Now you sound like a schoolmistress – no, don't say another word. Think about it – and if you decide that I am not altogether unworthy of such a token you can leave it for me in an envelope, sealed and marked "Alexy".'

I felt rebuked. But I really do not like to encourage his infatuation, if that is what it is. He is sure to misunderstand my feelings of friendship, and to take them for something other than they are.

Friday, August 8th If Clara does not contain her intemperate remarks, I think I must put an end to our idyll. She does not like the idea of the Misses Thorpe taking charge of Alba. Very well, but what alternative do we have? She finally admitted that she has written to his lordship, not once but several times. She has had no answer, which does not surprise me in the least.

'Well, then, let us stay as we are,' she said.

'We cannot maintain a house which includes children of all ages, born at six-months' intervals; the servants gossip and we are the talk of the village. They believe that Shelley keeps a harem in the middle of Buckinghamshire, and they think his charity is meant as a bribe to prevent people from talking.'

'I cannot understand why it offends you so much to be talked about. I thought you were above petty gossip.'

'We live in the world, Clare; we cannot pretend to be completely indifferent to people's opinions. You are very childish to think we can.'

'I am not the one who is being childish. I think you are jealous – you put all sorts of constraints on your own behaviour, and then you are jealous of me for being free, and cheerful.'

'That is complete and utter nonsense. I do not put constraints on myself, I am constrained by my circumstances. I am about to have my second child; I run a household which includes children, servants, adults who behave like children, and friends who appear for meals and conversation whenever it suits their fancy. I am not jealous of you for being free; I think you show a want of sensitivity.'

'I see no reason for both of us to be prisoners of your need to manage everyone.'

I was now in a towering rage. 'I do not *need* to manage anyone. I am *forced* to manage because otherwise nothing would ever be done. I would like very much to see you manage for yourself; I have yet to see you take the first step towards doing so.'

'It is always a question of money, isn't it? Well, that is the difference between us; I care nothing about money, and it is all you think about. I cannot talk to you – you don't hear anything I say, and you don't care about me in the least.'

At this point she disappeared into the garden. She has the advantage of me there; at the moment she moves much faster than I do, and she has always been mistress of the dramatic exit, having had a great deal of practice at Skinner Street. She left me fuming, of course, and even more annoyed with myself than with her, since she had provoked me into saying things I did not mean.

And then Hogg appeared, as if on cue, and I had to pretend to be easy and unconcerned while he made love to me, and looked at me soulfully from his sad brown eyes, which remind me of nothing so much as a Shetland pony. He has now declared his love; he asked again for a lock of my hair, which I had to promise him before he would consent to leave me. I am indebted to him for his efforts on our behalf, but it is a trial for me to play my part in this charade, and I wish heartily that he would return to London.

Saturday, August 9th At last a letter from Papa. He has read my story; he thinks it is excellent, and he does not want a page altered. He has taken the liberty of sending it directly to book-seller friends of his, Lackington, Allen & Co., in Finsbury Square, and he is confident that they will respond favourably. 'I have been agreeably surprised by your manuscript,' he writes. 'The story moves forward from the opening pages to the horrific ending without pause; the writing is vigorous, the characterisation clear and sufficient for the purpose. The conception is highly original. In all, it is a remarkable production for a girl of nineteen. I am confident that it will appeal to readers of both sexes.'

This was high praise indeed. It is strange, but Shelley's enthusiasm did not mean so much to me; I half suspected that he was praising the story out of a desire to please me. But I know this is not the case with my father; he has no thought of pleasing me, but is concerned only to give me the benefit of his sound and experienced judgement.

Meanwhile I have sent the Journal of our European travels to Ollier, but I shall be surprised if there is to be any payment;

Shelley has had to pay for everything Ollier has published thus far, and it is a mystery where the copies go, for we never hear of them after the first set are sent out to friends and reviewers.

Papa's kind letter gave me the courage to raise a matter close to my heart. I have written him to say that I propose to name my child, if it is a girl, after my sister Fanny. I have been thinking of this for some time, and Shelley agrees with me. I cannot see that Papa could offer any objection, but it seems only courteous to inform him in advance.

This afternoon I told Mrs Peacock I would prefer Shelley not to accompany her to the houses of the poor. 'His health is not good; he will catch an infection.'

She gazed at me with her honest blue eyes. 'I have advised him against it, but he will not listen. He sees that there is suffering and want; he believes it is his responsibility to relieve it. You know that is his nature.'

She is such a good soul, such a picture of charity, with her grey bonnet and cloak and sturdy boots, her straw basket on her arm filled with cakes and fresh fruit; I do not like to argue with her. But I do not see why S. cannot relieve the sufferings of the poor without making himself ill.

In the evening, after supper, we had an interesting discussion about the proper grounds of action in human affairs. S. said he believes that we should act so as to increase the sum of human freedom. This applies to our smallest actions as to the larger; to our intimate domestic circle as well as our relations with the wider world.

Peacock: 'A noble ideal, but impractical in daily life. One wants to exercise restraint, to anticipate the consequences of any addition to human freedom which is likely to cause suffering to others.'

Clare said she thought we should act so as to make ourselves and others happy.

But I know that for myself the imperative is different; it is to refrain from acting in a way which one is likely to regret.

FIVE
August 1817
Marlow

I have no life, Constantia, but in thee;
Whilst, like the world-surrounding air, thy song
Flows on, and fills all things with melody.

Shelley, *To Constantia*

MARY
August 1817, Marlow

Sunday, August 10th I am too agitated to write – but I must clear my mind. I think my life has collapsed around me – yet nothing has happened. I may be dreaming, or perhaps I have been living in a dream – no matter, I shall write everything down as it happened.

It was just past eleven. Shelley and Clare had been gone for an hour. Each morning when it is fine, Shelley writes his Poem in his favourite seat in the woods, Clare and Peacock walk, or fish; so they have told me a hundred times. Hogg appeared, as usual. I felt a longing to walk down to the river, though I am hesitant to go far from the house at this time. But the day was so fine, and the lane down to the river is so inviting, and Hogg was so reassuring – he proposed to accompany me there and back, he even prepared some light refreshments, bread and cheese, fruit, and a cold punch. He took his spy-glass, his latest toy; we have been sighting birds with it in the garden and the nearby woods.

It is only fifteen minutes' walk down to the river, through the lane and along the footpath that crosses the river meadows. We stopped for some bread and cheese and shared a glass of punch, then we walked along the tow-path towards Temple Lock. There were swans on the river, and water-fowl, and cows standing or lying about in the meadows, and a mare and foal by the stile. We had gone as far as I thought safe, and were about to turn back, when I saw a boat that looked like Shelley's drifting among the willows along the opposite bank, just past Bisham church. I could not see clearly whether it was moored, or if someone was in it, so I asked Hogg for his spy-glass, and with some difficulty (for I cannot manage the spy-glass at all well) I looked through it, focusing first on the tree-tops, then on the church tower, and at last on the boat. I saw the dim shape of a woman, then as I adjusted the lens she came sharply into focus; it was Clare, and

Shelley was lying stretched full-length in the bottom of the boat, his head in her lap, and she was bent over him – she could have been singing to him – and the boat was not moored but was drifting slowly downstream. I gasped, and stumbled – Hogg caught me in his arms, and took the spy-glass from me.

'What is it, dear girl? Is something wrong?'

'Nothing – it is only Shelley and Clare in the boat.'

He led me to a bench, and we sat quietly. He too looked through the spy-glass.

'Do you see anything?' I said.

'I see only what you saw – they are in the boat. Shall I signal to them?'

'Oh no, dear Hogg, you must not try to catch their attention, they will not want to be seen.'

'Perhaps not.' Then, after a long pause: 'Do you think they are lovers?'

I felt that I would swoon. 'They are not lovers – they cannot be lovers.'

He was supporting me with his arm. He repeated my words softly, as a question. '*Cannot be lovers?*'

I could not speak, but clung to him. 'No, it is not possible.'

There were people about – I could not give way to my feelings. I thought of the child in my womb, and forced myself to remain calm.

'My dear Mary, surely you, of all people, must know that in matters of love, anything is possible. But I assure you, from my intimate knowledge of the one we both love best in the world, that he loves you and you alone. If he and Clare are lovers that is a separate thing; it has nothing to do with you. I do not say it is impossible – but if your worst fears were true, it would be a matter of no consequence. Trust me – I know his heart.'

I think this is what he said. I could not really follow his remarks, and they seemed to mean nothing. All my energy was concentrated on one object: to return safely to the house, and to blot out what I had seen. After a while I felt strong enough to walk, and we returned slowly, retracing our steps across the field, and along the lane. When we reached the house, Will came running to me, wanting to play, but I asked Elise to take him, and I went upstairs to rest.

I could not rest; I have been writing my Journal instead. It makes very little sense to me – I know what I saw, but I am sure it signifies nothing. Then why did Hogg instantly leap to the same conclusion? Perhaps he guessed my thought. But then why was he so unconcerned? I feel that I have had a blow from which I shall never recover. But it is just as likely to be nothing. Probably it is nothing.

Clare thinks of one thing only: taking Alba to Italy and resuming her liaison with his lordship. This is her *idée fixe*; she has room for no other. She keeps Shelley company only as a diversion from her overriding passion. She has admitted as much; we all tease her about it. No doubt Shelley loves her, as a brother and a friend. He has said so to her, to me; there is no question about it. I know that he loves me passionately – I have never doubted it.

Then why do I feel as though my heart has been pierced through?

My thoughts are going around in circles – I feel dizzy, as if I am standing on top of a high mountain, or lost in a maze, unable to find the way.

I must rest – I must set my mind at rest. Perhaps Hogg can explain these mysteries to me – he seems so confident in his judgement. He is reading in the library – I shall go down to him.

He leaped up when I entered the library. Again he declared his love, and promised to wait for me. He would wait as long as necessary. When I was ready, I must come to him. He knew it was only a matter of time.

'I expect nothing, dearest girl. I want you simply to know that I am here, I am happy to serve you, I am entirely yours. You are the most wonderful creature – I love you beyond measure.'

'You are very good,' I said. I was utterly bewildered.

He flung himself at my knees, took my hand and covered it with kisses. 'My darling, my sweet love, my angel—'

I had not the strength to put him away from me. He embraced me, kissed me – I could not prevent him. Then I sobbed convulsively, and rested in his arms, while he stroked my hair and whispered, 'My love, my dearest girl, adorable one.' His eyes shone. He laid his finger on my lips: 'Not a word of this to the others, my angel – it must be our secret. But after the baby is born, after you are fully recovered, then you must come to me and you shall see what kind of lover I am.'

I protested feebly: 'My dear Hogg—'

'No, do not try to speak – you are overwrought, you need time. I understand you better than you know. Do not say another word.'

It was hopeless. I extricated myself as best I could, and suggested that it might be wise for him to leave before the others returned. He agreed, and at last he was gone, but not before taking another long kiss, and a promise to do I know not what.

When they returned, Clare had a wreath of wild briony in her hair; she looked happy and pleased with herself. I waited until she and I were alone, then I asked as if casually whether Peacock had gone with them in the morning.

'No, he was attending his mother on her rounds of the cottagers,' Clare said. She spoke quite naturally, as if we had never quarrelled, as if she had a spotless conscience. 'Shelley finished his canto, and then we took the boat to Temple Lock, and drifted among the islands, under the willows – it was very beautiful. Shelley said it was like his idea of Paradise.'

I felt again that stabbing pain in my heart. I have a terrible feeling that this cloud will not lift – it is of my own making, and I must suffer in silence.

Tuesday, August 12th A short note from Papa. 'You will do no such thing – it would be tempting fate. Even you and Shelley must realise that you cannot give an innocent child the name of one who has taken her own life.'

I am more crushed by this than I would have thought possible. He is right, of course; we were fools not to think of it.

They are now taking it in turn to accompany Mrs Peacock on her charitable rounds. Peacock is planning to include the poor in his next novel; Clare thinks of writing an indignant piece on the unemployed lacemakers of Marlow for Hunt's *Examiner*, and Shelley plans to adopt at least half a dozen children and educate them. I cannot describe the anger I feel at their well-intentioned efforts. The poor have enough to do to feed and clothe their children without having their hopes raised to the skies only to be dashed again to earth.

I cannot speak to S. about this, or about anything. He asked me if something was troubling me. 'Many things,' I said shortly.

'Can I not do anything for you?'

'You have done enough.'

He turned pale, but did not pursue the subject.

Marianne has still not been able to find a nurse for me in London, though I asked her six weeks ago. I refuse to have a local woman; I would rather do without. I shall suckle the child myself, in any case.

Friday, August 15th I told Clare I do not want her to go out with Shelley in the mornings.

'Why not?'

'I need you here. There is too much to do, and I find it tiring if I am left to do it myself.'

She agreed; I had left her no choice. Then she had one of her Clare-ish changes of personality – she was all sunshine, chattered away, cut and sewed a smock for Will from the muslin Marianne sent, and was altogether as helpful and considerate as I could wish.

This lasted two days; on the third day she announced that she was walking with Shelley to Henley, and before I could protest they were off.

Hogg advised me to say nothing. 'You cannot order her about. Try to put it out of your mind. You are tormenting yourself, and it is all for nothing.'

'It is so unfair.' We were walking slowly about the garden. It was hot, still and humid; unpleasantly warm out of doors, but chilly and damp in the house.

'Do you think I am wrong, to want to be cared for just now? It is not an easy time – I have all sorts of fears, for the baby, for myself.'

'But no one thinks of you as someone who needs to be cared for. It is your own fault, you always appear so strong and competent.'

'But I am not strong now. Perhaps I was before, but I have a kind of terror now, which afflicts me at night, especially. I am afraid to be alone, yet I am afraid to be with anyone. Probably it is a foolish fancy, but I seem to hear my mother's voice, as if in the next room, talking so quietly that I cannot hear the words, but her tone is so gentle, so reasonable, that I am comforted.'

'What does Shelley say to this?'

'I have not told him – I have not actually spoken to him alone since . . . that day.'

'You should speak to him. He must know that something is wrong.'

'Let him guess what is wrong, then.' I cannot imagine any circumstances in which I would interrogate him about his relations with Clare. My pride would never permit it. If there is something he needs to say, I will listen. But the thought of asking questions, probing, prying into his affairs – oh, I could not think of it. But I did not like to say this to Hogg.

Indeed, Hogg has been very sensitive to my feelings – he has not pressed his suit, he has not attempted to make love to me, and I feel kindly disposed to him in consequence. But I have suggested that he and Peacock refrain from visiting in the evening. The truth is that I find general conversation tiring, and I feel a compulsion to observe Shelley and Clare together, without the distraction of the others.

Certainly their manner to each other is as natural and affectionate as ever; if I were not watching with a suspicious eye I would see nothing to alarm me. But my nerves are attuned to each nuance of feeling; I register it with a shock whenever their fingers touch, when Clare's arm brushes against his, when she smiles at him. I hate myself for this, but I am possessed by a demon – I feel as though I have a viper in my bosom, which will not release me from its suffocating clasp.

Pleading exhaustion, I go upstairs early, leaving them in the library, reading or playing at chess. I cannot sleep; I lie awake for what feels like hours, listening for the sound of footsteps on the stairs.

Then Shelley comes in to see if I am awake, and if I want him to stay. This is the hardest moment. I want with all my heart for him to stay, yet I cannot bring myself to say so. Nor can I bear it if he leaves me. I pretend to be asleep. He waits, listening to my breathing. He must know that I am only pretending. How unhappy I am! What misery I am causing him! I am half inclined to whisper his name, to open my arms to him – but it is impossible, I cannot move, I cannot say a word. I am torn between willing him to stay, willing him to go. At last he tiptoes out, but he leaves the door ajar, in case I should want him during the night.

I can see that I am making him desperately unhappy. He does not say anything, but he is waiting – waiting for me to accuse him of some nameless crime, waiting for the thunderclap, the lightning bolt. He is reluctant to leave me, refuses to take the boat out, he follows me about anxiously, or waits at a distance, within earshot, playing forlornly with Will for hours. I am pleasant to Hogg, I force myself to be civil to Clare, but to my own love, my best Beloved, I cannot say a word, I am growing cold as ice. It is horrible; I shall die of it.

SIX

Autumn 1817
Marlow/London

So now my summer task is ended, Mary,
   And I return to thee, mine own heart's home;
As to his Queen some victor Knight of Faery,
   Earning bright spoils for her enchanted dome . . .
                    Shelley, *Laon and Cythna*

CLARE
Autumn 1817, Marlow

Thursday, September 18th At last, *finalmente*, a letter from his lordship to Shelley. He is definitely *not* coming to England, he is to remain in Venice for the present, and he asks, actually *requests*, that Shelley arrange for his small daughter to be brought to him in Italy. He suggests that she be christened 'Allegra', denoting 'merry' – though perhaps he also intends an allusion to Montalègre, our little lakeside villa in Geneva. I take this to be a happy sign. 'Allegra' is most musical, and suits the Babe very well.

Thus all things conspire to move us towards a change of life. My heart calls: to Italy! Albion House has become cold as a tomb; everyone is suffering from colds and catarrh and rheumatic aches and pains, and Shelley believes that his life is in danger from the combination of frost within and without.

But I have been very remiss, and must bring my Journal up to date.

Mary was delivered of a fine girl-child on September 2nd, three days after her twentieth birthday. I am godmother to this small creature, who is named Clara Everina, in hope of a bequest from the quarrelsome Irish aunt. A week after her confinement, Mary was reading Tacitus and correcting proofs of her novel, having recovered completely from the minor inconvenience of childbirth. She is a remarkable human being, with a will of iron.

Shelley has finished his Poem, and we have been favoured with a reading each night after supper. The poem is dedicated to Mary, who is praised extravagantly for her 'ample forehead' and her 'gentle speech'. I was tempted to protest at the last of these, but exercised a noble restraint. The epic has a most terrific ending, in which the heroine is burned at the stake, and her spirit is transported to the heaven of democrats and atheists, where she is reunited with her lover and her illegitimate child, and all three serve for ever after as beacons to mankind. We did not have the whole of the epic, but enough to have a sense of its general character. The act of love, which occupies the whole of Canto 6, lasts two days and two nights. This, I believe, is called Epic exaggeration.

The completion of the Poem should have been an occasion for rejoicing. But poor Shelley is as unhappy as I have ever seen him. He can do nothing to alter Mary's implacable resentment. This is directed chiefly at him; I seem to have escaped her wrath, for reasons which are not entirely clear to me. Evidently she does not consider me worthy of her anger. And what is it all about? She must have seen something, suspected something. Whatever it is, she will not say anything, and I must pretend that all is as before.

Shelley and I had a sad conversation on the subject, in a moment of privacy, which has become a very rare thing. (I have a constant sense of being watched, which is most disagreeable.)

'As for the two of us, you know it is finished,' he said.

'I am sorry you have been made to suffer so.'

'Do you have any regrets?'

'I have regrets only about Mary. It is unfortunate that she must take it in this way. And of course I wish us to remain friends.'

'I cannot imagine that you and I will ever be anything but the best of friends, my dear. It is a great help to me.'

Well, I shall try to be a good friend to him. I wonder if it is true that my feelings tend to be shallow. It is easy for me to act on my affections, I am quick to laugh, quick to forget. But Mary is far more passionate, her feelings run deep, she cannot forget, cannot forgive. What puzzles me is that she does not actually *know* anything about our relations. Neither of us would say anything to add to her sense of injury, and she is far too proud to ask a direct question. But I fear that it is enough for her to suspect – and nothing will now persuade her that there are no grounds for suspicion. It is a thing we all have to live with.

Unfortunately, her instincts are preternaturally sharp. She was certainly right to warn Shelley against visiting the poor; he has an eye infection which is extremely troublesome, and does not heal. She was also right to warn him that he must settle the debt to the coachmaker for Harriet's carriage; a Mr Wright from Maidenhead has been lurking about the house, and we are sure it concerns the carriage, which cannot be paid for until December at the earliest. This seems most unnecessary, since we do not even have the carriage; but Shelley has some notion of bringing it here, and possibly even keeping horses. What it means for the moment is that he must once again be in hiding, with the ever-present fear of being arrested.

Mary was also right in predicting that I would not finish my Novel, but I would not give her the satisfaction of telling her.

To add to our troubles, there is definitely something amiss in Albion House. One would never guess that the rooms were papered less than a year ago; in the library and the drawing room the paper is curling away from the wall in a dozen places, and the upstairs rooms all have great blotches of damp, with signs of mould and mildew on the ceilings. My poor piano is sadly out of tune, from the continual changes of temperature. There is also a sweetish-sour smell, unpleasant and persistent, which Peacock says must be the drains. Now that the sun is low in the sky, the garden is in the shade all day; the only pleasant prospect is the road in front, with its bustling human traffic. But this is not the best thing for privacy, which Mary insists upon. We keep fires going day and night, but all the heat goes up the chimneys; the warmth reaches only those who are directly in front of the fire. In the morning the mists and miasmas rise from the river and the river-meadows; at night the cold air comes down from the great beech woods, and drifts in through the windows, not one of which closes properly. We are forced to endure one another's company as best we can – but even Peacock finds it hard to raise a smile among these melancholy faces. The children too are irritable – Will has developed a cough, and Alba is cutting a tooth, and cries miserably and must be carried, and Mary complains that she does not have enough milk for Clara, and that asses' milk disagrees with her – and so we go from day to day.

But I hold fast to one thought: if all goes well we shall be in Italy by the spring, and under sunny blue skies all things will once again be possible.

Saturday, September 20th Now Mary has dismissed Hogg, her ardent suitor and constant companion of the past two months. She is unrelenting – if she goes on in this way she will turn everyone out of doors. What was his fault? Too great a love of Shelley, whom he defended against her bitter criticism. So he told me – for he is as indiscreet as ever.

'She will only hurt herself if she persists in treating him like a pariah,' he said. 'I do not complain of her treatment of me – I do not matter, I am merely an incident. But Shelley deserves better of her; and she will not see the harm she is doing. He must have affection, it is his life's blood. He cannot understand her coldness; he is cut to the heart.'

'Did you tell her this?'

'She will not listen. She has set her mind against him, and against all of us.'

And so he has returned early to his chambers in town.

Peacock too has been exiled. He has not been forbidden the house, but if he comes to tea Mary stays upstairs and refuses to join us.

'What is wrong with our fair Maid Marian?' he asked me.

Shelley was reading a story to Will in the nursery; Peacock and I were waiting for tea in the library, regarded, or I should say disregarded, by the blank gaze of Apollo and the pitiless stare of Venus.

I decided to tell him the truth. 'She does not approve of my relations with Shelley. She thinks we have grown too intimate, and wishes to put a stop to it. She is convinced that you have aided and abetted us – hence you too are under a cloud.'

'But my dear Clare, surely this is a misunderstanding! Why do you not tell her the truth?'

Here I blushed, and remained silent. 'There is a difference of philosophy between us,' I said at last.

He did not understand at first. Then he looked very disapproving. 'You surprise me,' he said. 'I did not think you were a
convert to our friend's theories. You did not encourage me to
think so when I proposed a change in our relations.'

'You were talking about marriage,' I said. 'I am not interested
in marrying you or anyone else.'

'You are an odd girl. A destroyer, I fancy. You do not seem to
consult anyone's interest but your own.'

'Who then is to look after my interest? I have a child whose
existence I must keep a closely guarded secret; I have a mother
who wants nothing more to do with me while I am under
Shelley's roof. I have one friend only – and are you saying I am
not to comfort him? Not to make his life a little pleasanter? It is
Mary who is the destroyer, not I.'

I did not say to Peacock, whose sensual life is limited to a glass
of cold ale and the occasional mutton chop, that it is hard for a
man whose being is intensely sensual to live entirely celibate
during his wife's pregnancy and the first months of the new
infant's life, when she has pressing physical claims on her attention. This is a truth which the world recognises but does not
discuss, and it explains why so many men seem to live con-
tentedly with two wives, though society recognises only one of
them. I am sure this is the case in the Hunt ménage, and
Marianne shares in the benefits of it, since her sister does
everything for her and the children. It is a pity that Mary cannot
see the matter in a more philosophical light; but she must have
sole and exclusive possession of her lover. This is the law of her
being, and she cannot reason herself out of it.

Monday, October 6th More alarums and excursions. Now Mary
too is afraid Shelley is to be arrested for debt; she has packed him
off to the Hunts, in Paddington, where he is to stay during the
week, returning to Marlow only on weekends, when he should
be safe from arrest. He is under instructions to consult the
celebrated eye surgeon Sir William Lawrence about his eye
infection. He must also help Godwin resolve his affairs; and in

between these tasks he is to see to the proofs of the Journal of their European travels, and to supervise the printing of his Poem, which Ollier will do for a price.

But I hope he will attend to my affairs too – that is, to set in motion our move to Italia. I have asked Milly if she will come with us; she sees this as a great adventure, and I have promised to teach her Italian as soon as I master the language myself. She asked if she could take an extra day to say goodbye to her children; of course I agreed. She says the children are very happy with her mother, and hardly seem to miss her; but she has become so attached to Alba (which I can well understand) that she would be very loath to lose her, and this is her chief reason for coming with us. Elise of course is delighted; she despises the English, loathes the English climate, cannot bear English food, and wants nothing so much as to return to the Continent. I am sure we will be able to arrange for her to visit her little girl, who is now seven in Geneva. Mary too seems to accept the necessity of a European trip, and talks of next April, when Clara will be weaned. Then she surprised me by suggesting that we might go sooner, possibly as early as November, to escape the English winter.

'I do not see how we shall survive the damp in this house,' she said.

It is true that Albion House has lost all its charm as autumn closes in. The dark cypress trees and the great cedar in the garden are oppressive to the spirit – they are like brooding presences, foreboding death and disaster. We must light the lamps by four o'clock, and everywhere there is a feeling of gloom. It rains every day for at least an hour or two, the meadows are flooded, and are likely to remain so for months, and our favourite walks are blocked by fallen trees and rivers of mud. Even Peacock is defeated by the rain; he thinks of going to London for the winter, and may even seek paid employment, possibly, he thinks, with the East India Company.

Thursday, October 9th Alarming letter from Shelley. He has been to Sir William, who advises him to rest his eyes completely for at least a month; he is to do no reading or writing at all. The condition is dangerous; he may lose his sight. Furthermore, his old kidney complaint has returned with a vengeance. All in all, he says he must live in a mild climate or he will not survive the winter.

Therefore he asks Mary to tell Madocks to put the house up for sale immediately, and to pack up and come to London – this very weekend, if possible. He will find us lodgings, he says. If we sell the lease of the house and the furnishings we will be able to pay off our debts; if not, we can let the house furnished, and Hunt's friend Horace Smith will lend us the money for the trip to Italy.

I cannot remember seeing Mary so distraught. 'This is madness,' she said. 'What am I to do? I cannot pack up in two days and travel to London with an infant of four weeks, leaving everything here to sort itself out. We have accounts with every tradesman in town; we must at least pay for the milk and eggs, if not for the curtains and carpets. He seems to have no idea of the extent of our borrowing. I doubt very much that Madocks can sell the lease, or rent the house furnished – it had been empty for years when we took it; he could hardly believe his luck when Shelley agreed to a twenty-one-year lease.'

She seemed to have forgotten her anger in her anxiety over this latest development. 'I must persuade him to return home – or perhaps I should go to him. I suppose I could wean Clara – but I do not like to wean her so soon . . .'

She was holding the letter in her hand. I waited for her to show it to me.

'He sounds very frightened. He has a violent bowel complaint, and pain in his side, for which I am sure he will take laudanum. He writes that we must spend the winter in Italy, his health requires it – not on his own account, for he does not fear death for himself, but only for me. He is convinced that he is suffering from a consumption, which he conceives would soon be fatal in this climate.

'Then there is his terror about Will – he is sure that if the Lord Chancellor's judgement goes against him, after this last appeal, they will try to take Will away from us. This is another argument for going to Italy. But I do not see how we can discuss these things rationally when he is in Paddington and I am here.'

'If you are reluctant to go to London,' I said, 'would you like me to go?'

'Certainly not. You give in too readily to his wild ideas – it would not be at all helpful.'

She did not offer to show me the letter, but she left it lying on the table, and I glanced at the first page, which began: 'My dearest and only love.' I had to suppress a smile – to be reduced to such stratagems! But it is the only way – to repeat over and over again, until it is believed, a formula that is at best a half-truth.

My journal entry for the 10th of August is written on a separate sheet of paper and folded away in a second, unmarked notebook. I shall probably destroy it – but not just yet.

Sunday, August 10th As I walked up the path into the woods, S. was sitting on a fallen tree, writing in his notebook. When he saw me, he put the notebook aside and opened his arms, and I flew to him – dear man, he is so kind, so gentle and loving, I cannot bear to see him hurt. He held me, and I kissed him, and we stayed as we were, close and tender. Then I could feel his sex hard against me, and I would have released myself, as I have done before, but this time I delayed, and I did not do anything to suggest my reluctance. After a minute or two he put my hand there, and he said, 'That feels better.' 'O my dear,' I said. It was a strange and exciting sensation, like holding his life, throbbing in my hand. 'How good you are, Clara mia,' he said.

Afterwards he spread his cape on the fallen leaves, and when we lay together it seemed very natural and inevitable, we were entirely private and what passed between us had nothing to do with anyone else, it was between the two of us only, and I felt loving and content.

My feelings for him have not changed in the least, but there was a question hanging in the air between us, which has now been resolved, and I am glad of it. As S. says, we two are children of nature, the setting of our love is river and woods and sky and sun, and we shall not bring our passion indoors to Albion House.

Our first care, we agreed, must be to protect Mary, whom S. loves more than his life.

Wednesday, October 15th. Lisson Grove, Paddington After all the fuss, here I am in London, staying with the Hunts in Lisson Grove. It was a struggle, but in the end Mary had no choice but to send me in her stead, with strict instructions to bring Shelley back as soon as possible. When I left Marlow, she gave me a very strange look, as if to say 'Take him' – or, 'You can see that I trust you.' Or 'It is too late, in any case, it no longer matters.' Well, I cannot think too closely about this. I intend to be good, I would have told her so if these matters could ever be talked about openly, but they cannot, and there's an end on't.

Meanwhile we have been enjoying ourselves; we have been to see the Elgin Marbles at the British Museum, and we have gone with Hunt to the opera to see Mozart's *Don Giovanni*, which is performed in English, an excellent idea for those who cannot understand Italian, and we have taken tea with Hogg in his rooms at 1 Garden Court. He described the dinners in Hall – venison and turtle, and an array of fine wines; he said the judges, who are called 'benchers', invariably fall asleep over their port but the young bloods have a fine time drinking until all hours and singing bawdy songs. His Inn has just had a ballot on whether to rent out accommodation to ladies, a proposal which was turned down by a vote of 37 to 2. What a masculine preserve the Law is, along with the Government and the universities; only Queen Elizabeth has ever dined in Hall. How can change ever be brought about in this country if the fathers simply pass on their power and pride of place to their sons?

Shelley seems to have had a miraculous recovery from his various ailments, though he still insists that he is dying. I think privately that he had a surfeit of Someone's bilious temper; this made him very ill indeed, and the cure was to remove himself from the scene.

I think I am at heart a city-lover. It is certainly far more diverting to take in the great scenes of bustle and varied human activity in London than to sit in Marlow observing the waters gradually reclaiming the land, and the birds shivering forlornly in the dripping trees. It seems pointless to struggle endlessly to keep warm and dry in a house that defeats all efforts to keep out the elements. Hunt's house, which he shares with his brother John, is tall and narrow like many London houses, with the kitchen below ground level and the children and servants in the attic, and the intervening rooms, apart from the bedrooms, devoted to music, reading and writing, and conversation, a sociable and civilised arrangement which suits us all very well. Marianne is soon to be confined and stays close to home; she has made over some of her prettiest gowns for me, and she is so clever with her needle that you would never guess their original shape, designed for someone tall and thin – which alas I shall never be. She says that with my high colouring I should wear rich colours, like scarlet and cobalt blue – and I now have a gown of each kind.

Tuesday, October 21st We have a great deal to do before we can return. I had not realised how important a part Shelley's epic Poem plays in his thoughts. He told me it is his bid for immortality, as *Childe Harold* was for Albé. He has been convinced for several months that he has not long to live, and he put all his convictions about love and society into this one work, in order to leave something worthy behind him.

'It is true that *Queen Mab* was the product of youth,' he said. 'But I have seen no reason to change my views. I still believe in equality and liberty and disinterestedness, and I am still convinced that the Xtian dogmas lie at the heart of all tyranny and injustice. If men and women are taught to accept their suffering as the will of God, they are prevented from acting to change their conditions. If I can do one thing through my poetry, it is to encourage readers to imagine a world better than the one they inhabit.'

I think it is wonderful that he retains his faith in humanity, much as he has suffered from the malice and vindictiveness of his enemies. This would be beyond my own powers, I am sure. I have a very low opinion of humanity; I think it is only the rare and exceptional person who rises above the common level.

Ollier is to publish the Poem, but he has already made objections to its atheism (which Hunt says is not atheism but a form of Deism found in writers from Plato to Rousseau). He is also unhappy about the fact that the hero and heroine are brother and sister. This he thinks will offend readers, and may lead to the book (and, more important for Ollier, the bookseller) being prosecuted. He is worried about the laws against blasphemous libel, which have been used against several of the more liberal booksellers, and I fear Shelley may have to yield on these points. But Hunt is to publish an excerpt in his Journal, and he and Shelley have agreed between them to include the stanzas beginning: 'I had a little sister.' Shelley says the echo of the Song of Solomon is deliberate; the Bible is the model for his own celebration of sensual and spiritual love, which together have the power to transform the world. His revolutionary heroine, Cythna, is drawn from the heroic women of the Old Testament, like Deborah, Judith, and Esther, who were prepared to sacrifice their lives to save their people.

Mary's Novel will be published in December, but she insists that her name must not appear as Author. Shelley has written an introduction, 'by a Friend', which he hopes will increase its chance of success; the title is 'Frankenstein: or The Modern Prometheus'. The Journal of their travels will also be published anonymously in December. The Poem is to appear under his own name; the title is not yet fixed, but Shelley thinks of calling it 'Laon and Cythna; or, The Revolution of the Golden City: A Vision of the Nineteenth Century'.

Then there is the problem of Godwin. His affairs are more obscure than ever, and he has entangled all his friends in their complications. We visited them yesterday at Skinner Street, and while Shelley spoke with Godwin in his study, I had a conference downstairs with Mama, in which she tried very hard to be amiable.

'I am pleased to see a great improvement in your general appearance, Jane,' she began. 'At last you are wearing your hair in a becoming fashion, and your dress is in this year's style and shows your bosom to advantage; if I am not mistaken, you are even wearing stays, which I thought you had sworn never to use.'

'Since I am in town, and we go about in society, I do not wish to shame my companions,' I said.

'That is a sensible attitude. If I had given you the same advice you would no doubt have laughed at me. But I thought you would eventually come round to a more practical way of regulating your life. You are a good girl at heart, I have always thought so.'

If I am now *a good girl*, I thought, who is *the bad girl*? I did not have to wait long to find out.

'Why do you not come to visit us when Papa next comes?' I asked.

She sighed, and looked very glum and self-pitying. 'Mary does not want me to visit.'

'I am sure that is not true.'

'I do not blame her; she would rather have her father to herself. I would only be a burden to her; she would feel obliged to talk to me and to consult me on domestic matters. But I know she does not want to see me; if she did, she would write to me directly. She has not written to me once since they were married. She is still angry with me; she thinks it was I who prevented her father from speaking to them when they came back from the Continent. I assure you that was not the case. He had very firm convictions on the subject – as he does on all issues of principle.'

'Well, I cannot speak for Mary,' I said.

'No, I do not think you can. I am sure you have all you can do to keep things easy between the two of you. I do not envy you; I would not want to be on the receiving end of her frosty silences or her sharp tongue. Good luck to you, I say, and I hope you know what you are doing.'

Thus did I receive my mother's parting blessing.

We did not mention to either of them our plan to go to Italy; this would be a blow to Godwin, and the cause of bitter recrimination. Godwin assumes he is to be Shelley's pensioner for life; this becomes more difficult if we are abroad.

We took a meal with them; I saw no great improvement in Mama's cooking, but there was a dish of boiled broccoli in Shelley's honour. Godwin is dyspeptic; he takes only a little beef, and a glass of ale. But he seemed to relish the pudding: tapioca and stewed plums, which Mama cooks every day, on the doctor's recommendation. Godwin is over sixty, and looks like an old man, shrunken and deeply lined, dripping gravy on his napkin; he and Mama preside at opposite ends of their table like the Gog and Magog of stewed mutton and cabbage. He complains that no one ever asks his opinion on matters of current interest; his old friends occasionally call to chat, but I suspect that he feels very much like a relic of the last century. He praised Mary's Novel, which is dedicated to him. He longs to have conversation on intellectual subjects with Shelley, but he cannot stay away from the subject of money.

They asked if I would stay the night, but I said I was quite comfortable at the Hunts. Godwin was impressed, in spite of his avowed contempt for newspaper people, whom he considers prisoners of their own party and slaves to each crisis of the day. I have not slept at Skinner Street since Fanny's death; if I were to do so I am sure I would wake up screaming in the middle of the night. Shelley says it is foolish to believe in the old superstition, but I feel her restless spirit everywhere in the house; she seems always to have just left the room we are in, or just about to appear, in her worn brown frock, with her thin pinched features and her reproachful gaze.

After we left them we talked about Godwin's sad decline. I told Shelley I thought it odd that although Godwin has visited us two or three times in Marlow he has never expressed the slightest curiosity about Alba, nor, evidently, has he discussed her existence with Mama. It is certainly convenient for me, but it puzzles me that a philosopher who has written so eloquently on the intercourse between the sexes, and the freedom of women, should be so indifferent to those matters which concern women most directly.

'Much as I owe to Godwin,' Shelley said, 'I suspect that his intellectual life came to an end when Mary was born and her mother died. His life since that time has been a continual struggle against domestic realities, quarrelling women and young children, and the insurmountable problem of making ends meet. It is difficult if not impossible to attend to abstract thought under such conditions.'

Was he thinking of himself as well as Godwin? I did not like to ask. It occurred to me that his exhaustion is not only physical but spiritual.

We return to Marlow a week from Friday. Shelley is determined to remove from Marlow as soon as he can persuade Mary to leave. 'It is a disaster,' he said.

And so when we return we shall begin the cheerful labour of packing up everything that we have accumulated in the past year, books and babies, pictures and statuary. After which, we can bend our thoughts towards Italy.

MARY
October 1817, Marlow

Saturday, October 25th I find October the most melancholy month, though it is also in some ways the most beautiful. Everywhere I have the sense of an ending. Whether it is the steady rain, or the great beech trees shedding their leaves, or general feelings of low spirits as the days grow shorter, and one is less and less inclined to venture out of doors – whatever the reason, I find myself sitting idly by the fire in my study or the nursery, my work loose in my hand, day-dreaming, wondering what the future holds for our fragile, strife-torn household.

Clare writes that there are ghosts at Skinner Street. I think they are here as well. My mother died twenty years ago, on the 15th of September; Fanny put an end to her troubles last year on the 9th of October. Now that a year has passed, I suppose that I must add Harriet to this sad roll-call. She took her life in November – and although she was a foolish and selfish girl she did not deserve to be abandoned by all her friends. Her family shut their doors against her when they discovered that she was pregnant; she was alone in the great unfeeling city, loneliest of places. I cannot imagine how she had the strength, heavy with child, to take that last fearful walk, in the cold November rain, past the gaily lit shops and into the dark and deserted Park, and so to the silent brimming lake, there to cast herself from the low bridge into the icy depths below.

When my mother died in her long agony, so poignantly recorded in my father's Diary, she did not want to die; she had everything to live for. She loved and was beloved by my father and was surrounded by friends; she had a small daughter whom she cherished and a new-born baby; she had just embarked on half a dozen projects for books and essays. But Papa said she had sought death twice, once before and once after Fanny was born. On each occasion she believed herself to be abandoned by those whom she loved best in the world, and so she lost hope.

Fanny's death I shall never understand. I shall never forgive myself for failing to respond to her cry. She wanted only to come to us; I put her off with transparent excuses. I still think that if she had seen one of us when the coach changed horses in Bath, or if her resolution had weakened and she had decided at the last minute to stop with us, or if Shelley had reached her sooner – then she would be with us still. Even when she arrived at Swansea she may have had a glimmer of hope remaining; if Aunt had been waiting for her, or if Papa had arrived in time, she would have had some evidence that she was mistaken in think-ing her life meant nothing to others. But as it was, she died convinced that she was sparing us further trouble on her account – this was her last thought.

I brood on these events even as I am sitting with the children, nursing the baby, watching Will and Alba at their play. Since Shelley and Clare have gone I have had no one to talk to except Elise, and so keep returning to my own thoughts. I cannot bring myself to sit in any of the rooms downstairs; even with fires it is impossible to banish the chill air, and with all the lamps lit there are still dark shadows in every corner. Apollo and Venus preside over a vast emptiness; I cannot bear their blank stone looks. I have asked Cook to serve meals in the nursery – we can be cosy here, and free of ceremony, instead of sitting at opposite ends of an immense polished table. Elise sews or reads, Milly chatters away, without expecting any conversation in return, and that suits my mood.

In spite of my melancholy, it is really very pleasant to be tucked away upstairs. When I suckle Clara, I love to have Will in sight, playing with his wooden blocks on the floor, conversing seriously with Alba, interpreting her gurgles and translating them into his own language. Alba is a delicious child, full of spirit. She has her father's eyes – blue-green in their depths, fringed by long dark lashes. Clare does not want to give her up – she can see the necessity of it, but does not believe it will happen. I too have grown accustomed to having her about. She adores Will, who tolerates her passion for him with good humour but now seems more interested in Clara, placid as she is; he loves to caress her tiny fingers and toes. Perhaps it is the male instinct to discard the old favourite for the newest toy, or perhaps he knows she is his sister, while Alba is only a cousin, of sorts.

I find that I have very different feelings towards this second child. I am much calmer, less profoundly interested, if I may put it so; my feelings are tender but not so all-consuming. I think I am happier with this baby, though unhappy in my wider relations. Each new accomplishment of Will's seemed a small miracle; Clara is not a continual source of amazement to me in the same way. I cannot tell if this is a difference in her, or in me, though I am sure she is more placid and contented than Will ever was. I would not have thought of weaning Will so soon; the first time I left him was in Geneva, when we travelled to Chamounix, and I had to tear myself away from him, and rush back as soon as possible. I remember how hurt I was when he seemed to prefer Elise to me on our return. I doubt that I would have weaned him even then if I had not been reluctant to allow

Clare to travel alone with Shelley, which she would most certainly have done. I think my instincts were right, and I am sorry now that I have not kept her under lock and key.

Another difference between the first and second child is the effect on sexual feeling. After Will's birth it was only a month or so before I felt the return of physical desire. His presence seemed to make our love more visible and real. But it is now two months since I was confined with Clara, and I feel no signs of returning desire. On the contrary, I feel numb, passive, almost repelled. No lover could be more tactful or more delicate, but when S. touches me, I recoil from him, in spite of myself, and I have not been at all sorry that he has been in London these last three weeks.

I cannot tell if this represents a normal absorption in maternal activities, or whether my physical feelings have been affected by my unhappiness. Certainly it seems that people who read a great deal, like our small circle, tend to underestimate the importance of natural instinct in human affairs. It may be that women are meant to be breeding machines, and men, once they have served the purpose of propagation, can be dispensed with. But then why do we long, always, for something more?

I know that S. loves me, and places my happiness and wellbeing above his own; this is not in question. But my feelings have changed; something in me has died. I am acting a part. Perhaps through repetition and force of habit, feelings of sexual love will regenerate themselves.

But I know that I cannot, will not, accept a shared love. If I am driving my Beloved away from me by rejecting a *participated* love – well, I cannot change my nature.

Monday, October 27th Yesterday two of Shelley's pensioners came, a young farm labourer and his wife from Hambledon. They walked all the way. They said they did not want anything but heard that we were leaving, and came to say goodbye to the odd young gentleman who had befriended them. I said we would be here for some time yet. How does this news get about? There must be eyes and ears behind every haystack. They asked how old Clara was, and said I must be very pleased to have such a fine, fat baby. I gave them a sack of clothes, and asked Cook to give them the leftover stew. I saw as they went out that the wife was pregnant; she could not have been much more than seventeen.

Wednesday, October 29th This morning Harry came to say there are rats in the barn and he has set traps; he caught two the first day, and thinks we had better have a 'rat shoot' for the village lads. He knew there were rats because all the potatoes were eaten.

I said he should do whatever he thought best, I wanted to know nothing about it. I have no one to consult on this or any other matter to do with the house. I was not expecting Peacock to call, since I made it clear that his visits were unwelcome. But I am surprised that Mrs Peacock has not been to see us – I did not think she would be a slave to the prejudice that puts a son's injured pride before the claims of friendship.

Saturday, November 1st The travellers returned last night, Clare very cheerful, and full of news and gossip. She insisted on waking Alba to kiss and hug her, and of course the little one was up for the night, so our talk was much interrupted. But her account of life at Skinner Street made me feel guilty that I have not been to see Papa, and that I have not urged him to visit me to see his new grandchild. Shelley said Papa is very pleased that I have dedicated my Novel to him.

S. seems completely exhausted, he is even thinner than he was when he left, and still very agitated. He has negotiated a post-obit loan for £2,000, payable at £4,500 three months after Sir Timothy dies (in the unlikely event that that should occur); half of this is to go to Papa, the remainder will pay off the debt for the carriage, and part of our debts here. So for the moment the danger of arrest has receded.

I was hoping that on their return I would feel easier, but the cloud is still there. S. saw it immediately, and I could see the reflection of my altered feelings on his face. I longed to embrace him with my old love, to hold him to my heart – and instead I kissed his cheek as if he were a distant relation, and held myself away from him with unmistakable coolness.

Clare took Alba up to bed with her, and S. and I sat by the fire for some time longer, talking about money. This is very dreary. I left him by the fire, and when he came upstairs he went into the study.

Tuesday, November 4th Today Madocks showed us the advertisement in *The Times*, which brought tears to my eyes:

BUCKS. GREAT MARLOW. To be LET, furnished, or unfurnished (or the Lease and Furniture, which is modern and new, to be disposed of), a HOUSE, containing a good dining room, library 36 feet by 18, drawing room 30 feet by 18, study, 5 best bedrooms, 2 large nurseries, each 30 feet by 20, water closet, 6 or 7 attics, convenient offices, good garden and pleasure-ground, with immediate possession; 4 acres of land may be had. Apply to Mr Madocks, carpenter, Great Marlow.

Madocks said he doubted that we would have many answers to the advertisement, especially at this time of year. But Shelley professed great satisfaction at seeing it appear in *The Times*.

'One way or another, we must leave. If the house is not sold, we can leave the cook here, with Harry, and eventually there will be a purchaser. Madocks will sell off the furniture – all we need to take with us are the books and our writing desks. But we must go to Italy. It is no longer a matter of health, it is a matter of life and death.'

In truth I have been quite alarmed at his state. He suffers from an exhaustion of body and spirit which cannot be relieved by sleep, even though he sleeps very heavily, and for long hours. But it is a drugged sleep that does not leave him rested. He is often in a state of extreme torpor, in which he cannot read or take the slightest exercise, but lies on the sofa, watching the children through half-closed eyes but not joining in their play as he is wont to do. It is as if he is surrounded by an invisible barrier which prevents him from hearing any speech or feeling any emotion. Then he has periods of unnatural excitement, in which he cannot remain still, cannot eat or sleep, and is intensely irritable. He described his painfully heightened sensations to me – each blade of grass is present to him in minutest distinctness; he sees the distant boughs of the trees as if he is observing each detail of the bark through a spy-glass. I fear that his body cannot tolerate the strain of these alternating states. Something must be done, and he seems convinced that his only hope lies in travelling to Italy as soon as possible.

He brought the final proofs of my Novel, which I have been correcting. I am pleased with it – but it now has a separate existence, I think of it as a child that is grown, and must be sent out into the world to fare as best it can, on its own merits.

Shelley has written an Introduction which I have just read for the first time. There is much in what he writes for me to ponder. He praises the tale for its originality, for the steady interest with which it drives towards the catastrophe, for its refined analysis of the human mind, but above all, for its 'powerful and profound emotion'. There is too much praise here – but at the same time I realise yet again that there is no human being on earth who understands me as my Beloved does.

And so I too am now an Author.

Monday, November 10th We are all in a state of shock – this morning we received a letter from Hunt with horrifying news. Three of the Pentridge men have been hanged and beheaded on Nun Green, in front of Derby Gaol, and their heads displayed to huge crowds. This is to prove that the law is truly impartial, for High Treason can now be committed not only by noblemen but by poor labourers. By gracious remit of the Prince Regent, the sentence of quartering was rescinded. Of the other men, six were sentenced to various terms of imprisonment, thirteen to transportation (six for life), and the remainder, mainly younger men and boys, were released. Brandreth killed a man, but the others were stopped before anything occurred. Everyone knows that the uprising was planned by the Government spy Oliver, who then informed on the men so they could be intercepted and arrested, and we cannot understand why the defence lawyer failed entirely to mention this important circumstance. Hunt writes that he must have been under the strongest pressure from the ministry, and was probably persuaded to sacrifice Brandreth, who was portrayed as the incarnation of the Devil himself, in exchange for lighter sentences for the others.

The *Leeds Mercury* has reported fully on the case, and Hunt has reprinted all the articles in the *Examiner*; and *The Times* reprinted the trial verbatim in a special edition, though reporting was forbidden while the case was being heard. Brandreth was dignified on the scaffold – he had refused to shave while he was in prison, and must have presented a most impressive appearance. But Turner and Ludlam, who were both stone-masons, were evidently in a state of terror, and Turner cried out loudly, as the executioner put the rope round his neck, 'This is all Oliver and the Government!' No doubt there will be a Government inquiry in six months or a year, exonerating all public officials.

Just before this terrible news arrived we learned that Princess Charlotte had died in childbirth. This is seen as a national calamity; her coffin lies in state at Windsor while the nation mourns – though neither she nor her father the Prince Regent ever did anything to benefit the masses who weep for her death. In Marlow, too, Elise says the women are all in floods of tears, there is already talk of a subscription for a memorial.

Shelley fancies that it is Liberty who has died – driven at last to despair as each brief flicker of hope has been extinguished. Long exiled from her earliest home in Greece, cast out of her bright asylum in Italy, most recently banished from France, her ancient rights forever destroyed in England, she has drowned herself in the dark waters of the Thames, and her corpse is carried through the London streets, like Ophelia fantastically wreathed in flowers. It is Liberty for whom the great bell of St Paul's is tolled, it is Liberty, promised bride of Albion, for whom the people of England mourn.

Tuesday, November 11th Whether his anger at these events distracted him from his private troubles I do not know, but Shelley is suddenly much improved, less agitated, more like his usual self. This morning he wrote a pamphlet on the death of the Princess, comparing the official public mourning for this creature of state with the public execution of Brandreth, Ludlam and Turner, engineered by hired Government agents. Thus does the state decree praise and honour for its puppets, shame and dishonour for those who dare to oppose its injustice. It is a most powerful piece of prose; I trembled violently when I read his account of the exhibition of Brandreth's head to the assembled multitudes. He ends with a call to the people of England to 'weep – mourn – lament – for "a beautiful Princess is dead, she who should have been the Queen of her beloved nation" – her name is LIBERTY – and she has been murdered by MAN.'

He is sending the pamphlet to Ollier with instructions to print it as soon as possible, and to send twenty copies to the press. It is signed, like his pamphlet on reform, 'The Hermit of Marlow'.

It is true, as S. writes, and as Hunt has so often said, that this Government is the worst in recent history, the most repressive, the most indifferent to the condition of the poor, the most determined to maintain itself in power at all cost to the nation. But I still believe the chief enemy of human happiness is the tendency men and women have to injure and enslave themselves, freely and by choice. There are many things that it lies in the power of men to amend – but too often they stubbornly persist in the course they have set until it is too late, and the damage is irreversible.

Thursday, November 13th I have agreed to go with Shelley to London next week, to tell Papa in person of our plans. Clara is safely weaned, and thrives on cows' milk; we sold the ass, who was in foal, and no use to us. Although I am not happy about leaving the children, Clare assures me that she will see to all their needs, and I know that Shelley is anxious for me to accompany him. I dread the prospect of plunging into the bustle and commotion of the city, and breathing the dirty air of these grey November days. But I think I must do this for my Beloved, if we are to return to the frank comradeship of our early days.

Last night, when he came upstairs, he knocked at my door, entered and sat by the side of the bed. 'Are you recovered, my love?' he said with his old tenderness. I clung to him, and he kissed my tears, whispering 'my best girl, my only love'. Later we lay together, and when he came into me I was as before, and wanted him passionately with all my heart. I feel whole once more, and healed, after a long absence from myself and from my love.

Saturday, November 15th I woke this morning in terror, from a dream which was so real, so entirely convincing that I cannot shake it off. In the dream, Shelley and I have been in London for a week, and are returning to Marlow, eager to greet our darlings. On arriving at Albion House we are met at the door by Clare, who says, 'A terrible thing has happened – try to be calm, I will tell you what it is – the children are gone.'

Gone? How gone? My first thought is that Will must have wandered off into the field, as he has often done before.

'It happened two days ago,' Clare says. 'We have searched everywhere. We have asked everyone in town, we cannot find a trace of them anywhere.'

Horribly, the truth dawns on us. They have in truth disappeared, Will and the baby, they have vanished utterly, *they are gone*. Clare was upstairs with Alba, she heard a cart stop in the road outside; she ran downstairs but the cart was gone, and the children were nowhere in sight. They must have been snatched up and bundled away – it is beyond belief. My heart is pounding, but I try to think clearly – perhaps they have been taken for ransom? But then we would have heard. No, the Westbrooks must be behind it, they have hired assassins, it is their final revenge. I think to myself, we shall have to have the river dragged . . .

And with this thought I woke up, trembling all over. I could not stop shaking. Yet I saw that Clara was safe in her cradle, next to my bed, and I clutched her to my breast. I tried to force myself out of bed to go to Will, but I could not move. I woke Shelley and sent him to look at Will, then when he returned I told him my dream, but he could not comfort me.

We have not talked further of going to London – it is now out of the question. I could not think of leaving the children, not for a day, not for an hour. But it is certain that we must leave this country idyll, which seemed once to promise a paradise and has now become a prison. We cannot stay any longer in Albion House, which is cold and damp and mouldering, and has become home to rats and beetles; we cannot remain in this town, which appears so kindly and hospitable but is a sewer of malicious gossip; we can live no longer in a country which hangs simple working men for Treason if they protest that they cannot feed their families. Even if we cannot sell the lease, we must leave as soon as possible; we are no longer safe here.

Friday, December 5th This morning, when we had almost given up hope, Madocks arrived and told us that the house is sold, with contents, for £1,000. We lose £400 at least, but this is nothing to the relief of knowing that we can leave when we like. It is bought by Colonel Vansittart of Bisham Abbey, cousin to Nicholas Vansittart, Lord of the Exchequer. Madocks says there is talk of using it as a school of needlework for indigent girls and women. This is not our concern, of course.

We also have had a letter from Hunt, informing us that Marianne was safely delivered of a son, whom they propose to christen 'Percy Shelley Leigh Hunt'. No doubt he is destined to be a scribbler. Hunt urges us most warmly to spend Christmas with them in Paddington.

Suddenly it is as if a thunderstorm has passed – or rather, a long season of fog and torrential rains. There are smiles all round, Elise and Milly are already packing their things. Shelley says we need not stay with the Hunts; we have money enough to rent commodious lodgings in the centre of town. It should be interesting to live a few minutes' walk from the British Museum and the Opera House – perhaps I shall learn to conquer my aversion to the city in the few weeks we shall remain there, while we arrange our trip to Italy.

Clare is happier than I have seen her for a long time – she hums to herself, hugs Alba and Will and Clara each in turn, pirouettes two or three times, and talks of nothing but Italian skies and sunshine, Italian mountains and rivers and lakes, the divine simplicity of Dante and Tasso, Raphael and Michelangelo. She does not mention his lordship, but he is so plainly in her thoughts, he is so clearly the ground of her happiness, that I begin to think I was mistaken last August. Is it possible that I was in error? I do not like to go back over this old history; I would like, with my Beloved, to tell myself that it does not matter, all that matters is that we love one another, and trust one another. If we cannot change the world, at least we can protect our own little circle from the cruelty of life.

I shall try to put that anger and bitterness behind me. Slowly but surely I feel my old love returning upon me; my senses are reawakening to the possibility of happiness, and I believe in my heart that all will be well.

Judith Chernaik is a New Yorker living in London. She has written three previous novels, *Double Fault*, *The Daughter* (based on the life of Eleanor Marx) and *Leah*, and is the author of a highly praised book on Shelley's poetry, *The Lyrics of Shelley*. She reviews for the *Times Literary Supplement* and other journals, and has written features and talks for the BBC. She is a founding member of "Poems on the Underground," an organization that displays poetry in the London subway.

She is married with three grown children.

A NOTE ON THE TYPE

The text of this book has been set in Goudy Old Style, one of the
more than 100 type faces designed by Frederic William Goudy
(1865–1947). Although Goudy began his career as a bookkeeper,
he was so inspired by the appearance of several newly published
books from the Kelmscott Press that he devoted the remainder of his
life to typography in an attempt to bring a better understanding of
the movement led by William Morris to the printers of the United
States.

Produced in 1914, Goudy Old Style reflects the absorption of a
generation of designers with things "ancient." Its smooth, even color
combined with its generous curves and ample cut marks it as one of
Goudy's finest achievements.